GAY COURAGE

The music stopped. In the midst of the tumultuous applause for an encore, the pirate swung her through a doorway to the foyer where an electric fountain spouted its crystal spray through softly changing lights.

"You go with me," he said, "when the clock strikes twelve. My ship's on the river."

Ship! River! Go with him! Why not go with the man whose nearness sent her heart skyrocketing to her throat? But the lights, the dancers, the perfumes, the cigarette smoke, the fight between her heart and her loyalty to Bruce had become unbearable. She ran down the broad steps. The pirate! Was he following her?

A hand caught her arm; a rough voice said, "Did ye think to escape? You're coming with me."

He threw his cape about her and held her in one arm as he hurried her to a roadster in the shadow. She struggled as she was unceremoniously lifted into it. She sat quietly. Dare she go further with this aching awareness of him tugging at her heart? She did not protest as they sped away into the darkness. . . .

Gay Courage

Emilie Loring

BANTAM BOOKS
Toronto • New York • London • Sydney

*This low-priced Bantam Book
has been completely reset in a type face
designed for easy reading, and was printed
from new plates. It contains the complete
text of the original hard-cover edition.*
NOT ONE WORD HAS BEEN OMITTED.

GAY COURAGE

*A Bantam Book / published by arrangement with
Little, Brown and Company*

PRINTING HISTORY

William Penn edition published 1928

Grosset & Dunlap edition published June 1947

Bantam edition / October 1968

2nd printing . November 1968	*7th printing . . . . . April 1971*
3rd printing . . . . March 1969	*8th printing . . February 1972*
4th printing . . . . . June 1969	*9th printing . . . . March 1973*
5th printing . . December 1969	*10th printing . . . August 1974*
6th printing . . February 1970	*11th printing . . . August 1976*
	12th printing . . . May 1982

Cover photograph courtesy of Freelance Photographers Guild

ISBN 0-553-20569-2

Published simultaneously in the United States and Canada

PRINTED IN THE UNITED STATES OF AMERICA

21 20 19 18 17 16 15 14 13 12

To
Mary Valentine Loring

GAY COURAGE

Chapter 1

"Hi! Boy!"

As the two stoutly shod feet kicking idly on top the load—the hay of which was bulging over the sides to the exclusion of traffic from the narrow country road—ceased not one iota of their activity in response to the hail, Geoffrey Hilliard sounded a deafening, strident demand to pass with the horn of his car.

The echoing and re-echoing protest achieved immediate results. Results exceeding his most hopeful expectations. Not only did it produce a flushed face in place of the waving feet, it startled the unseen horses into a run. Their frenzied leap ahead loosened a portion of the load which slid smartly to the ground bringing with it a flash of green, glinting copper, ivory, which coördinated into a laughing clutching passenger who landed in front of the closely following roadster with a crash and a breathless;

"Well, here we are!"

Hilliard's face was white under its bronze as he ground on the brake. He was out of the car in an instant looking down into radiant brown eyes in a flushed, uplifted face. A face topped by ruddy chestnut hair stuck through and through with wisps of hay. A girl! He had thought he was hailing a boy. A girl and not such a young girl, either, the man appraised. Perhaps twenty-five or so. One who knew her way about, decidedly. Her lovely mouth was curved in an enchanting smile. The lines of her chin and neck were beautiful, the little hollow at the base of her throat was fashioned for a man's lips. Good Lord, did she divine what he was thinking? A curious expression had ousted the radiance from her dark eyes. Fright? No. Dislike? Intense dislike. Why should a person whom he never before had seen dislike him? Conscious, even through his solicitation, of the faint fragrance of sandalwood about the girl, he dropped to one knee beside her and inquired;

1

"I hope you're not hurt?"

A defiant note jangled through the charming voice in which she answered;

"Hurt! Absurd. That is my usual expeditious, if unconventional method of alighting from a load of hay."

Hilliard regained his feet with dispatch. Two tiny flames in the depths of his cool, slightly cynical grey eyes, responded to the sparks in the brown eyes as he suggested with a hint of drawl in his voice;

"Do you usually select the moment for acrobatics when a storm like that is aproaching?" He indicated a sullen cloud spindling stealthily across the patch of blue sky above them.

With a startled exclamation the girl scrambled to her feet. Her green sweater, her short skirt of the same shade, even her stockings of the sports variety shed hay. She listened. From far ahead drifted back the clatter of wheels. She observed lightly;

"Those temperamental horses seem to have departed for Sunnyfield and points west."

Thunder growled in the distance. Drab clouds closed in above. A big drop of rain kicked up the dust with a "Plop!" reminiscent of the sound of a bullet burying itself in a French road. The girl looked up at the sky, down at the spot of moisture and accused;

"Now see what you've done with your silly horn."

"I have done nothing which can't be speedily remedied. Jump into the car and I'll take you wherever you were going."

"Thank you. I prefer to walk."

"Don't be silly. You'll be wet through before you have gone two yards. Get in while I pull up the top."

He was conscious of her eyes upon him as he began to unfasten the straps which held the covering. Evidently she intended to take her time about getting in. It would serve her right to get soaked, he thought wrathfully. With that innate sense of propriety so maddeningly characteristic of thunderstorms the heavens selected the moment when a hasp stuck to break wide open and pour their accumulated moisture down upon him. With pardonable exasperation he shouted above the din;

"Come and help!"

As no hands appeared in answer to the call he wriggled his head from under cover. The girl had gone.

"That's appreciation. Just like a woman. Did she think I'd do this for myself?" Hilliard growled at the engine, but the engine remained discreetly non-committal. The top, which never before had been called into action, balked at every strategic point. Minutes passed before he pulled a raincoat from under the seat, slipped behind the wheel and started the car. He drove slowly peering into shrubs and behind such tall trees as bordered the country road. Showy trilliums, lobelias, even those sturdy ferns bent under the torrential downpour. Something disquieting in the atmosphere tautened the man's nerves. He must find the girl. He was responsible for her fall but who in heaven's name would suppose that in these days there could be found anywhere horses of sufficient unsophistication to bolt at sound of an automobile horn?

The sky went black. Thunder pealed. Sharp outlines blurred into foggy shadows. A length of fiery chain crackled the western sky wide open. It banged shut with a deafening crash. A copper glow shot through the darkness overhead. Lightning stabbed at the tree-tops, thrust at the cowering ferns. The world seemed uncannily still between flash and detonation. Nearer and more continuous rolled the thunder, nearer and more continuous blazed the blinding flashes. With ghoulish shrieks the wind tore at dead tree arms and wrenched them from their age-worn sockets. The rain hissed in sheets. Torrents of grey water surged along the gutters sweeping tipsy flotillas of fallen leaves on its turbulent course. Metallic rivulets dripped from twig and branch. Near-hail beat the gravel of the road into strange patterns.

As his anxiety for the girl's safety increased Geoffrey Hilliard's exasperation at her perversity kept step. Where the dickens was she? There hadn't been time for her to get far. Would she know enough not to stand under a tree in a storm like this? In an instant's lull which presaged a burst of pyrotechnics he shouted.

No answer. He shouted again. Listened. He drove at snail's pace for fear he might miss her. Peering into an endless wilderness of rain he discerned a dark shape plodding doggedly ahead. He stepped on the accelerator. As he came alongside he stopped the car with a jerk. The green and copper and ivory of the hayrick passenger had been drenched to neutral tints. In an instant he had thrown the raincoat over the girl's shoulders. He caught her in his arms and deposited her in the roadster with as little ceremony as he might have bestowed upon the bundle of hay which so recently had betrayed her. Before she could regain her breath which apparently had been beaten out of her by the storm, he was behind the wheel. He observed crisply as he started the car;

"People who don't know enough to take care of themselves have to be taken care of."

Little rivulets were cavorting down the girl's face. She brushed a saturated lock of hair away from her eyes. Her shrug was more of a shiver as she countered;

"And who appointed you guardian of the world at large?"

Hilliard regarded her with an incredulous scowl;

"Look here! What's the matter? I've apologized for jolting you from that load. When I saw your feet and legs kicking up there I thought you were a boy. I shouted for the driver to stop hogging the road. I'm . . ."

"Why is it that one feels impelled to kick on a load of hay. A point for the psychoanalysts, isn't it?" Hilliard ignored the flippant interruption:

"I'm doing all I can to make up for the fiasco. Your voice sounds as though you'd caught me stealing sheep or deserting from the army."

"Aren't you a deserter?"

"A deserter! What do you mean?"

"I'm Nancy Caswell."

The man's dark brows met in a puzzled frown above his fine eyes. His voice was maddeningly tinged with amusement as he responded;

"It is a pleasure to have you crash into my life even in this informal way, Miss Caswell, but, your tone connotes . . ."

"If you knew anything of the village which provides your bread, butter and marmalade, said marmalade being a figure of speech for rare books, cars, boats and polo ponies. . . ."

"Only one pony. Interesting and stimulating as you are

I can't permit you to exaggerate. You implied that I should know you."

"I'm the clergyman's daughter at Sunnyfield."

Sunnyfield! The clergyman's daughter! Caswell! Geoffrey Hilliard remembered a letter he had received recently signed N. Caswell. It had called his attention to his selfish neglect of his own people living next door to the writer, at Valleyview, the Hilliard estate. His face burned now at the memory of its curt frankness. Camouflaged as it had been in chilly politeness, nevertheless it had been a denunciation. He had thought after reading it;

"Darned meddler, N. Caswell! He's the clergyman at Sunnyfield. Lives in the parsonage. If father needed me he'd send for me, wouldn't he? He can't be lonely. He has Aunt Serena and Aunt Sally. Luke Small practically runs his paper mills. Of course he doesn't miss me. If he did, why didn't he tell me to come home when I finished the course in Business Administration? Why did he encourage me to globe-trot, air-trot, to become a connoisseur of old books?"

Mentally he threshed out the same argument as he drove through the rain with the silent girl beside him. He pulled himself up. He was indulging in self-justification. He hated it in anyone else. Why didn't he acknowledge frankly that he had dreaded coming back to the village which had been the scene of heartbreak and bitter humiliation for him? That also he had side-stepped the possibility of stirring up Luke Small's animosity by his return? Why didn't he acknowledge that N. Caswell's letter had pricked at his conscience until he had cancelled all September engagements that he might spend the month with his father and aunts at Valleyview? The remembrance of the sports, the polo, the companionship he was missing crisped his voice as he repeated;

"The clergyman's daughter?"

"Then you are not asleep? I began to wonder if I had better take the wheel."

"You'll never take the wheel in my car. To return to the clergyman, if the father shows the sympathetic courtesy displayed by the daughter he must be a power in the community."

Lovely color crept to the girl's wet hair.

"I'm not much of a credit to him, am I? He isn't at all like me. He's a—a saint."

Hilliard was uncomfortably certain that a mist of tears had followed in the wake of the color. His voice warmed as he suggested;

"Let's bury the hatchet, Miss Caswell. I don't know why you should flourish it, but, I suppose there's a reason. Tell me something of what's happened in Sunnyfield. I was abroad for three years. When I landed on this side my father and aunts met me in New York. They are not letter writers. My father cables, wires, or 'phones. My aunts send little notes, no news, just reports, sunny reports as to the state of their health and the Squire's. I am sure that if there are clouds you'll have the courage not to spare my feelings."

A dirty dig, he thought, with a sting of self-contempt. But the girl after a sidelong glance above the collar of the raincoat, elected to take him literally.

"Why should your feelings be spared? You're thirty-three. I know because your father has shown me photographs of you from the cradle on. The parsonage, The Manse, is next door to Valleyview."

"I haven't been so long away that I've forgotten that. It's a pity that you should have been afflicted to the extent of having to admire photos of me."

"Don't worry. I haven't admired them. I loathe conceit. I've looked at them because I adore your father. I don't wonder that the villagers and mill workers call Peter Hilliard 'The Squire,' he looks the part. He's so—so darned proud of you and for what? Collecting books doesn't seem to me to be a full-sized job for a man of your age."

Hilliard jammed the brake on his temper. He might have answered, "Possibly he's proud of me because of an honor or two at college, my baseball and football letters, a citation treasured in his desk." Instead he laughed;

"Call that burying the hatchet?"

"I haven't agreed to bury the hatchet. It hurts unbearably to see your father holding his handsome head high and blithely explaining your ignoring of home while all the time . . ."

"Go on! Why hesitate? Now that you have your knife in finish the operation. All the time—what?"

"The business of the mills is falling off."

"Off! How can it? He has gilt-edge contracts to supply newsprint besides regular customers for the finer grade paper we make."

"He has lost one of the newsprint accounts."

"How do you happen to know?"

"I happen to know Luke Small."

"Why didn't that little tin-god of a manager nail the account?"

"He tried to—he says. But, he's had an advantageous offer to go with the Upper Mill and . . ."

"The Upper Mill! Hm-m-m!"

"Were you commenting or just growling? I didn't mean to intimate that Luke is planning to leave your father, he was rather proud of the offer, that's all. You can't justly condemn him if he takes advantage of a chance to better himself, can you?"

"Considering the fact that when Luke's father lost all he all had put into the Upper Mill and died years ago, my father gave the boy a job in our mills summers, kept him at school winters, sent him through college and then gave him a permanent position, I can condemn him, but I won't. The rain has stopped as suddenly as it began. Better throw off that coat and get dry."

The sun shone wanly through the breaking clouds like a child trying to smile after a storm of tears. Stealthily the thunder heads, spongey now, retreated. The sapphire blue of sky spread and spread and spread. The slanting sun blazed out at its early-September best. A soft breeze shook crystal showers from trees and shrubs. The air was fragrant with the smell of rainwashed earth and drenched wild blossoms. Birds twittered. From the green gloom of distant woods rose the song of a thrush. High. Ecstatic. Heart-breakingly sweet.

Geoffrey Hilliard drove swiftly along the red dirt road now mirrored with shining, shallow puddles looking for all the world like bits of isinglass set in a Turkish scarf. He stopped the low-slung car before the white picket gate in front of the Manse. Above the fence nodded a welter of bloom sparkling with brilliants left by the shower.

Marigolds, a gold mine of them. An occasional tall spike
of larkspur lingering long beyond its time as though loath
to give way to its rival, purple monkshood, giant masses
of it. There were patches of deepest orange. Tall pink
lilies. Drifts of white cosmos, nuances of pale rose against
dark greens. Gladioli in gorgeous profusion. Cloud mists
of gypsophila. Brilliant color massed in the middle of the
border shaded down to cool tints at the ends. Droning
bees tumbled drunkenly from flower to flower, their
bodies gold with pollen. A humming-bird skimmed
through the scented air. It serenaded its stately sweetheart
with the rhythm of beating wings as it thrust its head,
ruby throat deep, into the gold-veined chalice of an Auratum lily.

A lawn, green as an emerald, soft as the transparent
velvet of a woman's frock, was flung like a choice rug
between the flower border and the white cottage. There
were little rabbits with upstanding ears cut in the yellow
shutters. Gay orange and white awnings shaded the
porches, boxes spilling over with yellow and white and
purple blooms, adorned windows without, snowy muslins
were visible within. As the car stopped the girl jumped
out. Her damp clothing clung to her slim body, her
drenched hair was plastered to her head. Her voice was
chilly;

"Thank you for bringing me home."

Geoffrey Hilliard regarded the white house as he followed her from the roadster.

"Are you the miracle worker? I remember the Manse
as a drab structure, in color a depressing blend of granite
and clay. It had a rubber-plant perennially at the window, gobs of scarlet geraniums on a scraggly lawn."

Nancy Caswell's laugh was delicious;

"Scorn not the flower-grower's best friend. Blooms may
come and blooms may go but the geranium keeps on . . ."

From behind the house interrupted a rich, sonorous
voice declaiming;

" 'There were forty craft in Avès that were both swift
and stout.
All furnished well with small arms and cannons round
about;

And a thousand men in Avès made laws so fair and
free

To choose their valiant captains and obey them loy-
ally.' "

A lovely light warmed the girl's eyes.

"That's Dad. He orates on all occasions, especially
when he's shaving. Sometime I expect to find him with an
ear hanging by a thread."

"Nan-cy!"

She waved her hand in response to the hail as a man
came around the corner of the house. Coatless and hatless
he was armed with rake and hoe. He dropped the tools,
slipped into a coat of shabby brown velveteen which he
appeared to pick from a tree, pulled off white cotton
gloves and approached the two standing by the roadster.
He had aquiline features, clear skin tinged with healthy
tan, white hair matted in moist silky rings close to his
finely shaped head, great dignity of presence. A wonderful face, Hilliard thought. He was erect, lean. On the
border of sixty? Perhaps the shady border. His black eyes
softened to velvet, his rich voice was solicitous as he
inquired;

"Nan, where have you come from? After Sandy had
landed the hay in the Valleyview barn he was stunned
with amazement to discover that you were missing. He
had raced home to get ahead of the storm. 'I canna hae
drapped her off,' he kept muttering. Give an account of
yourself, my dear."

The girl re-bowed the broad, dangling ends of his
near-windsor tie before she slipped her arm within his
and explained;

"I did drop off. Quite unexpectedly. Dad, this is
Geoffrey Hilliard. He picked me up out of the road."

With the remembrance of that angrily ignored letter
pricking at his conscience Hilliard was unprepared for the
cordiality of the clergyman's greeting. His dark eyes lighted with pleasure as he extended his hand;

"Our young neighbor! 'The way of the gods is full of
providence,' to quote old Marcus Aurelius Antoninus.
You're needed next door, boy. I'm glad you've come."

"Thank you, sir. I—I apologize for not having answered your letter, but . . ."

"My letter? I have never written you a letter."

"Aren't you N. Caswell?"

"Yes. Noah Caswell."

Geoffrey Hilliard's eyes interrogated the girl. She made a little face at him from behind her father's shoulder and colored pinkly. So—she had written that letter. Why? It was apparent that she disliked him cordially. Why? Was Luke Small responsible? Even from boyhood Luke had been furiously jealous of him. Would he try to prejudice this girl against him?

"Won't you explain about that letter?"

Noah Caswell's question snapped Hilliard's attention back to the present. He hastened to admit lightly;

"Of course I'm mistaken. I mixed you up with someone else."

Chapter II

Those "Whys?" still intrigued Geoffrey Hilliard as a few moments later he drove between the two stone lions which for fifty years or more had guarded the entrance to Valleyview, the family homestead. Was anything ever designed more ugly than the house which his grandfather had built to replace the Colonial structure which had been burned, he wondered, as he looked ahead at the Mansard roof with its cupola crawling with curlycues, dotted with excrescences in the most approved, wedding-cake manner. Beds of cannas bordered with red geraniums starred, crescented and circled the plushy lawns. In the middle of one green expanse poised a white dog with black spots. Tail pointing, long ears drooping, nose sniffing, he stood as he had stood since long before the man who was regarding him had been born.

"Good old Spotty!" Geoffrey said aloud.

A wave of emotion swept him as he looked at his one-time playmate, emotion which startled him. He had thought himself coolly impervious to sentiment, except where his father was concerned, yet his blood had quickened to fever-heat at sight of a hollow in a girl's throat and now an old iron dog had set memory tugging at his heart. Had the sights and sounds and smells of the town where he had grown up exorcised the spell which disillusion had cast upon him when he came back from France?

At the top of the porch steps he turned to look out over the valley from which the Hilliard homestead took its name. Nothing ugly about that. A meandering river, nooking, curving in shining loops, iridescent in the afternoon light, foamed in spots where the water was swift. The world was so still that plainly he could hear the dull roar of the dam above the paper mills and the nearer overtones of rush and splash and ripple of water. He could see fields yellow where the ripe grain had been cut, pas-

11

EMILIE LORING

tures sectored by stone walls, green hills flaming with darts of maple where a young, a very young Jack Frost had touched them with chilly fingers, in the midst of the white village the slender apex of a church spire pricking the sky. Everywhere the summer mellowing into autumn.

As he entered the house he stopped with a sense of strangeness. Changed. The black walnut hatrack with its intricate convolutions, which had adorned the wall ever since he could remember, was gone. On the floor below where it had hung stood a brass-bound chest. Who had salvaged that from the attic?

"Anyone at home?" he called.

With startling suddenness two women appeared in a doorway. Serena Hilliard, tall, gaunt, with skin as yellow as old ivory, hazel eyes set deep in Websterian hollows, high-bridged nose and delicate lips, was in marked contrast to her sister Sally. She was short, plump, fresh-skinned. There was an engaging twinkle in her young blue eyes; a dusting of powder of her retroussé nose, a mere suggestion of artificial color on her still girlish lips. Both women were white haired. They regarded their nephew for a stunned instant before they chorused;

"Geoffrey!"

Their incredulous delight gave a twist to the thumb-screws of self-reproach which the last hour had attached to young Hilliard's conscience. He put an arm about the thin shoulders, an arm about the plump shoulders, and walked between the two women to the living room. He cleared an uncomfortable catch from his throat before he inquired gaily;

"Been elected to the state legislature yet, Aunt Serena? Aunt Sally, how do you do it? You haven't grown a minute older since last I saw you."

They beamed upon him speechlessly. They fluttered about him until they had installed him in a wing chair in front of an open French window. He looked out upon the garden, a garden luminous with color in the afternoon sunshine. Prim gravelled paths, set like pewter patterns in an emerald rug, were bordered by phlox in all shades and varieties. Where they crossed shimmered a pool in the center of which two iron children crouched under a dripping iron umbrella. He turned to forestall Sally Hilliard as she was about to move a table.

"Let me do that. What's the use having a big husk about if you don't make him work?"

"Oh, Geoff! It's so wonderful to have you here!" The plump woman's soft voice wavered betrayingly.

The thumbscrews tightened. It would have been such an easy thing for him to week-end at home occasionally, her nephew reproached himself. He watched her spread a cloth of superfine texture.

"Does it really make a difference?"

Her laugh was like the coo of a pigeon. Two deep dimples dented her roseleaf cheeks as she teased;

"Now you're fishing, Geoff. Here comes Nora with tea. When she sees you . . ."

Serena Hilliard caught up the sentence;

"The Lord save the china. She . . ."

She was in turn interrupted by a crash. The tray the entering maid carried followed the law of gravitation as she flung up her hands in surprise;

"The Saints be praised! If it ain't Master Geoff!"

Hilliard bent and kissed her ruddy cheek as she caught his two hands in her rough ones. She had been a maid at Valleyview when he had made his entrance into the world. She had remained scoffingly impervious to the lure of the eight-hour day and the five-day week. Her white print dress dotted with black was stiff with starch and decorously covered her ankles. Her coarse hair streaked alternately with red and grey was drawn so tightly back that her brows reared. Her little green eyes snapped continuously as she accused;

"Now, Master Geoff, ain't thet jes' like yer to scare a body's if yer was a ghost?" She frowned down upon the sisters who on their knees were holding a post mortem over the tray;

"Don't yer go to worritin,' Ma'ms. That's the blue teapot went broke, bad cess to it. Lucky I didn't put old Madame Hilliard's on. I knew Miss Nancy wouldn't be in—she went hayin' with Sandy—so I didn't use the comp'ny china."

With the dexterity of long experience in handling domestic casualties, she swept the débris into her immaculate and capacious apron, settled the tray upon the table and started for the kitchen.

"I'll be back wid more tay before yese can tell a prayer," she encouraged and vanished. With stiff-back dignity Serena Hilliard seated herself at table. Sally hovered over it settling cups and sugaring saucers.

"Nora is such a trial," deplored the elder woman. "We keep two village girls to help her, Sally has trained them beautifully, but she bursts into a temper if they serve tea. She considers that her prerogative. She's been spoiled by the young people. They flock here for tea so that she may tell their fortunes from their cups."

Sally broke a lance in the maid's defense.

"She may be a trial but she's a wonderful cook. When you think of the trouble the summer people have with servants who work only on schedule time you'd better go down on your knees and thank the Lord for Nora, hadn't she, Geoff?"

"I'll say she had." He lifted the cover of a china beehive.

"Honey! Hot scones! Now I know that I'm at home."

Home! He looked about. For the first time he saw the room, he had only felt it before. Changes here too. When last he had seen it, it might have been transferred bodily to the American Wing of the Metropolitan as a perfect example of the design-atrocities of the black walnut era. Now its contents would wring tears of envy from the eyes of a lover of antiques. He remembered the high-chest across the room as the attic receptacle for first, his butterflies, then shells, then stamps. He had been born with a collecting complex, most boys were, he suspected. The satin finish of a pie-crust table reflected the polished brasses on the hearth. There were chairs by the choice pair, a huge braided rug was on the floor. Rare Chinese vases had been transformed into charming lamps. The piano, which he remembered as closed, was open. It looked as though it were used. Restful wall spaces, had replaced a former scatter of small pictures. His great-great-grandfather's portrait hung above the fireplace. There were two curious brass candlesticks on the mantel below it, nothing else. Only the shelves and shelves of books remained unchanged. Ponderous volumes from which emanated the faint scent of old calf-skin.

His aunts had kept pace with the changes in the room. Their gowns were silvery grey with a suggestion of modishness. Sally's was much shorter than her sister's. She must be at least ten years older than his father. In his boyhood he had felt nearer to her in spirit than to her sterner sister.

"You are noticing the changes, Geoffrey? You don't mind?" Serena Hilliard inquired anxiously.

"Mind! I like them."

"So does your father, in fact he is really responsible. We had kept the house as your grandmother left it, but he showed Nancy Caswell this old furniture in the attic and asked her what could be done with it. She was so enthusiastic about it that . . ."

"We sent the black walnut upstairs and brought down this," Miss Sally tripped into the explanation. "We do like it better. Now Nancy wants us to . . ."

"Does Miss Caswell run this place as well as the Manse?" her nephew interrupted in his turn. The crispness of his question made no dent in Sally Hilliard's serenity.

"I wish that she did. I'm not the only one who'd like to have her about all the time. Luke Small . . ."

She stopped speaking with a significant lift of her eyebrows as Nora crackled into the room with a Canton teapot in one hand a plate of cookies, thin, crisp, golden-brown wafers, in the other.

"Is Mr. Geoffrey's room ready for him?" Serena Hilliard inquired.

Having deposited her burdens with a minimum of clatter—for her—the Irish woman planted hands on hips. With rearing eyebrows twitching, green eyes snapping accompaniment she protested;

"Shure, Mam, ye know yerself, 'tis. Don't we kape it always ready? An' ain't it yerselves what's always sayin' ter me;

"'Nora,' says you, 'Be shure the curtains is crisp an' fresh in Misther Geoffrey's room. He may come droppin' in an' surprise us.'"

Three years since he had come "droppin' in." He might

not have been here now if the officious Miss Caswell
hadn't written that letter, Geoffrey reproached himself.
His voice gave no hint of his remorse as he commended
gaily;

"I've been around the world three times and I've never
tasted anything so good as your scones, Nora." He heaped
a crisp, flaky morsel with comb which oozed golden
honey.

"An' I'll bet ivery time yer wint round yer kissed the
blarney-stone, me boy. Go way wid yer! Flatterin' an ould
woman like me. Save that fer Miss Nancy. There's a gurl
for ye. Don't yer let her throw herself away on thet
spalpeen Luke Small. He's smooth an' he's edicated an'
smart at the mill but underneath he ain't different than he
wore whin he used to come into my kitchen an' say you'd
sint him fer cookies when yer hadn't. Wurrah! Wurrah!
That was Himself slammed the door. I'd better be afther
gittin' busy fer supper." She departed kitchenward stumbling over a footstool in her exit. Serena Hilliard winced;

"In all the years Nora has lived with us we've never
been able to teach her to move quietly. She sets the very
walls to vibrating. Sally, meet the Squire in the hall and
tell him that Geoffrey is here." As her sister left the room
she explained; "If your father were to walk in and see you
the surprise might set his heart pounding. We've been
warned to look out for that."

"Why haven't I been told, too? What's the matter with
him? I thought he looked wonderfully fit when you all
met me in New York the day I landed."

"He has aged."

"He's only sixty. Young, as men appear and accom-
plish these days. Has he been working too hard?"

"Land sakes, no. Work never kills. It keep folks
young. Worry's the murderer, not work."

"What's he worrying about?"

"Don't get panicky, Geoffrey. Last spring the doctor
told him to keep away from the mills, take up golf and
live out of doors. He obeyed and left Luke Small to run
the business. He ought to be competent. He grew up in
the mills under your father but . . ."

"But what?"

"You'll think I'm crazy when I tell you but Nora is hipped on the subject of Luke. You heard her just now."

"That was absurd, harking back to school days."

"I know—but—she saw signs of the treachery of a dark man in your father's tea-cup."

Geoffrey shouted. He disciplined his mirth to a chuckle and demanded;

"Do you believe in Nora's tea-cup fortune telling, Aunt Serena? I'm ashamed of you."

"Laugh if you like, Geoffrey, but Nora's prophecies have an uncanny way of coming true. Of course, it isn't the tea-leaves, it's a sort of psychic sense. Anyway, your father is troubled."

"About money? If so why didn't he cut my allowance?"

"That would be the last thing he'd do. Here he comes. He mustn't suspect that we've been talking about him."

The thumbscrews tightened uncomfortably on Geoffrey's heart as his father greeted him with incredulous delight. For the first time he noted his own resemblance to Peter Hilliard, "The Squire," as the head of the Hilliard family had been called for the last five generations. His nose was straight and clear-cut, mouth slightly grim. His black hair was identical in color and texture to that which he himself confronted in the mirror every morning, except that there were patches of silver above the elder man's ears. His father's grey eyes had the same trick of half shutting when he was intent. Bodies built on fighting lines, both of them. Hilliard senior was too heavy, his skin was too ruddy, his son decided uneasily, but his voice was refreshingly young as he rejoiced;

"It's great to have you here, Geoff!"

"It's great to be here, Squire. I was afraid if I didn't come back my place would automatically grow together and crowd me out."

"Silly boy," Miss Sally murmured fondly and patted his arm. "I'll go and make sure that Nora is having what you like for supper."

"Oh Sally." In response to her brother's call the plump little woman poised on the threshold like a plump little robin ready for a take-off. "Tell the maid to set another place at table. Luke Small's coming. He got back from

New York too late for me to see him at the office. I'm at
the wheel again at the mills. No more vacationing for me
for a while. I won't wait till tomorrow to hear the result
of his trip."

"Then I'll 'phone Nancy Caswell to come over? Luke
hasn't seen her for a week. You won't talk business at
supper."

"Why ask her if Luke Small is coming?" demanded
Geoffrey sharply.

"Because if they are not engaged Serena and I expect
they will be soon." His aunt flung the information over
her shoulder before she started in quest for Nora.

Chapter III

"Know the penalty for forgery, Miss N. Caswell?" Geoffrey Hilliard inquired a few hours later in a voice attuned only to reach the ear of the girl at the piano in the living room at Valleyview. She ran her fingers lightly over the keys as she countered;

"Preparing a How Much Do You Know quiz to submit to the village weekly?"

Her tone set off a flare of anger.

"Don't quibble. You wrote that letter signed N. Caswell knowing that I would think it was from your father, didn't you?"

" 'I seen my duty an' I done it.' " She executed an impudent little scale on the keyboard. Geoffrey saw red. He thrust to hurt;

"To use your own words of not so many hours ago, 'Who appointed you guardian of the world at large?' Perhaps, though, that word duty is a smokescreen. If you were so eager to meet me, why didn't you wire or write in your own name asking me to come? I should have broken my neck to get here, believe me."

Incredulity, anger, fury, rushed one another in rapid succession in the brown eyes which blazed up at him. The girl sprang to her feet.

"Oh, you—you . . ." Words failed her for an instant then she accused stormily;

"Just because one girl disappointed you, you think all others are of the same calibre. You've cultivated that attitude till it's become a perennial. You trade on it. Oh, yes you do," she persisted in response to his growl of denial. "You like to have your aunts sympathize, 'Poor Geoff!' I say 'Darn,' every time I look at that photograph of you, the one with the hint of a skeptical smile."

"Why look at it?"

19

Only a faint increase of lovely color indicated that she had noted his cool interruption.

"You like to have your father treat you as though you were a tender plant which must be protected from too hard a rain, too hot a sun. Do you know how I think of you? As a patch of hard-caked earth which needs a tremendous stirring before it will produce anything worth while."

"And you feel it your Christian duty to do the stirring? Thanks lots."

Hands thrust into the pockets of his blue coat, Geoffrey Hilliard leaned against the piano and watched the color surge to the uneven line of the girl's brown hair. The glow from the softly shaded lamp set little copper lights aglint in it, enriched the hue of her filmy topaz-colored frock. It deepened the alluring hollow at the base of her throat. He swallowed hard. Why the dickens should that softly pulsing bit of flesh set his blood to rioting? One would think that never before had he seen a girl's throat.

Peter Hilliard and Luke Small were absorbed in a business discussion on the porch. The hum of their voices, the scent of their cigars, the evening symphony of innumerable crickets, wafted in through the open windows, windows open to a night as warm as summer. In the room Serena and Sally were battling over a game of checkers quite unconscious of another battle raging by the piano. Geoffrey couldn't remember having seen in years a girl blush as Nancy Caswell was blushing. He had supposed the trick was not only démodé but a lost art. He laughed as he encouraged;

"Don't stop. Now that you've recovered your breath, go on. You first called me a deserter. Second, hard-caked earth. Anything to add to that?"

"You'd be surprised how much! I won't waste another moment talking to such an insufferably conceited person."

Geoffrey caught her before she reached the door. He held her arm in a grip of steel as he announced;

"You'll waste a good many moments talking to me. Understand?"

With a quick twist she freed herself and dashed into the hall. Her tone, her words had fired him with a determination to crash through barriers he hadn't felt since war days. Her aversion maddened him. Coming back to Sunnyfield had certainly done things to his hard-won philosophy to laugh where once he would have winced.

By the time he reached the porch she was standing on the lowest step. There was a tinge of breathlessness in the voice in which she insisted;

"But I must go. Phyllis, the maid who looks after Betty, is going to a party. She's party mad. It wouldn't do for Betty to disturb Dad if she wakens. He's working on his sermon for Sunday. No, Luke. Don't come with me. I'm going through the cut in the hedge, but...." Geoffrey would have taken oath that her eyes flashed to the shadow in which he was standing before she went on persuasively, "but do come over on your way home. Remember, I haven't seen you for a week and I have heaps to consult you about and a letter from Bruce to read to you. Say good-night to Miss Serena and Miss Sally for me, Squire. I didn't want to interrupt their game to say it for myself. So glad that the wandering boy has returned. I'm sure he'll prove a comfort. Good-night!"

Geoffrey waited until he heard the opening squeak, the closing clang of an iron gate before he took possession of the Gloucester hammock and pulled out his pipe. A reddish gold moon rose in stately dignity in the east. Luke Small stood with eyes peering toward the hedge evidently restraining with difficulty a desire to follow the girl. As at a word from Peter Hilliard he resumed his seat, his head was silhouetted against the glow of a lamp in the drive. A good-looker in spite of a suggestion of veneer, Geoffrey grudgingly acknowledged. He had hands like John Barrymore's, eyes of the sheik variety, nose straight and patrician, a small dark mustache, chin pronounced. With all his mind, with all his soul, with all his strength he loved himself. How women fell for the type!

He looked from him to Peter Hilliard. The glow from his cigar lighted the troubled eyes above it. As Small stopped in his monologue of explanation Geoffrey inquired;

"Hope you don't mind my listening-in on this conference?"

Before his father could answer Small patronized;

"Not in the least. What we are discussing must be Greek to you. As I was saying, Squire, I couldn't get near that purchasing agent. He's a hard egg. He was too busy to see me."

"You should have stayed in New York until he did see you, until you found out why he didn't renew the contract. That was the biggest account we had for newsprint. When did he turn us down definitely?"

"Oh—I felt that it was coming a month ago."

"Why didn't you tell me then?"

"Well, you see, as you had been ordered not to think of business I decided not to trouble you about the matter."

"Trouble me! Great Scott, what do you think you're doing now when it's too late to do anything about it? From this minute on, I'm back on the job, full time."

"Why don't you talk with that purchasing agent, Squire?"

Geoffrey could see Luke Small's eyes smolder with anger at his suggestion. Peter Hilliard answered his son;

"I will. We won't discuss business any longer, Luke. Can't have Geoff's visit spoiled by my problems."

Small rose and flung away the end of his cigar. Its light glowed on the lawn like a sinister eye. Because of the formation of vines behind him the head of his shadow spouted Satanic horns. Nora's tea-cup prophecy as to the treachery of a dark man wormed its insidious way into Geoffrey's mind. The manager's voice was double-edged as he agreed to his employer's suggestion;

"You're right, Squire. He'll be flitting in a day or two then we'll get down to brass tacks. I'll run over to the Manse. Nancy misses me when I'm away. She's grown to rely on my advice. Good-night, sir. Good-night, Geoff."

Fury at the man's smug declaration of the girl's reliance on him, the assumption that his visit would be short, choked Geoffrey for an instant before he heard a voice—a cool voice—could it be his own?—answering;

"You're wrong, Luke, about my flitting, I mean. I'm here to stay. Good-night!"

With a short laugh of incredulity, Luke turned on his heel and crossed the lawn. Father and son were silent until they heard the clang of the iron gate in the hedge between Valleyview and the Manse. Then the elder Hilliard questioned gravely;

"What did you mean by, 'I'm here to stay,' Geoff? Was it a theatrical gesture because Luke annoyed you?"

The son considered. That pronunciamento had been hurled by his subconscious. Had the sudden determination to stay been but a tidal wave of impulse set in motion by Small's smugness, which would recede as quickly as it had surged? From behind the house swelled the Ch-chunk! Ch-chunk! of frogs, the shriek of a tree-toad. Good Lord, what lonesome sounds. Little old New York City would be a-glitter at this time of night. He visualized irregular towers of skyscrapers spangled with hundreds of lighted windows—towers of Babel perhaps, but incredibly splendid—swarming humanity surging through the swift currents of the thoroughfares to ports of pleasure, drama, dreams. In imagination he looked down from the apartment he had recenlty leased on top of a mammoth building,—an anchor to stop his wandering—upon skeletons of steel and cement, upon canyons which were streets. Within he could see Taka, his soft-voiced, catfooted Japanese servant moving about the rooms filled with trophies of his travels. As though staged to emphasize contrast came the clatter of pans rolling down the back steps. Rattle! Rattle! Rattle! A tinny roll and bang. Peter Hilliard groaned. He tossed away his cigar and rose;

"Noiseless Nora in action. Don't answer my question now, about staying I mean, Geoff. Let it stand for a month at least, if you can endure the country that long. Don't make a momentous decision on impulse. It is a momentous decision, as you'll realize later. I could see that Luke irritated you. He's trying to draw me into a pool with other paper manufacturers. He's as reliable as the sun. I trust him absolutely but I prefer to remain independent even if we don't produce over twenty-five thousand tons of newsprint a year. He was prickly to-night. As a rule he's mighty good company."

"Evidently Miss Caswell finds him so. Aunt Sally intimated that she and that Main-streeter were engaged."

"The girls—Serena and Sally will always be 'the girls' to me though they're both in their early seventies—hum the wedding-march if a man calls once on a lady friend.

Small town stuff. Luke is often at the Manse. Nancy's brother Bruce and he were classmates at college. When her father broke down in health and was ordered to the country, the son wrote to Luke to inquire if a pastor were needed in this neighborhood. He turned the letter over to me and I engaged Noah Caswell at once. He's accomplished miracles with the mill people. They love him."

"Where is young Caswell now?"

"In South America. Going through hell. Just another tragic triangle. His wife, Sybyl, is getting a divorce. Through no fault of his, I'll wager. They came to the Manse for a short visit last year. I got a slant on her then."

"Is she beautiful?"

"Not a face to launch a thousand ships but more than pretty. While she's Renoing their five year old daughter Betty is here with her grandfather and aunt. Nancy gave up her work in New York—she's what they call a garden-maker—to come here with her father two years ago."

"Curious that neither you nor the aunts have ever written me about the family except that they were in the parsonage."

Peter Hilliard's laugh was slightly shamefaced.

"Have we ever written you about anything? As correspondents we're a total loss."

"Is Mr. Caswell better?"

"He's in great trim. I love that man, Geoff. Never supposed that I could care so much for one who didn't belong to me. He's the old-fashioned type of pastor. Has time to rejoice with, sorrow with, comfort his people. Don't find so many of that kind these days. He's quixotic to a degree. Having inherited a small income he has spent the best years of his life in a poor parish in the city. I love the classical allusions with which he sweetens or peps his conversation—his humorous, theatrical bursts into declamation. I like his shabby velveteen jackets, his flowing ties. I had a college education, but, since I've delved at business I've given mighty little time to books, painting, music, the real beauty of life."

"You've delved and encouraged me to globe-trot. I've waked up to a few things. Won't it be tough for the family at the Manse when the mother takes the child?"

"The mother can't have her. Bruce Caswell chilled to steel on that point. He made his wife sign a contract that she would give up all claim to the little girl if he let her plea for a divorce go uncontested. I understand that there's another man waiting to marry Sybyl, but—on condition that she doesn't bring the child."

"He's made a condition! He can't be much in love with the mother. He—good Lord! I wonder . . ."

Alec Pryde! The name blazed into his mind as though set there in electrically lighted letters. He had heard that Alec had been playing round with a married woman named Caswell. The condition sounded like his selfishness. So, the trap had sprung. Alec was caught at last. He had nibbled at so many domestic cheeses and escaped. He had been his friend once. Only two days ago they had met at a houseparty. He had suggested that if Pryde were motoring near Sunnyfield he stop at Valleyview and try the shooting. Nice mess if he came. He was a fascinating companion. No wonder a silly woman would go off her head about him. In college days he had spent a vacation at Valleyview. Serena and Sally Hilliard had fallen helpless victims to his charm. Of late years Pryde and he had drifted apart. He wouldn't keep the pace of his crowd. And now a child was to be set aside for Alec. He voiced his thought;

"Poor little Betty. Unwanted."

"She's wanted by her grandfather and aunt and the girls are crazy about her. They keep her here every moment she'll stay. She's revolutionized their lives. She was a disobedient little savage when she came but Nancy won her heart and she's improving."

"How does Miss Caswell occupy her time? After living in New York I should think she'd go mad for something to do. Most of the young people have left the village."

"Something to do! She's the busiest woman in town. The more she does the more she seems able to take on. She has started a community chorus, she plays the organ in church, she's the town tennis champion and she keeps on with her profession."

"Making gardens for the summer people?"

"Yes. I shall have her change this geranium spattered lawn when I get the girls worked up to the idea. But she also makes garden spots of color, gaiety, beauty, happiness in our hearts. Most of the summer residents come and go leaving no beneficent impress on the life of the village but she has been a miracle-worker. It must have been hard for her to give up her business, her friends and the city which she loves, but, you'd never suspect it. 'Nancy has such gay courage,' her father says. I wish—that she could plant a little seed of interest and faith in women in your soul, Geoff. Feeling as you do you're an easy mark for—for a golddigger. Forgive me for butting in but sometimes I lie awake fearing . . ."

"Don't worry on that score, Squire. As far back as I can remember I hated cheapness. My dream of marriage was of something beautiful. The dream steered me straight between the Scylla and Charybdis of temptations in France. I came back to find it not worth a darn. In spite of that, deep down in my heart I've clung to my vision of beauty. Nothing cheap shall take its place."

"Thank you for this confidence, Geoffrey, I know that it has been hard. We Hilliards don't bare our hearts easily. You've taken a big load from my mind. You're the last of the name, remember. Good-night! See you in the morning. It's—it's great to have you here, boy."

Geoffrey lingered on the porch after his father had gone in. His throat had contracted uncomfortably in response to the emotion in the elder man's voice. It seemed as though every experience of the day had given a stir to what Nancy Caswell had called a patch of hard-caked earth. At least he had set the Squire's heart at rest about his choice of companions. All the old bitterness was gone, but, it had left his heart so cold that a seed of faith would be mightily chilled before it could send out roots.

He thoughtfully rapped his pipe against the vine-clad trellis. Nancy Caswell had accused him of trading on his disappointment. Was it strange that after two soul-searing, heartbreaking years at "the Front of the Front," with nerves stretched to the snapping-point, he should have turned to stone under the shock of discovering upon his return, that the girl to whom he had thought himself engaged, the girl who had been writing him impassioned letters, was already married? Her excuse that she hadn't had the heart to tell him that she loved another man while he was in the heat of the conflict, hadn't helped in the least.

Why dwell on it? All that was behind him. The realization that he had hardly thought of the girl in the last three years made Nancy Caswell's accusation the more unbearable.

He dropped his pipe into his pocket. How still the world was. The indigo dome overhead was pricked through and through with golden points of light. The frogs had ceased their chorus. The river crooned drowsily over the dam. A slight breeze, fruity with the breath of ripening apples, rustled the vine leaves. Could he stand it here? Had Nancy Caswell hated the country at first? But she kept busy. His father had said;

"She also makes garden spots of color, gaiety, beauty and happiness in our hearts."

A garden-maker! She'd stirred the patch of hard-caked earth she called his heart sufficiently to plant a choice collection of nettles, thistles and all things prickly, he'd tell the world. Was she equally interested in Luke Small's . . .

His eyes half closed. Luke Small. Was he double-crossing his employer? Was there something back of the magazine company's refusal to renew the contract? Had he evaded when the squire had put the straight question;

"When did he turn us down definitely?"

Geoffrey throttled the suspicion. It was absurd. Was that darnfool tea-cup reading of Nora's getting him? Hadn't his father said that he trusted Luke absolutely? If he were going to be suspicious of the trusted manager of the Hilliard Mills he'd better wind up his visit and return to New York. Luke didn't like him any too well now. His jealousy dated back to school days when the village boys had banded together as buccaneers and elected young Hilliard their chief. He had been sullenly resentful then, had tried to stage a mutiny, but the pirate crew, led by stocky, Irish Mac Donovan, had refused to follow him.

Mac! He hadn't thought of him for years. Coming home seemed to have turned his mind upside down. All afternoon memories of old days had been slipping through like grains of sand in an hour-glass. What had his father meant by;

"It is momentous, as you'll realize later."

With his hand on the knob of the door Geoffrey looked out over the valley spotted with lights, somnolent under the stars. Vague night sounds stirred the fragrant dusk. His glance rested on the moon-silvered roof of the Manse. "Such gay courage," his father had said. A solitary frog ch-chunked. He laughed and addressed the waterside ventriloquist softly;

"No use. Neither you nor Small can frighten me off. I'll keep tactfully in the background—for the present—but I'll stay."

Chapter IV

"Coo-ee!"

The call came from the direction of the iron gate in the hedge between Valleyview and the Manse. Geoffrey Hilliard stopped in his thoughtful pacing of the lawn, stopped trying to solve the problems which had rolled up like mountains of cumulous clouds on his clear horizon during the last twenty-four hours and looked up in response to the hail.

A little girl was swinging on the gate which squeaked excruciatingly with every motion. Her gingham frock, the shorts under it which revealed her dimpled knees, matched her eyes which were the color of larkspur, not quite blue, not quite violet. Her hair was pale gold, her skin as soft, satiny, pink, as the petals of a butterfly rose. Nipping at her heels was a wirehair terrier. He was white except for the smooch which blacked one eye and one floppy ear. He stopped nipping to bark furiously as Hilliard approached. The child stopped swinging.

"Hulloa!"

"Hulloa!" Geoffrey responded.

She regarded him for a moment before her lips curved in an enchanting smile which showed white teeth, small, even, gleaming like pearls. She started the gate again with a quick movement of her fat little stomach. She swung back and forth to a squeaky accompaniment as she volunteered;

"I know who you are."

"Who am I?"

"The Prod—Prod'gal Son." She swelled visibly with pride over her achievement of pronunciation. Geoffrey felt the angry color surge to his hair as he thought, "So, that's what Miss Caswell dubs me in the bosom of her family!" Bigger and bluer grew the child's eyes as she demanded;

"What you getting so red for? Isn't it nice to be a
prod'gal son? Didn't he get the best robe an' the fattest
calf? My gran-farver, Gran, I call him, reads that story to
me when I'm tucked in bed. I asked Nanny why your
name was Prod'gal Son an' she said 'twas 'cause you
wasted your her'tance in *ri'*tous living. What's *ri'*tous
living?"

"Better ask your aunt, she seems to know so much
about it." The response wiped the light from the laughing,
radiant face. Geoffrey repented. Why should he hold the
little thing responsible for the disagreeable traits of Nancy
Caswell? He dropped to one knee to pat the terrier who
twisted himself into an S of ecstasy in response. He smiled
up at the child;

"Nice dog you have here?"

Steel to magnet. She jumped from the gate and ran to
him.

"You look ever so much nicer when you smile."

"Do I? Then I'll try always to smile at you. My name
is Geoff. What's yours?"

"Betty Caswell, Gran calls me Betty Blueskin 'cause I
al-*us* wear blue clothes, I guess. I live at the Manse,
Sunnyfield. I have to know that case I'm lost." She
dropped to the lawn beside him and clasped the vocifer-
atingly resisting dog in her chubby arms. She dug her
dimpled chin into the top of his fuzzy head as she informed;

"His name's Scooty."

Geoffrey nodded in the direction of the iron dog.

"His name's Spotty."

"Is he your dog?"

"Yes. He was my best friend when I was as little as
you are."

The child hitched nearer to lean contentedly against the
man's shoulder. He slipped an arm about her. She snuggled close.

"I'd like to see my Daddy." With a control far beyond
her years she steadied her little cupid's bow lips and went
on, "You're nice, Prod'gal Son. Tell me a story about
Spotty an' you when you were little like I am."

With slight confidence in his powers as a juvenile enter-
tainer Geoffrey plunged in the good old fashion;

"Once upon a time there was a little boy . . ."

"Betty! Bet—*ty!*"

The call came from the Manse side of the hedge. The child hitched a degree nearer her companion.

"Don't stop, That's only Phyl-*us.*"

"Who is Phyl-*us?*"

"She's the cook-lady's daughter at our house. She's s'posed to look after me. I never mind her 'less I want to. Go on, about your dog Spotty."

Hilliard promptly set the child on her feet and regained his.

"You'll mind her this time. Come on."

He caught her by the hand. As she skipped and hopped to keep up with his long stride, she protested strenuously;

"What you makin' such a fuss 'bout, Prod'gal Son? Oh—oh, there's Nanny," she shrieked as they passed through the gateway. The child dashed toward Nancy Caswell standing in the middle of the stepping-stone path. Hilliard disciplined an impulse to retreat and stopped. His eyes were coolly cynical as he regarded the girl. She stood straight and slim in her green sports frock against a background of clear pale yellow in the flower border. The air was spicy with the scent of old-fashioned cinnamon pinks.

The structure of anger against her which he had been erecting in his heart tilted a bit as he noted the shadows about her eyes, the faint droop of the vivid lips. She swayed under the impact of child and dog as they flung themselves upon her. Barbarians! Couldn't they see that she was tired? She acknowledged his presence with a curt little nod before she inquired;

"Didn't I hear Phyllis calling you, Betty? Where were you? Not off the grounds, I hope."

The culprit inserted a grimy finger between her pearly teeth. She dug into the turf with one stubby shoe. Scooty, on his haunches, head cocked, regarded her judicially from his blackened eye as she explained;

"Not really off, Nanny, I was swingin' on the hedge gate—it's got such a nice squeak—an' it opened itself, an' then the Prod'gal Son came an'—what you getting so red for?" she demanded as Nancy Caswell's face turned a

lovely pink. There was a glint in Geoffrey Hilliard's voice
and eyes as he explained;

"She's blushing with annoyance because she didn't think
of that name for me herself."

"But she did! I told you she did," protested the child
eagerly. She danced up to him and caught his hands. With
her two dirty little shoes braced against his immaculate
white ones she swung like a chubby boat at anchor,
abbreviated blue skirts, pale gold hair flying as she announced;

"I'm the Prod'gal Son's sweetie. Aren't I, Prod'gal
Son?"

"Sweetie! Where did you pick up that word?" demanded
her aunt.

"I didn't pick it up. I heard it. Phyl-*us* said you were
Luke Small's sweetie an' . . ."

Nancy Caswell caught the child by the shoulder.

"Betty! Let her go please, Mr. Hilliard." As Geoffrey
released the little hands she turned her small niece firmly
in the direction of the white house with its yellow shutters. "Go in to your supper at once."

Head on one side the child regarded her. She parleyed;

"You cross 'cause I'm the Prod'gal Son's sweetie, Nanny? Phyl-*us* said when he came next door . . ."

"I'm not in the least interested in what Phyllis said. She
talks altogether too much."

Geoffrey Hilliard caught the child's warm, dirty little
hand in his and encouraged softly;

"I'd like to hear what Phyllis said."

Betty looked from one to the other appraisingly. She
capitulated to the man's smiling, intent eyes.

"Phyl-*us* said when you came yesterday;

" 'Ain't he the han'some Sheik! He's a knock-out. Miss
Nancy won't like him though, he's too lazy. She likes 'em
peppy.' Are you lazy, Prod'gal Son?"

Hilliard's laughter-brimmed eyes met the defiant eyes
of Nancy Caswell as he declared;

"Sometimes, Betty, but not when I've made up my
mind that I want a thing. Run to Phyllis now." As the
child lingered he added gravely, "If you're my sweetie,
you've got to mind."

"Do sweeties mind?"

"Mine do."

Betty's tone was wistful.

"Have you lots of sweeties, Prod'gal Son?"

He caught her up in his arms. He pressed his lips against her soft neck faintly fragrant of scented talcum and whispered;

"It's a secret. You're the only one."

She gurgled and wriggled and laughed.

"You—you tickle."

She flung her arms about his neck. She pressed her soft cheek against his. With a child's quick change from gay to grave she approved solemnly;

"You're mos's nice as my Daddy."

Geoffrey deposited her on the porch and figuratively into the waiting arms of the indignant Phyllis. She was a plump, shapeless girl whose skin suggested a diet of chocolates, whose slightly open mouth bespoke adenoids. Her eyes, seen through the thick lenses of horn-rimmed spectacles, shifted beneath direct gaze with dog-like evasion. Her not too slender legs were encased in shimmering near-silk hose of incredible thinness, her painfully bright blue dress was protected by a scrap of apron spattered with roses of a size and color to make the ghost of Burbank quaver with envy. She seized the child's hand. Her carelessly slurred words were not unkind, merely impatient as she reminded;

"Don't you know that this is my night for the movies, Betty Caswell? An' you late to supper! Ain't life humorous! I'll get you in early tomorrow an' I don't mean maybe."

The high-pitched childish voice floated back from the hall;

"All dressed up in your bestest dress, Phyl-us? Goin' wif your boyfrien'? I'm somebody's sweetie too."

With a laugh Geoffrey Hilliard turned to the girl who still stood in the path looking at the doorway through which her niece had disappeared.

"Hear that? Somebody loves me—unless the lady turns fickle like the majority of her sex." Pain from an old wound long since healed surged in his voice. Nancy Caswell's face was white as she protested vehemently;

"No! No! Betty isn't fickle. She—she mustn't be!"

Hilliard's eyes widened in surprise. Why should she take his cynical thrust, of which already he was ashamed, so seriously? Then he remembered. Her brother's wife, the child's mother, was "Renoing." The girl's evident distress toppled his barricade of anger.

"Look here, Miss Caswell, can't I help? You look dead tired."

"I am. Ever try to do anything and have someone combat you at every step? I've been superintending the planting of an iris bed. The work didn't tire me, it was shouting at the owner who is deaf and who has views of her own on planting. I fought and died over every bulb that went in because I knew if it wasn't done my way, it wouldn't come up as it should, then where would my reputation as a garden-maker be?"

His eyes warmed into sympathetic laughter.

"Take me on as an assistant. I'll do the fighting for you. I don't know an iris bulb from a potato but I'm husky. I can dig. You see, I'm offering the olive branch."

"The olive branch! Yesterday you were burying the hatchet."

Gold stars of laughter lighted the depths of her brown eyes. Geoffrey had the sense as of an elixir stealing through his veins, warming him, breaking up the ice of disillusion, much as the spring breaks up a frozen stream. Little as he liked girls, much as he distrusted them, he'd admit that she was adorable when she smiled, he told himself. He hastened to profit by her unexpected friendliness;

"You owe me something for that Prodigal Son tag. Betty will never forget it."

"I pay my debts."

"Mean it? Then play tennis with me tomorrow at the Club. I'll call for you at three. After the game we'll . . ."

He left the sentence suspended to stare at an Hispano Torpedo, sportiest of the sporty which stopped in the road. The two standing side by side in the path watched without speaking as a man alighted from the car, opened the gate and approached hat in hand. Hilliard recognized his blond good looks, his arrogant carriage which proclaimed an attitude of convinced superiority. Alec Pryde! In response to his invitation. He glanced at the girl beside him. Did she recognize the man who had broken up her brother's home? She was curiously still. A set smile curved her lips. He had a feeling that her spirit even was holding its breath. Would she turn her back on the intruder? He must get him away, he decided, in the instant before Pryde greeted him buoyantly;

"They told me next door that I'd find you here, Geoff. Got beastly sick of our noisy crowd, of doing the same old things in the same old way. Decided to accept your invitation."

He looked from Hilliard to the girl beside him with an assured smile. Waiting to be presented, was he? Well, he wouldn't be. Geoffrey ignored the suggestion in voice and manner, slipped his arm through Pryde's and turned him in the direction of the front gate.

"The aunts will be pleased to see you, Alec. Come on."

The girl laughed.

"Your friend's manners are not of the best, are they, Mr.—Alec? I'm Nancy Caswell."

"That name will give him pause," Geoffrey thought. But Pryde gave no hint that it held significance. To be all things to every attractive woman he met had become a science and an art with him. He responded with flattering eagerness;

"Geoff's a cold fish. Youth, beauty and charm have no appeal for him. He thinks everyone else is like himself. I'm Alec Pryde at your service. Very much at your service."

Now what? The girl must know the name of the man her sister-in-law was planning to marry. But not even so much as a wisp of a cloud dimmed the brilliance of her laughing eyes. Her smile was radiant as she encouraged gaily;

"Don't be reckless with your promises. You're to be our next door neighbor for a while. I shall be horribly tempted to put you to the test. Good-bye—for the present."

She ran along the path and dashed into the house as though pursued by the Furies. Hilliard looked after her.

" 'Ain't life humorous!' " he muttered under his breath.

Pryde linked an arm in his.

"What are you growling about, old scout?" He squared

his shoulders, set his costly Panama hat at a rakish angle
as he approved;

"I certainly had the right hunch when I turned in this
direction."

Chapter V

The flicker of crimson on the living room ceiling of the Manse faded to a pink tinge. Twilight stole softly in. Shadows on old mahogany deepened. Outlines of books on tables, books on shelves, blurred. In a filmy green gown which made a lovely note of contrast among the tans and browns of the room, Nancy Caswell looked out upon the garden, a blotch of pastel colors in the dusk. A canary in a gilded cage hanging in a plant filled bay, trilled response to the sleepy twitter of a retiring feathered tenant of a gnarled old apple tree outside the window. In a corner a clock, ceiling high, ticked off the minutes ponderously. A cheery fire crackled an invitation, sent out the faint smoky tang of burning wood.

The girl's eyes lingered on the western sky where silver-gilt isles floated in a rosy sea of afterglow. Her thoughts were on the indistinct rumble of her father's voice in the room overhead as he read to Betty. She pictured the child in her little white bed, lids ever so slightly drooping over blue eyes, a chubby hand clutching Scooty's ear as he stretched out beside her, unashamedly asleep.

She crossed to a table and picked up the framed photograph of a man who looked enough like her to be a twin. Bruce! Her heart ached unbearably for him in his trouble. Another day gone of the wife and mother's self-elected exile. Did Betty miss her? Since the first week of her arrival at the Manse she had not mentioned her. Bruce had said that the child had been left day after day with a maid while Sybyl danced and teaed and bridged. For weeks she had cried at bedtime for her Daddy. What a mess! What a tragedy! Even if she had ceased to love her husband how could a mother give up that adorable little girl? Betty was like a plant wrenched up by the roots, its life threatened by a major operation. Sybyl had been the

victim of a brain-storm, that must be the explanation. She
had been brought up by an aunt to marry for money.
When she chose a man without any she had been cast off
with an elaborate wedding, nothing else. The aunt had
had other views for her. Was she financing this divorce?
If not where was Sybyl getting the money? Not from
Bruce.

Seated at the piano Nancy's supple fingers charmed the
still ivory keys into rippling sound, she improvised a soft,
flowing accompaniment to her thoughts as they surged
on;

Had the other man financed the divorce excursion? Her
face whitened with disgust at the suggestion. The first she
and her father had known of the sordid matter had been
when Bruce had appeared at the Manse with Betty. It had
seemed as though she couldn't bear that such unhappiness
should smirch her brother's life. He and she had been
devoted comrades in spite of ten years' difference in their
ages. While she had had his companionship other men
had counted with her not at all. It had been hard enough
to give him up to Sybyl and now to have him unhappy—
it was unendurable. She expressed her feeling in a culmi-
nating crash of chords.

"Whom did you think you had under the piano keys
then, Nan?" her father laughed as he entered the room
with a book in his hand.

"I wish I had had Sybyl. I was thinking of the excuse
Bruce gave for her marrying as soon as her divorce is
granted;

" 'What else can she do? She has no money, no business training.'

"Think of a woman or girl marrying to be taken care
of in this year of Our Lord. It seems as though I couldn't
bear the sordidness of it for Bruce or Betty."

Noah Caswell pulled the chain of a lamp and flooded
the room with a soft glow.

"That's better. We'll face our problems in the light. It
seems as though I couldn't bear having this extra responsibility of the child laid on your shoulders, Nan. You've
mothered Bruce and me since your mother died when you
were sixteen, you've had the anxiety of this upset of
mine—oh, I know how the doctors frightened you—you

gave up your work in town. You've taken on care and
borne disappointment with gay courage but I know what
it means. An I've-a-right-to-live-my-own-life individualist
like Sybyl, usually lives her own life by dumping her
burdens on another's shoulders. The situation is searing us
all but think what Sybyl is doing to herself." With the
book still in his hand he dropped to the wing chair by the
fire.

"Sing to me, dear."

The girl pushed a stool under his feet and returned to
the piano. She struck the rich, deep opening chords of the
hymn her father loved. Her voice was clear with a beautiful resonance in its fuller notes. Her eyes were on the
afterglow, her thoughts with her brother as she sang;

> " 'Day is dying in the west;
> Heaven is touching earth with rest;
> Wait and worship while the night
> Sets her evening lamps alight
> Thro' all the sky.' "

Her hands fell to her lap. Her father's voice roused her
from thoughts of Bruce.

"Thank you, my dear. There's a thread of buoyancy in
your voice to which my spirit responds as to a bugle
call." There was evident an attempt to speak lightly as he
inquired;

"Do you know what Betty Blueskin calls our young
neighbor, Geoffrey Hilliard?"

His daughter forsook the piano for the arm of his
chair.

"Yes. I'm responsible for that. She overheard me calling him the Prodigal Son to you yesterday."

"Except for the rejoicing of the household across the
hedge I can see no resemblance in his return to that of the
Biblical renegade. He shows no indication of riotous living. There isn't a suggestion of dissipation of any kind
about him. I ought to be a judge, I diagnosed the symp-
toms often enough in my city parish. Indolent on the
surface he may be, but he has unplumbed depths of power,
I'll warrant. His mouth shows that and temper, but, temper thoroughly under brake control. A lovable mouth.

Where did he get the impression that I wrote to him? In spite of his denial I have a feeling that he still thinks I sent that letter."

Nancy's voice was slightly muffled as she confessed;

"I wrote it."

"You! And signed my name?"

She felt the blood burn in her cheeks as she became absorbed in the bowing of her father's tie.

"Not quite so bad as that, Dad. I typed the letter and signed, 'N. Caswell.' I won't deny that I hoped he'd think you wrote it. I realize now that it was a silly thing to do, but, I had been having supper with the Hilliards and the one subject mentioned by the Squire and his sisters had been, 'Geoffrey.' 'Geoff' likes this. 'Geoffrey' said that. They touched tenderly upon the disillusion of his broken engagement. That happened years ago. He should have recovered from it by this time."

"From the heartache, yes. But, remember, he had been in the thick of the World War, he had endured about all mortal nerves can endure overseas. He was young. He was in an abnormal state. The shock of dicovering the girl's perfidy on his return was the last straw."

"Evidently it was. His aunts are troubled as to his future. They adore him. That little cynical smile which just touches his lips and eyes, the perfection of his clothes, the perfection of his hand with that curious seal ring, in the photograph in the living room at Valleyview got on my nerves. Every day when I looked at it ..."

Noah Caswell interrupted bluntly;

"Why look at it?"

"It has a sort of hypnotic attraction."

"Um-m, I see. Go on about the letter."

"On my way home that night I considered sending a nice, little ladylike bomb which should jolt him into a realization of his selfishness with his people. Then I thought of asking you to write him. Then I knew that you wouldn't. I wrote myself. I'm stiff with mortification when I think of it."

"You have reason to be. I never knew you to dip your fingers into the affairs of another person before. Your 'bomb' exploded as per schedule. He's here. He must think me an interfering old Fix-it."

"He doesn't. He knows that I wrote the letter. When you appeared dazed at mention of it he third-degreed me with his eyes. Of course I blushed furiously. I'd never made a successful diplomat or detective, I'm too darn transparent."

"I'm glad that he knows. Betty Blueskin has succumbed to his charm. I don't wonder. He's delightful. She told me tonight that she was his 'sweetie.' "

"You're not the only one to whom she announced the glad tidings. She told Geoffrey Hilliard himself. Phillis is devoted to Betty, takes excellent care of her but we must do something to combat her argot. One year as salesgirl in a New York department store basement has crammed it full of slang. Doubtless by this time it is quite out of date but its effect is the same on Betty as if it were the current vintage. Since the child came to us I've used a fine-tooth rake on my own vocabulary. I retain 'darn.' It lets off steam. You've no idea how it helps. I recommend it. Did Betty keep awake while you read?"

"A little droopy at the close. She insisted upon my reading the Parable of the Prodigal Son. So early she has learned to appreciate one of the greatest short stories in the world. 'And a certain man had two sons,' " Noah Caswell quoted in his rich voice.

Nancy laughed and smoothed the silken silver of his hair.

"I hate to discourage you but I'm afraid that its literary merit doesn't count with her. She likes the color, the drama of the story, the robe, the ring and what she calls, 'the fattest calf.' "

"At least she is learning to know the greatest book in the world. It is the inalienable right of all children to be grounded in that knowledge. If later they elect to ignore it, at least they have been given their chance. I want Betty to have hers at all the fine things of life. Then, if temptation attacks her, as it has her mother, she'll have a firm grip on a higher standard."

"You and I will cultivate and seed the soil in which her character takes root until it sends forth lusty plants of goodness, honor, sweetness and gaiety. You see, I can't help thinking in garden terms." She rested her cheek

against the top of his white head, "Life seems just one
problem after another, doesn't it?"

"Sometimes it does, my dear. And yet, I'd rather spend
my days in this sweating, bleeding, blundering old world
than in those Fortunate Fields or the Isles of the Blessed
whither mortals favored by the gods were transported to
enjoy an immortality of bliss. Remember Moore's song;

> " 'I come from a land in the sun bright-deep,
>   Where golden gardens grow;
>   Where the winds of the North, becalmed in sleep,
>   Their conch-shells never blow.' "

"Wouldn't it be boring never to hear the modern
equivalent of a conch-shell, an automobile horn?" Nancy
returned to the piano bench. Hands gripping its edge she
leaned forward as she asked;

"Whom do you think walked in through our gateway
today?" She answered the question in his eyes;

"Alec Pryde."

Noah Caswell's clear skin darkened with anger.

"What did he want?"

"He was looking for Geoffrey Hilliard. He had dropped
down on Valleyview for a visit."

"Doesn't young Hilliard know?"

"From his expression as of a suddenly awakened sleep-
walker when Pryde appeared I should say that he did.
But what does such a contretemps mean in this world
where ditched husbands and wives attend the same house-
parties? However, he did try to get him away without
presenting him to me."

"Did he succeed?"

"I introduced myself."

"Nan! Why?"

"Because I had an inspiration. Suppose Alec Pryde
stays on here for a while? Suppose he were to become
even slightly interested in someone else?—he must be a
congenital philanderer or he wouldn't have made love to a
married woman—Suppose he were to change his mind
about marrying Sybyl on her triumphal return from
Reno? Bruce and Betty would be spared the disgrace of
her immediate marriage, at least."

"And so would Sybyl. Don't forget her, Nan."

"I don't. I think of her constantly. When I succeeded in getting the best of my furious jealousy of her—oh, I know how hateful I was about Bruce's engagement—I liked her. I can't help feeling that she's the victim of a heart-storm, first cousin to a brain-storm, the sort which makes people do crazy, queer things. If she divorced Bruce to marry another man how long will she be satisfied with him? Even if she loves Alex Pryde to distraction let her wait a decent interval to make sure that this isn't another mistake. If she marries him at once, because she has no money, I believe that she'll start on a swift toboggan slide to tragedy."

"What is Pryde like?"

"Good-looking. About Geoffrey Hilliard's build. Blond. Cruel eyes. You're-the-only-girl-in-the-world manner and a plushy voice."

"I understand your plan, Nan. I don't like it. Suppose you fell in love with him? I've made inquiries. From long practice his technique with women has reached superb perfection. His past is littered as thick with the skeletons of affairs as a covered wagon-trail of the Forties was scattered with whitening bones."

"A hardy perennial charmer, is he? But what does one get out of life if one never takes a chance, Dad. If he really loves Sybyl my plan won't do any harm. If he doesn't, and she is to be just one more skeleton left to bleach it's worth a try. I don't mean to deliberately try to vamp him. I'll just be nice to him."

"Hmp! I've seen you 'nice' to people. Luke Small haunts this house."

"I'm Luke's confidante. He talks to me—mostly—of himself, when he isn't slamming Geoffrey Hilliard. He monologues by the hour on his ambitions. . . ."

"The soul of man searching always for his Eden, his Atlantis, the lost land lying to the westward," interrupted Noah Caswell.

"You're an incorrigible optimist, Dad. To borrow from the phraseology of the incomparable Phyl-*us,* I'll tell the cockeyed world that Luke's Eden is paved with gold, his lost land lying to the westward is a mirage of business success. Power! Power! Power! is his battle-cry."

"He won't be a power if he deserts Peter Hilliard, the man who has given him the chance to forge ahead."

"Luke contends that he has no chance there, that it's a dying concern. He hasn't said so, but I have the feeling that always he has feared the son's return to take a hand in the business. But to go back to Alec Pryde. We'll ask him here. We won't let him suspect that we know that he touches our lives. I can camouflage my contempt but I'm a little afraid of you. You're a good deal of a fire-eater if you are a clergyman."

"This time I'll dissemble, Nan. For the honor of the family. If we succeed in preventing Sybyl's marriage to him until a fairly decent interval has elapsed we will have accomplished something, we will have given her a chance to think things through. This off with the old marriage and on with the new while the divorce decree is red-hot seems to me so tragically wrong."

"Wrong or right it's tragically cheap. Remember, you're to watch your eyes and voice."

"I'll remember. If I feel that I must blow off steam I'll confide in Peter Hilliard. I love the man. He stands for the best. The thought of his being worried financially hurts unbearably."

"It hurts me, too. That's one reason why I am so furious with his son. Spending his youth collecting books!"

Noah Caswell tenderly smoothed the testament he held.

"But, books are so worth-while. Don't be one of those narrow-minded persons who see in collecting only a fad. Think what collectors have done for this country. They've enriched it with untold treasure from an older civilization. They've preserved for its own, historical objects from country taverns to pewter bowls, paid for out of their own pockets too."

"I realize that, but I resent Geoffrey Hilliard's spending the best part of his life on those things when there are humans in this town who need developing and a lot of history forcibly fed to them. What will happen to the mills which mean so much to this community if his father breaks down? Why doesn't he come here and follow the business? Can't he see that the Squire needs him? Can't he see ..."

"He can," assured Geoffrey Hilliard from the threshold.

Surprise set Nancy's heart to thumping until it seemed to shake her body. She set her lips hard in an effort to control it. It had clamored like this yesterday when she had looked up from her fall to see the eyes of the photograph which had seemed to hypnotize her gazing down into hers, to see the hand with its curious seal ring held out to her. Then she had accounted for the tumult by fright at her fall, but, here it was again—darn! She sensed her father's amused appreciation of the situation. Was he laughing at her? The younger man's cool, challenging eyes met the elder man's as he explained;

"I knocked and knocked. No answer. Hearing your voices I walked in. Opportunely, I judge. The telephone is on strike so the aunts sent me over to ask if you both would have supper with us tomorrow night to meet . . ."

"Mr. Pryde?" Nancy supplied, as he hesitated as though loath to have the name cross his lips. He was a poor dissembler. She slipped her arm within her father's and administered a reminding squeeze.

"Tell Miss Serena and Miss Sally that we shall be charmed to come. Your friend looks as though he might be great fun and what Phyl-*us*, the discerning, would call 'peppy.' Dad, you'll admire him. He's Apollo Belvedere in the Vatican come to life."

> " 'Bright-haired Apollo! Thou who ever art
> A blessing to the world—whose mighty heart
> Forever pours out love and light and life.
> Thou . . .' "

As Noah Caswell paused in his theatrical quotation for a word Geoffrey Hilliard cut in crisply;

" 'Forever pours out love' is right. Alec's a glittering testimonial as to the *n*th power to which philandering may be raised."

"Nancy tells me that she has explained to you that I did not write that letter."

The lightning of anger in the electrically charged atmosphere ran harmlessly off through Noah Caswell's rich voice. The air cleared. His daughter laughed.

"Fools rush in where angels fear to tread. I've confessed to Dad that I was the butter-in and received absolution. Will you forgive me, Mr. Hilliard?"

"Judgment deferred. Case under consideration. How does my father seem to you, Mr. Caswell?"

"Much better. Months at golf instead of the mills have been worth all the business worry which I suspect has followed. Your little visit will help set him on his feet. While you are here his problems will drop off much as Christian lost his burdens. When he turns to pick them up some of them won't be there. When you go . . ."

"I'm not going. I'm here to stay."

Nancy experienced the sensation of being dropped several floors in a lift. Here to stay! Was she responsible? When she had written that letter to him, which now she realized had been an unwarrantable piece of interference, her motive had been to make him appreciate what an occasional visit from him would mean to the family at Valleyview. Here to stay! What effect would his staying have on the manager of the mills? She met his eyes. He commented curtly;

"You look frightened. Because I'm staying? Little girls shouldn't set sparks to fuses unless they're game to watch them go off. Good-night!"

He departed as suddenly as he had appeared. A too emphatically closed door shook the firearms. Noah Caswell regarded his daughter quizzically as he confessed;

"I was about to vociferate my opinion of Pryde and my refusal to meet him when I remembered our compact. I blew off steam with that flowery quotation. It was a near explosion." His lips twitched as he observed irrelevantly;

"Strangely potent this thing we call, for want of a better name, 'attraction,' isn't it?"

Chapter VI

Arms crossed on the shaggy cedar railing of the bridge, Nancy Caswell gazed down at the brook while the blue of the sky overhead deepened, shadows crept higher on the suntipped trees, a fat old spider craftily wove his gossamer ropes from twig to twig. The swift water sang and hummed and tinkled as it tumbled over moss-green boulders, purled over broad flat stones, eddied over pebbly bottoms or in dark pools beneath overhanging willows. The banks of the stream were gay with color. Flames of sumach, enormous nuggets of goldenrod, purple asters, tall russet brakes, dwarf crimson maple, clumps of burdock rioted against a towering background of spruce and firs. The girl's sweater, skirt and soft hat were the only spots of clear green in the landscape.

A glorious world, she thought. Why need it be cluttered and choked with the weeds of dishonor and greed and faithlessness until one wondered if ideals were as old-fashioned as the flowers of early nineteenth century gardens had been for a time. But, the hardy perennials had come into their own again. Perhaps living up to high standards of honor and courage would come back into fashion too. Hasten the day.

She sniffed ecstatically. Mint! She loved the pungent fragrance. She watched a cloud of golden butterflies rise from a clump of dried burdock and float away in twos and threes till they faded into a delicate yellow mist. She smiled down at a water-strider, skipping over the surface with his three pairs of legs casting six oval shadows, silver rimmed, watched it disappear, reappear. As it darted out of sight she returned to her contemplation of the brook which widened two hundred feet below the bridge, where it divided to encircle a miniature island. It united again in a small cascade—from which rose a glamorous mist of spray shot through and through with rainbows, red, orange, yellow, green, blue, indigo, violet—before it plunged on to join the river glinting in the distance.

Nancy regarded the island curiously. How had that towering mass, which looked like a heap of field-rock, come there? Washed up by the brook? The bit of water enclosed land was a tangle of vines and bushes, brilliant with bittersweet. The most glorious she had ever seen. Its berries shone as though burnished. She visualized great bowls of it in the tan and brown living room at the Manse. Could she get it? She leaned far over the rail. A worn path ambled from the end of the bridge along the bank till it met a broader trail which shot off at right angles as though it knew right well where it was going and was on its way. Where the two paths met a felled tree made a bridge between shore and island.

Almost too easy, Nancy thought as she started down the declining path. Her hat caught in a swinging rope of wild grapes, heavy with fruit not quite purple, not quite green. She nibbled at a bunch as she picked her way along to the tree trunk. She tested it with her foot. The small end rested on the island. Fairly steady. She looked across at the bittersweet. It was even more desirable than it had seemed from the bridge.

She started across. Half way over the log rolled treacherously. Her arms described a parabola as she struggled to maintain her balance. The tree-trunk steadied. Better go on now that she'd started. Step by cautious step she went forward. At the island end the log seemed to cling by a mere breath. Would it turn again under her feet? She jumped. The sudden release of her weight spun the log free. The swift water caught it, whirled it exultantly, shot it down the cascade, on toward the river.

Speechlessly, incredulously the girl watched it go. She looked upstream, downstream, about the island, measured the distance to the shore. Not far but she had no idea of the depth of the water. It looked treacherous and— extremely wet. The brook tinkled and tumbled as though mocking her. Would it like to sweep her along as it had the log? Nothing doing. She'd wait until someone passed on the bridge road. Would anyone pass? It was a private way between Valleyview and the mills through the Hilliard estate. The Squire and his son used it. She would wait until dusk, if no one came before she would wade across.

The air chilled. The declining sun deserted the treetops. As Nancy culled great masses of bittersweet her thoughts returned to the subject which was never far from her mind. Bruce. It was the middle of September. Not quite two weeks since Alec Pryde had appeared at Valleyview. Serena and Sally Hilliard were obviously fascinated by his charm. They urged him to stay on and on. Was it because they enjoyed him or did they fear that his going would curtail their nephew's visit?

Since he had hurled that defiant, "I'm here to stay!" in the Manse living room she had heard nothing more of Geoffrey Hilliard's plans. She didn't care for the glint in his eyes when they met hers. Did he see through her flimsy scheme to show Alec Pryde in his true colors, to give Sybyl a chance to think things through, or did he index her as one more victim of his friend's fascination? When they were together perhaps she was a bit more friendly to Alec than necessary, she intentionally beamed upon Luke. Luke was a puzzle. Why should he resent Geoffrey's presence at Valleyview? Apparently the Hilliard son and heir was indifferent as to what happened to the business. When he and Luke were together he gave the impression of Paul at the feet of Gamaliel. Quite as though he were looking for information and counsel. Of course he wasn't. Undertones. She was conscious of them whenever the two men were together.

She deposited the bittersweet on the ground that she might investigate the mass of field-rock. A cave! Facing the river! High enough, broad enough to accommodate a half dozen persons. The entrance must have been overgrown with bushes for half of it had been recently cleared. From where she stood she could see across the breeze rippled river. Someone had been at work inside too. The jutting roof had been stripped of vines of Virginia creeper which grew riotously on the outside. The floor was covered with freshly cut spruce boughs, the place was spicy with their fragrance. Who had done this? Bootleggers?

She hastily returned to the pile of bittersweet and dropped down beside it to watch the bridge. She consulted her wrist watch. Four o'clock and growing darker and colder in the brook every moment. If only the Squire would appear. Often he walked back and forth. Even if he couldn't get to her he would send someone who could throw a dead tree across, do something. Rather good fun to wade if someone were on the other side.

She thoughtfully chewed a blade of dry grass as she reflected on Peter Hilliard's light-heartedness. Was the change due to the companionship of his son? Geoffrey never seemed to be doing anything constructive. His manner was intolerably indifferent, when it wasn't cynical. Except with Betty. That affair was progressing by leaps and bounds. She obeyed him without argument. He was her oracle. He told her stories of the rollicking adventures of the boy buccaneers on the river, he read to her, carried her through the opening in the hedge to have dinner with his aunts—the Misses Hilliard still dined at noon and with pre-war abundance—brought her curious things he had picked up on his travels. Now they had a secret. A mysterious secret. The child adored him. Pity he couldn't have been the man—if there had to be one—whom Sybyl had elected to be Bruce's successor. Disgusting thought! Much as she disliked him, much as he infuriated her, she'd admit that he would no more carry on an affair with another man's wife than he would steal.

She sprang to her feet. A rustle! A human rustle among the willows on the bank. Had she been right in her suspicion? Had bootleggers taken possession of the island? Wide-eyed she watched as a man appeared in hunting togs with a gun over his shoulder and a knife in one hand. Geoffrey Hilliard! Across the swift-flowing, foaming water he regarded her with cool, aloof eyes as he observed;

"I've been watching you for the last few minutes while I was cutting willow for a whistle for Betty. I'll bet a hat you were thinking of me. I've learned to recognize the disdainful curve of your lips when you're meditating on my sins of omission and commission."

Nancy felt the betraying color steal to her hair. Would she ever, ever outgrow the imbecile habit of blushing, she demanded of herself furiously. She opened her lips to refute the charge. He anticipated her reply.

"Don't jeopardize your chance of heaven by denying it.

Before Pryde appeared on the scene I thought for a mad moment that you and I would be friends. Not a chance." For the first time he noticed the absence of the connection between shore and island; "Good Lord, how did you get over there?"

"On a tree-trunk."

"Where is it now?"

"Flowing safe to sea with the river, I suspect." She held up the mass of bittersweet. "I came across for this. Jumped when I felt the log turn and—here I am. I've always been curious about that heap of fieldrock. I've had plenty of time to investigate. Now I know what it is. The bootleggers' retreat."

He laughed.

"Nothing so modern. The boy buccaneers built that over twenty years ago. How we tugged at those stones. How our families fumed to think that that labor couldn't be turned in on lawns and flower beds." He rested his gun against a tree and dropped his knife into his pocket. "I'm coming over for you."

"No. No! I'll wade across."

"Wrong wave-length. You'll do nothing of the kind. The stream is swift here, the rocks under it treacherous and the water—wet."

Nancy clutched her armful of bittersweet. Nice predicament she had landed herself in, she scoffed mentally, as she watched the water swirl about his knees. He held out his arms as he put one foot on the shore of the island.

"Come on."

"W-what are you going to do?"

His eyes widened in amazement.

"Do? Carry you of course."

"I'm—heavy."

He looked her over appraisingly.

"Are you? Put your arms about my neck. Drop that bittersweet. I'll come back for it."

She clutched her treasure closer.

"Oh no, I . . ."

He picked her up as unceremoniously as he had the day of the storm and waded into the stream. Half way across he slipped on a mossy stone. With instinctive effort at selfpreservation the girl dropped the bittersweet and

caught him about the neck. Close against his shoulder she
could hear the furious thumping of his heart. She was
heavy. She looked up at him. He was white under his tan;
the light in his eyes tripped up her breath. He stopped for
an instant to observe;

"You deserve to be dropped into this stream."

Instinctively she clung tighter. The muscles of his jaw
set before he swished on. She avoided his eyes as he
released her. She was humiliated beyond words at the way
she had clutched him when she thought he was going
down. She looked at the bittersweet bobbing and floating
down stream. His glance followed hers.

"You sure hate advice, don't you? You don't deserve it
but I'll cross to the island and get you some more."

He ignored her protest and waded in. She watched him
cross. How sure-footed he was. Watched him as he
gathered the burnished berries, watched his return. Not a
slip this time. She held the brilliant mass close in her arms
as she acknowledged gaily in spite of a persistent thumping in her breast;

"Thank you. Next time my artistic urge and curiosity
lure me on I'll make sure there is a reliable bridge. Where
does this path lead?"

He picked up his gun.

"Straight as the crow flies to the garden gate of Valleyview. The buccaneers discovered it to be the shortest
cut from Nora's cookie jar to their fastness on the island."

Nancy went on without speaking. She could hear the
water slosh in his high boots as he followed. He fell into
step beside her as the path lost itself in a broad, wind-
swept field lapped by the ripple of the blue and green
river, bordered with clumps of willows and patches of
plants. Beyond the broad expanse of water humped low
hills broken here and there by valleys gleaming with
threads of silver streams. The field rose gently until it
seemed to fold the chimney tops of the Hilliard homestead in its mellow embrace. The silence became strained.
The more the girl reached for a subject of conversation
the more it eluded her. She plunged for a topic and
brought up the last one commonsense would have suggested;

"Where is your *Fidus Achates* this gorgeous afternoon?"

"You mean Pryde? First I'll state that he is not my *Fidus Achates*. We were at college together. Served in the same outfit overseas. We've drifted apart since. What impulse nudged me to invite him here the Lord—no, he couldn't have been responsible—the Devil alone knows."

"You are not over loyal to your guest."

"He is not my guest. In fact I made it rather plain that he was *persona non grata* to me. He is the guest of my aunts. As to where he is now,—we've been shooting. He hurried back with the dogs. Said he had a date with you for tea."

Nancy glanced at her wrist watch.

"Good grief, so he had. I'd forgotten. I'd come from planting bulbs when I stopped on the bridge and saw the bittersweet. I've been making a little spring garden-spot for the woman who does our laundry. She spends most of her time over washtubs but she's pathetically eager for a flower. She'll be able to see this from the shed where she scrubs. A few purple and white crocuses; trumpet daffodils, clear golden yellow; white lady narcissi, a dozen or two; clumps of single early tulips, yellow, rose-pink, silvery white; and then Darwins, Clara Butt, who blushes so adorably, heliotrope, Rev. H. Ewbank, and off in a corner where he can't dim the delicate beauty of the others, Bartignon, all fiery red. I've only made a beginning in what Betty calls 'the wash-lady's garden.' Each year I'll add to it."

"Then you are not planning to return to New York now that your father has regained his health?"

"Not while we have Betty with us. We think this a better place for her. Dad knows that he is helping here though he yearns for his down and almost-outers in the city. Sometimes I feel as though I must break away, as though I'd been caught in a back-water."

"You're planning to break away and I'm planning to stay and take a shot at business. To borrow from Phyllis, 'Ain't life humorous?'"

"But, I shan't break away. When my business increases I'll keep a little apartment in New York so that I can go there at times for mental stimulation. Wasn't it the giant

Antaeus who renewed strength every time he touched his mother Earth?"

"Suppose you marry?"

"Marry! With Bruce's experience as a horrible example?"

"You are not like his wife, are you?"

"How do I know what I'm like? I've never been tempted. The men whom I've met are much like the men with whom Sybyl played round. I prefer them with higher, more uncompromising standards. The rich and idle don't appeal to me."

"You don't care how you cut, do you?"

"I have the habit. Pruning is as indispensable a factor in good gardening as cultivating and feeding."

"And, may I suggest, is the least understood of all horticultural processes. I don't know much but I've picked that bit of knowledge up in my travels. Through here!"

He swung the garden gate wide. He followed Nancy along the gravelled paths through the opening in the hedge into the Manse grounds. He stopped. The girl glanced up at him. His eyes startlingly black, looked straight down into hers. His nice lips, she had to admit that they were nice, were set in a hard line. If he knew her expression when she thought of him, she knew his when he thought of her quite as well. The living room windows were lighted. Alec Pryde must have arrived. Suddenly she felt an intense aversion to seeing him alone. He who at first had been patronizingly friendly—man of the world and country mouse attitude—was showing perturbing signs of interest. She mustn't snub him yet. Sybyl was doubtless on her way east. Impulsively she invited;

"Won't you come in for tea?"

Geoffrey Hilliard glanced at the lighted windows, down at his wet boots. He moved one foot experimentally;

"I think they won't mess up the rugs. Thank you. I'll come."

"Inescapable Destiny stalking me," the girl thought with an hysterical catch in her breath as he entered the house directly behind her. As she crossed the threshold of the living room the canary burst into a deafening fanfare of greeting. She spoke to the occupant of the wing chair by the fire as she began to arrange the bittersweet in a mammoth copper bowl on the piano;

"Sorry to have kept you waiting, Alec."

But the man who sprang to his feet was not Alec Pryde.

"Luke! You at leisure at tea-time!"

Red rag to a bull. Of course she had said the wrong thing. Small scowled and angrily resented;

"Why shouldn't I be here at tea-time? Why shouldn't I play the gentleman of leisure? Why slave my fingers to the bone making money for other people to squander?"

Geoffrey Hilliard laughed as he backed up against the mantel.

"You've mixed your metaphor, Luke. You don't work with your hands, do you? Much more to the point to say that you're scheming your head bald in my behalf while I'm—I'm scouting round the Upper Mill for—birds."

"What were you doing round the Upper Mill?"

"I said—birds. What were you?"

Small merely glared an answer. He resumed his seat as Nancy took the chair behind the tea-table. Had his face gone white at Geoffrey's curt question or had she imagined it, the girl wondered. The atmosphere seemed to sparkle and snap electrically with telepathic insinuations, suppressed aversions. She must break the tension. She cast an appraising glance over the tea-table drawn near the gay, whispering little fire. If only something were missing she could send Luke for it. But, the fat Georgian silver kettle was purring sociably among cups and saucers frail as egg-shells. Sandwiches, luscious rich red slices of tomato between snowy wafers of bread, flanked little cakes, Dresden plates of them. Cream—sugar—no lemon! The gods be thanked.

"Luke, please go and tell Phyllis that she has forgotten the—oh, here she is," Nancy supplemented as the "cooklady's" daughter, attired in a plaid version of the rainbow, entered. Beside her, threatening the safety of the tray the maid carried, hopped and skipped Betty Caswell. With a crow of joy the child flung herself at Geoffrey Hilliard.

"When did you come, Prod'gal Son?"

He dropped into a large chair and lifted her to his

knees. Luke Small indulged in a poorly restrained gust of laughter.

"Is that what she calls you, Geoff? What's that saying about fools and children speaking the truth?"

Nancy had a swift impression as of a panther preparing to spring as Geoffrey Hilliard parried curtly;

"What I'm called is no concern of yours, Luke."

"Hope you haven't eaten all the cakes," interposed Pryde gaily.

He stood on the threshold attired and groomed to perfection. A boutoniérre of bachelor buttons adorned the lapel of his grey coat. Nancy saw him glance at Hilliard in his well-worn tweeds, at Small in his unpressed business suit. His voice registered self-satisfaction as he loomed over the tea-table and suggested;

"Tardiness is its own reward. First come. First go. Get me, gentlemen?"

The gentlemen addressed remained mute as to their understanding of his pleasantry. Nancy's lips twitched as she observed them from behind the screen of her gold-tipped lashes. Luke Small's face was dark with fury. Geoffrey Hilliard was patently amused. He laughed at everything! What was he thinking? Alec Pryde contrived to touch her hand as he took the cup of tea she prepared for him. She didn't like that any better than she liked his host's smile. With an effort at being all things to all men Pryde spoke to the child curled up in Hilliard's lap to the imminent danger of his tea-cup;

"Hulloa, Kiddie!"

Betty regarded him with uncompromising blue eyes;

"Hulloa, Mr. Cain!"

"Betty! Don't you know that's not a nice name!" reproved her aunt. Nancy turned to Pryde who was pale with anger. "Dad is educating Betty in Bible literature and she airs her vocabulary on all occasions regardless of its pertinence. She . . ."

Her niece interrupted:

"What you makin' such a fuss about, Nanny? He looks just like the picture of Mr. Cain in my big Bible. I asked Phyl-*us* if he didn't an' she giggled an' said;

" 'I'll tell the cock-eyed world he does. Only Cain ain't

got such swell clo'ves nor so many of 'em. Ain't life hum'rous!' What's a cock-eyed world, Prod'gal Son?"

The atmosphere cleared in a general laugh. If only Betty could be removed before she made any more comments, her aunt wished wildly. She attempted to wireless the thought to Geoffrey Hilliard. His eyes darkened with surprise as they met hers. Would he understand? After an instant he rose with the child in his arms and announced;

"We are off to feed the rabbit."

Betty struggled to free herself.

"But I don't want to leave the tea-party. Put me down. I'll bring the baby rabbit here."

But her captor kept on his way. His voice drifted back from the hall;

"Feed a baby in the living room! I'm astonished at you, Miss Caswell. It just isn't done. Babies are always fed in the nursery."

"All righty, Prod'gal Son. If you . . ." distance spun out the child's high treble to a mere thread of sound.

Nancy sighed her relief. One out of the way. Whom could she dispose of next, she considered as she glanced from Small's obstinately set mouth to Pryde's hostile eyes. They were behaving like two combative dogs growling over the same bone. She flung a conversational shuttlecock into the air;

"Sandy McGraw found a baby rabbit when he was cutting hay and Phyllis and Betty are trying to raise it by the aid of a medicine dropper."

A silly shuttlecock of course, but they needn't have let it fall, Nancy resented as neither man answered. They sprang to their feet as she rose.

"If you have nothing to say I wish you'd go home, both of you," she suggested bluntly.

Pryde smiled sardonically.

"As Small was here when I came I naturally waited for him to leave first. In polite society . . ." he finished the sentence with a patronizing shrug. Oil on a smoldering fire. Small's rage flamed;

"Hang your polite society! Do you think you can land in this village and begin to sheik . . ."

"Luke!"

"Don't stop him, Nancy. His nose fascinates me. It

glows like a red stop-light when he loses his temper,"
tormented Alec Pryde. The girl turned on him wrathfully.

"I'll not let either of you go on. You'll go out at once."
As neither man moved she added; "You won't? Then I
will. I'll leave you to enjoy the tea—together."

She had intended to depart with a Lady Macbethian
stalk but she found herself running into the hall and up
the stairs. She was quite breathless as she crossed the
threshold of the nursery. To her excited fancy the wad-
dling geese in the frieze on the wall were doing the
Charleston. Hilliard, on a low chair, looked up from the
rabbit whose mouth he was holding open. Into the crevasse
slipped white globule after globule from a medicine-
dropper operated by Betty. The milk missed its target and
ran up Hilliard's arm as the child demanded;

"What makes you look so red, Nanny? Been quarr'ling
wif your boy frien'? You should worry. Phyl-*us* says, the
more you fight 'em the better they like you. Open the
rabbit's mouf wider, Prod'gal Son."

Geoffrey Hilliard broke into unregenerate laughter.
Nancy saw red with little green pin-wheels. How dared he
laugh at her! Her voice betrayed her anger as she commanded;

"Betty, put the rabbit back in the basket. It's time you
bathed your hands and freshened up for supper."

The child's lips set in a defiant little twist. She looked
at Geoffrey from the corners of her eyes. Her pouting face
flashed into a smile.

"All righty."

She solicitously deposited the rabbit in a basket and
departed. Her aunt gazed unbelievingly after her.

"Betty, leaving you and the rabbit without a scene? I
can't believe it. What's the answer?"

"To what?"

"To that obedience. Usually I have to fight and die
before she'll give in."

Geoffrey grinned engagingly.

"She's my sweetie. She does what I tell her to do."

His indifference infuriated the girl.

"Cave-man stuff. The dominant male. When she grows
older she'll understand that a man in your class . . ."

He took a step nearer. His eyes smoldered as he demanded;

"Meaning?"

"The horde of rich drifters." She brushed nervously at the base of her throat. "What are you staring at? Anything on me?" she brushed again. There was a disturbing quality to his laugh;

"Nothing you can brush off. You seem to like that example of a rich drifter down stairs, well enough."

His tone, his eyes sent her heart to her throat. She could feel it beating frightened wings. Absurd, she flouted herself, of what was she afraid? She laughed, a trifle shakily, but sufficiently tantalizingly to send that curious light in his eyes flaming.

"Alec Pryde, you mean? Oh, but he has so much pep, to quote the polished Phyllis. He quite sweeps one off one's feet."

Geoffrey Hilliard's smile paralyzed those beating wings.

"He does? And that's what you like?"

He caught her hands in a grip of steel. He flung an arm about her shoulders and drew her close. Twice he pressed his lips hard to the little hollow at the base of her throat before he released her. Even then he kept one arm about her shoulders as he demanded;

"Want to be swept off your feet again?" As she stood rigidly mute he added;

"This concludes the program of this interesting afternoon. G.H. signing off."

Chapter VII

Nancy Caswell looked up from the plan spread on the broad desk in her work room at the Manse. She nibbled a pencil reflectively. On the neutral tinted walls hung plans of gardens, watercolor sketches of gardens, photographs of gardens. At one end of the room tools of all descriptions stood erect or leaned in a rack. Great rolls of paper kept them company. The broad shelf of the secretary bookcase was scattered with open seed-catalogues. Late sunlight filtered in through a western window. In a bay which faced the south hung pots of ivy, vines of fragrant primrose-jasmine, green as the girl's smock. There were shelves of pots holding annuals just coming into bloom from seeds sowed in the summer, snowy patches of candytuft, calendulas, snapdragons, stock not yet budded, common mignonette, standards of heliotrope. Some of the plants were experiments, more of them true and tried friends.

Nancy's glance strayed beyond the window to the autumn tinted trees waving long tentacled arms against a sky, pink, lemon, mauve, blue. There were touches of jade like links in a bracelet. All the colors of the spectrum streaked the heavens. A soft flush crept to her hair. She put her hand to throat.

"It's unbearable! How did he dare!" she exclaimed under her breath as she had exclaimed a hundred times since the afternoon, three days before, when Geoffrey Hilliard had caught her in his arms.

She rose and crossed to the window. Silly, to sit there and think! She must force the man and his impertinence from her memory. Why had he kissed her? To show how little respect he had for any girl! Restlessly she returned to the plan on her desk and attacked it resolutely. Work! Work! Work! The only antidote she knew for unpleasant thoughts. Her mind snapped back like a ball on a stretched elastic. How had he dared? Was the feel of his lips burned forever into her throat?"

"Nancy!"

She sprang to her feet in answer to her father's voice. She swept a pile of catalogues with flamboyant covers picturing gigantic sweetpeas and gargantuan gladioli, from an armchair. She threw a piece of wood into the Franklin grate. It acknowledged the attention with a shower of sparks. She patted the back of the chair done in gay chintz.

"Sit here, Dad. A letter? From a parishioner? You want my expert opinion on it, I presume?"

Noah Caswell did not respond to her raillery. Seated in the ample chair he leaned his head somewhat wearily on his hand as he looked down at the letter he held.

"This is from Bruce's wife, Sybyl."

"Sybyl! Writing to you! What does she want? Not Betty? She can't have her. She can't. She promised."

"Quiet down, Nan. Sit in that chair opposite me. That's better. Relax. Don't take life so hard, child. You'll burn out."

"I know it, but, somehow, I can't do anything, feel anything with the tips of my fingers. Thank the Lord, I've never fallen in love. I plunge into things, even emotions, up to my elbows. What does Sybyl want?"

"Not Betty. She—read the letter. Read it aloud. It was such a surprise that I didn't take it all in. I came straight to you as I've been coming ever since your mother died."

Nancy pulled the chain of the floor lamp beside her chair. She took the sheet of paper with the tips of her fingers. Her father smiled.

"Don't hold it as though it were malignant. Remember that Sybyl is quite within her rights—as she and some of her post-war generation see life—and on the very crest of fashion."

"Thanks for that qualifying 'some.' It lets me out as I'm of the same generation. She begins;

" 'Dear Father Caswell—.' "

"Father! After her divorce!"

"Go on, dear. Let's get at what she wants. Let's suppress our own reactions for the present."

"Sorry. But Sybyl makes me so furious that I see little

fiery comets with scintillating green tails when I think of her. I won't interrupt again."

"'Dear Father Caswell—,
Knowing that you can't possibly be in sympathy with me it takes courage to write. I have the divorce. I am now known as Mrs. Howard Caswell.'

"Hmp! Quite proper. She was Sybyl Howard, before she married Bruce," exploded Nancy. Her father raised a weather-browned hand in reminder. She read on;

"'However, I shall not use that name long. I am to be married at once.'

"Darn! Three months' residence somewhere gives her the right! Pretty near legalized free-love, I call it!".
"Nancy!"
"I'm sorry!

"'We shall go to France, perhaps for years. I want to see Betty before I go. You needn't remind me that I have given up all claim to her. But, that promise didn't mean that I never was to see her, did it? Now, I'll give you a chance to show how real your Christianity is.'

"Insolence! She ..."
"Please."
"I'm sorry! Where was I? Oh, yes ...

"'how real your Christianity is. Will you invite me to visit you for two weeks? I know that Nancy will be furious at the suggestion ...'

"She doesn't know the half," Nancy interjected caustically before she read on;

"'I'd go to the Inn but I have so little money to carry me until I'm married that ...'"

The girl's lips were white as she expostulated;

"Dad, if I read one more word of that darned letter I shall choke."

Her father held out his hand. His voice was sympathetically tender;

"Give it to me, dear. I understand. You have been so adoringly devoted to Bruce that it was cruel to ask you to read it. What answer shall we make?"

"Answer! We! You're not considering having Sybyl in this house, are you?"

There was a quizzical gleam deep in the dark eyes which met hers.

"Unless my memory is tricking me, it wasn't such a long time ago that you were laying plans to prevent Sybyl from rushing into matrimony before she'd had time to think things through."

"That was when I—Good grief, Dad! Do you suppose she knows that Alec Pryde is in this village?"

"I had thought of that as an explanation of this extraordinary letter. That she should want to see Betty is natural, but to ask to come here . . ." he shook his white head.

"Do you suppose she suspects that he may not be so keen to marry her?"

"Isn't he?"

A tinge of color stained the girl's white face as she evaded;

"Even so, what could she gain by coming here?"

"Nothing. She'd lose, lose tragically. But Sybyl is too securely rooted in the consciousness of her power to attract to realize that. Let a man of Pryde's type suspect that he's being pursued and he'll side-step."

"But, he's in honor bound!"

"Honor!"

All the heart-break, all the humiliation, all the sympathy Noah Caswell felt for his only son whose life had been wrenched and twisted by a shallow woman was in the repetition.

"Does a man who will deliberately separate a wife from her husband, a mother from her child, know even the first letter of that word?"

"Then why consider having Sybyl here, Dad?"

"I am not considering having her here, in this house,

but I am considering sending her money for a month's stay at the Inn."

"The village would blow up with gossip."

"Let it. My plan is but an extension of yours. We've agreed that if possible we'll give Sybyl a chance to get a perspective on herself before she marries again, a chance to make sure that there is no mistake the second time. She is vain, impulsive, acquisitive. I doubt if she has ever given a conscious thought to law and justice. She thinks now that she is a very smart little woman, a votive at the shrine of realism, progressive, up-to-date to a degree.

"Very well, let her come here in pursuit of her quarry—I may be doing her an injustice, she may really want to see her child. Wasn't it Pliny the Younger who said, 'An object in possession seldom retains the charm it had in pursuit'? Whether that's a fundamental truth or not it is true of men of Pryde's calibre. This conservative town will hold a mirror up to Sybyl in which she'll see herself as law-abiding thoroughbreds see her. Mind you, I'm not listing myself with those who believe divorce is a crime —I have seen it carried through with beautiful dignity— nor with those who contend that the marriage tie should hold through misery, degradation of spirit, and abuse, but Sybyl had no such excuse. She allowed herself to drift into a love affair with a man—who, as it happens, has much more money than her husband."

Nancy gazed into the glowing embers of the fire as she observed thoughtfully;

"Wouldn't you think that she'd realize—Sybyl is no fool—that a man who hadn't the moral fibre to resist the attraction of another man's wife wouldn't have the moral strength to be true to her after he'd married her? I suppose even Sybyl with her advanced ideas would prefer constancy in a husband. I don't approve of your sending her money, Dad. You'll have to take it from the fund you're accumulating for that visit to Bruce in South America next year."

"The cost of four weeks at the Inn won't materially affect the fund. Even if it did I still think that we should make it possible for Sybyl to come."

"She'll upset Betty horribly. The child is just beginning

to obey—at least the third time she's spoken to. What would Bruce say if he knew?"

"He won't know until she had come and gone. It takes time for mail to reach the Argentine. He told me when he brought her to us that all decisions as to her welfare were indisputably in your hands and mine. Betty's welfare is, and always will be, indissolubly linked with her mother."

"I suppose so. You won't feel that you must ask Sybyl to the Manse, I hope?"

"No. Welcoming her in his house easily could be construed into a criticism of Bruce. He is my dear son. In spite of the difference in the beliefs of his generation he has always shown a courteous respect for and observance of the beliefs of mine."

"That's because in a secluded corner of your children's twentieth century hearts you early planted and cultivated a garden of nineteenth century ideals," Nancy acknowledged tenderly.

" 'I have set watchmen upon thy walls, O Jerusalem! Every person with high ideals of living is a watchman upon the walls of righteousness, Nan. Your recognition of what I have tried to do for you and your brother make all the personal ambition I may have sacrificed for those ideals worth while. Thank you, my dear. Bruce swore to me that always he had been true to his wife, that he still loved her. That he'd stake his life that she had been unfaithful to him only in spirit. Because of that belief I'll send her the money."

"After that, what?" Nancy queried thoughtfully. "Whenever I come to a crisis in life and hesitate, dreading for an instant to go on, I think of the three doughboys in 'The Big Parade.' Remember how shoulder to shoulder they pressed steadily forward through the forest? Snipers. Machine-guns. Traps. Comrades falling in horrible, huddled heaps. Yet on they marched, caution reconnoitering in their eyes, smiles curving their lips. What you called the other day, 'Gay courage,' the phrase has stuck in my mind. That's life, isn't it? We can't sulk. We can't run—and be soldiers. We've got to go straight on."

"Going straight on is the only situation in which I can see you, Nan. But, there are many who whimper and run.

Life catches them just the same. If Alec Pryde should stay after Sybyl comes ..."

"He won't! Of course he won't! He must have some sense of fitness. What is your plan? I suspect that you had it already mapped out when you came here with that letter."

"I thought that Phyllis could take Betty to see her mother every day."

"Suppose—suppose Sybyl were to kidnap her?"

"Kidnap her! She doesn't want the child. I'll take Miss Serena and Miss Sally into my confidence."

"Tell them about Alec Pryde?"

"No. We won't disturb their liking of him for the present. I'll ask them to call on Sybyl. To invite her there. They seemed to like her when she visited us with Bruce."

"All the more reason why they won't stand for what she's done. Not with their views as to the unbreakableness of the marriage tie."

"I think they will. Geoffrey will help."

"Oh. Geoffrey!"

Nancy could have bitten off her tongue for that contemptuous repetition. She avoided her father's eyes as he demanded;

"What have you against young Hilliard? You were furious with him because he didn't come to Sunnyfield. Now you appear to be furious because he did."

"I hate his type."

"What do you mean by 'his type'?"

"Rich and idle and sporty, with a collecting complex."

"You seem to be able to endure all that in Alec Pryde, though his collecting seems to be in the line of other men's wives."

"He's—he's different. He really isn't to blame for what he is. He was sent away to school when a mere baby. Had a guardian who couldn't stand him around."

"Nan! Are you making excuses for that cad?"

"I'm only trying to be as fair to him as you are to Geoffrey Hilliard."

"There is no comparison between the two. One is ..."

"Hush! Here comes Betty. She is all ears. She tells everything, everything she hears to her 'Prod'gal Son,'" Nancy warned, as she heard her small niece running down the stairs. Book under her arm, the terrier at her heels the child dashed into the room. With a crow of delight she wriggled into her aunt's lap. Scooty flung himself upon Noah Caswell and his daughter in turn before he flopped to the hearth-rug with a "woof!" of exhaustion. Back to the fire he closed one bright eye.

The child turned the pages of her book. Her grandfather lingered on the threshold to inquire;

"What's 'Alice' doing now, Betty Blueskin?"

"She's just gone to the Mad Tea-Party. Here's the place to begin, Nanny." She picked out the letters with a chubby forefinger as she spelled;

"T-h-e-r-e, there, w-a-s, was, a t-a-b-l-e, table . . ."

Noah Caswell interrupted with a laugh;

"That early Victorian method of learning to read would horrify a modern teacher, but it gets there, just the same. We'll discuss this letter again before I answer it," he added and left the room.

With Betty's soft gold curls against her shoulder Nancy read aloud from the story of Alice in Wonderland. She had read it so many times that her tongue glibly followed the printed lines while her thoughts reverted to the contents of that upsetting letter. Sybyl coming here! Coming into the neighborhood of her one-time husband's family! What would be Betty's reaction? She never mentioned her mother now. What would be Alec Pryde's reaction? He would hear at once if her father carried out his intention of asking the Hilliard girls to help. Ignorant that their guest was in any way involved they would pour out the news, Miss Sally would. Would he leave the village? Why should he? Sybyl was free. He could resume his devotion. Would he? She visualized his laughing eyes kindling into a blaze as they met hers.

"What you stoppin' for, Nanny, just's the Hatter's takin' his watch out of his pocket? Go on," commanded the child in her lap.

"Your talents are wasted in this village. You'd make an excellent slave-driver, Miss Caswell," her aunt observed dryly and read on;

" 'The Hatter had taken his watch from his pocket and was looking at it uneasily, shaking it every now and then and holding it to his ear.

" ' "I told you butter wouldn't suit the works," he looked angrily at the March Hare.

" ' "It was the best butter," the March Hare meekly replied.' "

The clock on the mantel chimed softly. Nancy closed the book.

"That's all for tonight, dear. It's a good place to stop, leaving that funny March Hare, with his long ears, insisting, 'It's the best butter.' " Her arms tightened about the warm little body as she asked tenderly;

"Betty dear, do you ever think of your mother?"

The child remained so still that Nancy wondered if she were asleep. Then she stirred her head with its pale gold crown from side to side in negation;

"Not much. Muvver was like the Queen in Alice, al-*wus* rushin' round. I miss my Daddy. Where is Muvver?"

"Would you like to see her?"

Betty considered.

"Yes. She's so pretty. My Daddy called her Beaut'- fulest. But I wouldn't want to see her if she would take me away from you an' Gran an' the Prod'gal Son. I couldn't leave him. Phyl-*us* says that a sweetie'd better stick by if she wants to keep her boy frien'. Wasn't Muvver Daddy's sweetie? Why'd she go off an' leave him?"

For answer Nancy cuddled her closer. The child went on soberly;

"I heard Phyl-*us* tell her muvver she guessed M's. Bruce Caswell'd get 'nuvver husband soon's she checked out on the first one. I wus bakin' mud pies an' they didn't know I heard but I saw Phyl-*us*' muvver look at me an' shake her head an' she said;

" 'Hush! The poor little kid'll hear you.' Why'd she call me a poor little kid, Nanny?"

Nancy blinked hot, stinging tears from her eyes. She tried to laugh as she exclaimed;

"You! Poor? Betty Caswell! You're a rich little girl with us all loving you to pieces, Daddy, Gran, Nanny and—and the Prod'gal Son," she added for full measure.

Chapter VIII

"Why'd she call me 'a poor little kid,' Nanny?" The child's wondering question rankled intolerably in Nancy's heart as the days went on. It flashed into her mind in the most unexpected places. It bobbed up as she sat on a rustic bench at the side of the tennis court at Valleyview. A green sweater was flung over her shoulders, a Lenghlen bandeau, white like her frock, bound her ruddy hair. She looked up at the branches of oaks spread like a golden-brown fan against the clear blue sky. Far overhead crows sailed like miniature black planes. From somewhere near came the "Tap! Tap! Tap!" of a red-headed woodpecker foraging for his supper.

"You're not a poor little kid! You're not, Betty!" she reiterated passionately in her thoughts. She blinked back tears as she turned to greet Alec Pryde and observed lightly;

"Only a week more of September and we're still playing tennis. What an autumn!"

He slipped into his sweater coat, dropped to a gay cushion on the ground and leaned on one elbow so close that his shoulder touched the girl's skirt. From the court where Geoffrey Hilliard and Luke Small were playing came the thud of balls against rackets. Cries of;

"Good!"

"Fif—thirty!"

"Game!"

With his eyes on the players Pryde produced a gold case from his pocket and complained;

"We ought to have won those doubles, Nancy. 6-4. 4-6. 8-6. Geoff's partner wasn't so good. He played like a demon though. Have one?" He offered the cigarettes.

She shook her head.

"I can't believe that you don't smoke. I'll bet you're the

only girl left in the world who doesn't. Does it shock you in others?"

"Not in the least. On the contrary I get a vicarious thrill when I see a woman manipulating one of those long enamel holders, especially if it is green. The fact that I am a clergyman's daughter carries with it certain obligations— in this community. Dad's parishioners would be horrified were I to smoke. Why not respect their prejudices?" She hesitated a moment before she went on, "Especially as my brother's divorce is a thorn in the flesh."

Had the man's color deepened or had she imagined it? There was no mistaking the keenness of his eyes as he observed cynically;

"Divorce as an indoor sport is becoming almost as popular as smoking."

"Sport! You call it that? You would."

"What do you mean by that 'You would'? Don't be a crab. Take it back." He laid his hand persuasively over hers on her lap. She shook it off.

"Don't! I don't like it. To return to the subject of divorce and Dad's parishioners, they are about to receive a shock. Sybyl, my brother's wife—I forgot, shall I say his grass widow—is here."

"Here? What do you mean by 'here'?"

Pryde was on his feet glaring down at her incredulously. His lips were tense. his face drained of color. His usually rather light eyes were black with astonishment. Nancy regarded him with raised brows.

"Now you are shocked. I agree with you that her coming is in rotten taste, but, she wants to see her little girl before she goes to France."

Pryde regained his poise. He whistled lightly.

"France! Lucky she didn't try for divorce there. Skiddy going now. Good old Reno's a sure bet."

"How did you know that she'd been in Reno?"

Cynical, a little cruel, his eyes met hers.

"No use trying to bluff, Nancy. You don't do it well. Your lovely color betrays you. You know who I am. You have known ever since I walked through the gateway of the Manse that first day, haven't you?"

"Of course. I read the papers. 'Mr. Alec Pryde, wealthy

bachelor, master of hounds, etc., etc.,' " the girl fenced glibly.

"Cut that out. I'll own up. Perhaps I did pay too fervid attention to your sister-in-law, your late sister-in-law. She's infernally attractive and lured me on till I was out of my depths."

"The woman tempted me."

His eyes blazed at her taunt. He caught her wrists in a grip which made her wince. He pulled her to her feet, carefully keeping between her and the tennis court. He attempted a tone of light irony as he demanded;

"Did you think me such a fool that I wouldn't see through your little game? I've heard how much you care for your brother. You deliberately flung yourself between Sybyl and me, didn't you? I'll admit that you haven't overstepped the border of cool friendship once, but, your plan has succeeded just the same. I'm crazy about you. I don't want Sybyl. I want you. I'm going to have you, but . . ." His grip tightened unbearably. "If, by any chance I shouldn't get you I'll run away with your late sister-in-law the moment you turn me down. Get me?"

Get him! She certainly did. He had known all the time. She had walked into his trap like a silly little fly. There had been occasions when silly little flies had escaped. There must be a way out. She wouldn't run yet. Her father's words recurred to her;

"Going straight on is the only situation in which I can see you, Nan."

She'd go straight on. She steadied her voice and flouted Pryde gaily;

"Bandit! You sound like the distant roar of an advancing crime-wave. Take my late sister-in-law if you want her and—she wants you. But, good grief, do have tact enough to leave Sunnyfield while she is here."

"It will be confoundedly unpleasant having her round, but, I won't leave you and give Luke Small his innings, Nancy."

"I'm surprised that you're not afraid to leave me to—to Geoffrey Hilliard?"

"I wish Geoff could have heard that. The scorn in your voice might have waked him up. He's a cold fish." He

tightened his hold on her hands. "You're the only girl I've
ever really loved."

"Love all!" the score from the tennis court drifted
between them.

Its timeliness set a smile tugging at the corners of
Nancy's lips. After all, perhaps it was better that Alec
should stay. If he snubbed Sybyl she'd have spirit enough
to resent it. Then what would his threat to run away with
her amount to? Relief showed in her voice as she suggested;

"If you will return my hands, Alec—I don't care to
sprain my wrists freeing them—that's better, thanks. Shall
we go in for tea? Miss Serena and Miss Sally are expecting us. They are dears. They insisted upon keeping Betty
with them while I played. I couldn't leave her at home.
This is Phyllis' afternoon out."

"You make a slave of yourself to that child."

She remembered the condition he had imposed on
Sybyl in regard to Betty. Her eyes hardened. She observed as though immensely surprised;

"Your growl would intimate that you don't like her."

He hastened to repair damage.

"She's a mighty bright youngster but I don't care for
kids. They're so infernally omnipresent. Whenever I want
you to myself, Betty's on the tapis. You have to do
something for Betty. Take Betty somewhere."

Nancy laughed up into his aggrieved eyes as he held
the house door open for her.

"Love me, love my niece," she paraphrased. She
slipped agilely from under the detaining hand he laid on
her shoulder. That was what she especially hated about
Alec, he was always trying to touch her.

Miss Serena and Miss Sally were already at their places
opposite each other at the big table in the dining room
when Nancy and Pryde entered. The portions of San
Domingo mahogany visible between exquisite white doily
islands shone like winey enamel. The brass samovar
reflected and lengthened Miss Serena's long, ivory-toned
face. Miss Sally's smiling, rosy countenance was shortened
and broadened ludicrously in the silver surface of a squatty teapot. The sisters were dressed in petunia colored

crêpe with curious old-fashioned brooches at the V necks of their modish gowns.

"Thoroughbreds," Nancy thought as she took the chair beside Serena. The fragrant aroma of coffee seeped from the samovar. There were silver jugs of cream, so thick that it could be poured with difficulty. Plates of delectable sandwiches of infinite variety inhabited the doily islands. There were dark cakes and light cakes, spicy cakes and plummy cakes, cakes with icings, cakes with fillings. It was abundantly evident that Nora O'Brien had been indulging in a baking orgy.

Luke Small, brown and taciturn, entered and backed up to the fire. Geoffrey Hilliard who had followed him in hastened to the help of Miss Sally who was struggling with the refractory lamp under the squatty kettle. Alec Pryde in a big chair by the window had Betty on his lap. He was showing her his wrist watch. Nancy caught back a little laugh as she remembered her flippant, "Love me, love my niece."

"He's making a valiant effort to live up to my terms," she thought as she watched the two. The child's eyes were like brilliant blue stars as she inquired eagerly;

"Will it open?"

The owner obligingly pried up the back cover.

"Sure. Want to see the wheels go round?"

"Let me hold it?"

"If you'll be careful not to drop it." He put the watch into her hands. Interested, but not too interested to chatter, Betty observed in her carrying voice;

"Phyl-*us* says you hav' a line would land a whale, Mr. Cain. What you want a line like that for?"

Pryde set the child smartly on her feet. He reddened at the chorus of laughter which greeted her observation. He scowled down upon her as he reminded;

"How many times must I tell you that my name isn't Cain?"

"Alec, don't be cross with her. She's such a little thing. Come here."

He obeyed Sally Hilliard's gentle command. She spoke to Nancy;

"Come to my end of the table, child. Serena can't have

you all the time." As the girl took the chair beside her she continued;

"The Women's Club wants to raise money for preservation of the old Inn and stagecoach. We'd rather do it than have Mr. Ford add it to his collection. Someone suggested a Charity Ball. Like the idea?"

"Wonderful! Why not have a masked costume party? We ought to have it next week before the summer places begin to close. Perhaps some of those who have left already will motor on from New York for it. It isn't far." For the first time since he had entered the room Nancy looked directly at Geoffrey Hilliard. She inquired in a charming voice, slightly spiced with sarcasm;

"Can we tempt you to stay over for the festivity?"

His eyes met hers. Except for casual greetings and comments it was the first time he had really looked at her since he had crushed her in his arms and—and—she put her hand to her throat. She heard him laugh softly. Did he know what she was thinking, she wondered furiously. Did he know that the memory had sent little flames licking through her veins? No wonder he hadn't spoken to her since. He didn't dare. She had a few, just a few things to say to him when he did. Before he could reply to her question Sally Hilliard answered for him;

"Of course he'll stay. How about you, Alec? You spoke last week of leaving. It would be wonderful to have you here."

"I wouldn't miss it. I'll bet now ten pounds of any candy she may select against a—a small favor to be named by me—that I'll recognize Nancy Caswell within five minutes after she enters the hall no matter how she is disguised."

The girl bit experimentally into a mushroom sandwich as she considered. She shook her head.

"I never bet. Can't afford it. Just the same, you won't recognize me especially as I've never danced with you. Luke, you're silent as the grave. Don't you approve of this threatened frivolity?"

"Sure, I do. I'll go Pryde one better. I'll bet anything you like that I recognize you the moment you step within the door of the hall."

"Smarties, aren't you? Mr. Hilliard, are you in on this wager? I'm taking on all comers."

The expression in Geoffrey's eyes as he answered sent a premonitory tingle along Nancy's nerve centers.

"I never bet on a certainty."

Miss Sally patted the girl's hand.

"Don't mind their teasing, child. I'll see that Alec doesn't recognize you, then you'll share that ten pounds of candy with me," she traded shamelessly. "Thank heaven I've reached the age when I eat all the sweets I want and let my figure go hang."

The laughter of the young people quite drowned Serena's shocked;

"Sally!"

Nancy squeezed the plump hand which still rested on hers.

"We'll fool them. Look at the grounds in my cup! I knew when you tucked the strainer out of sight you were preparing for a fortune-telling party. Call Nora, Miss Sally. Do you think she'd mind?"

"Mind! My dear, look in the bottom of this teapot. It's filled with leaves. She left them so that she would be sent for. Serena, ring for Nora."

"I don't approve of encouraging her in this silly nonsense, Sally," the elder sister protested at the same time that she pressed a bell under the table. As though waiting in the wings for the cue to enter Nora O'Brien appeared at the door. Her face shone from recent scrubbing, her white print dress crackled with starch. She rustled forward. Nancy held out her cup as she informed gaily;

"I've twirled it and wished according to formula, Nora."

The woman twisted the bit of egg-shell china round and round in her hand. Alec Pryde slipped into the seat beside Nancy. Geoffrey Hilliard put his hand on the back of her chair. The girl sensed Luke Small's intentness. Who would believe that a company of grown-ups would even listen to Nora's nonsense? It might be nonsense but some of it had an uncanny way of coming true, she remembered. The sibyl of the tea-cups shook her head portentously;

"Shure, Miss Nancy, it's a big mix-up ye have ahid of

yer. See that straight little thing like a stick? That's you. See it go runnin' back an' forth like a squirrel in a cage whin I move the cup? Looks as though ye was goin' to be ketched in something."

Nancy was quite unconscious that she had drawn a quick breath until the woman encouraged;

"Don't ye go to getting frightened. I don't see no tears in yer cup an . . ."

"Will I get out, Nora?"

"Shure, you'll get out. Ain't there a door to ivery cage?" She squinted her small green eyes speculatively; "Oi see a man stealin' up to open thet door. He's goin' to let you out an' thin . . ."

"What does he look like?" demanded Luke Small.

Nora tilted her head with the air of an insolent bird surveying a nice fat worm before gobbling it;

"A leetle taller than you, Mr. Luke, I'd say. Eyes lighter than yours an' . . ."

"Pure Nordic like me, Nora?" wheedled Alec Pryde.

"Go way wid yer Nordics, Mr. Alec. What's thim?"

"Don't mind him. Go on, Nora. What else do you see?" prodded Nancy.

"A journey. A suddint journey. A prisent. A square prisent . . ."

"That ten pound box of candy Alec will lose?" suggested Sally Hilliard with a chuckle. Nora hurried on with a tinge of excitement in her mellow voice;

"The Lord luv us! If this crool mess you be gettin' into ain't all because a blonde woman's a comin' into yer life. Yer'll have a quick decision to make . . . that's as clear as the spots on the iron dog's back. I see a letter. A long letter. It's a comin' over water. It may shock you."

Nancy's heart contracted. Silly to be affected by Nora's nonsense but could the letter be from Bruce? Was he in more trouble? From behind her chair Geoffrey Hilliard protested;

"You've been seeing that shocking letter in tea-cups ever since I can remember, Nora. You've got a great line but it's pure bunkum. Confess now, it is, isn't it?"

Nora sniffed her indignation.

"Confession is it? It ain't my day fer it, Masther Geoff. You laugh. You're always laughing, but, if I was to tell all that cup tells me 'bout yer future, you wouldn't be standin' there a grinnin'. You'd be jumpin' through that winder."

"Nora! What do you mean?" Serena and Sally Hilliard chorused.

"Shure, you wouldn't be believin' me Ma'ms, if I was to tell you. But ye'd best better watch yer step, Master Geoff."

"But, it's my fortune you're reading, Nora," protested Nancy Caswell.

"I know it. But that warnin' seemed to fly up at me whin I stirred thim leaves. As for you, Miss Nancy," she peered intently into the bottom of the cup and lowered her voice to a blood-curdling whisper;

"Watch out fer a dark man! A quare actin' man. Looks like a Dago. It's him yer'll be goin' on that journey wid." She placed the cup on the table.

"Is that all?"

"The saints luv us, what do you want more than that? Caged, a letter, a package, a journey an' a blonde woman an' two men in yer life? That ought to satisfy anybuddy. No, Mr. Alec, put yer cup down. I don't tell no more fortunes today. You're all a laffin' at me. Besides, I've left Betty in the kitchen. She's as proud as a paycock wid that watch Mr. Alec let her took. She won't need no supper whin she goes home, Miss Nancy. It beats me where she puts all she eats. She's a quare childer if ever there was one. Says she to me, 'Nora,' says she, an' thet knowin' pup settin' there fer all the world as though he was a weighin' ivery word;

" 'Nora, is this the best butter?' "

Nancy arrested the progress of a delectable bit of snowily iced cake on its way to her mouth. Something curiously familiar about that sentence, "The best butter." Where had Betty picked it up? The Mad Hatter Tea-Party, of course. What a memory the child had. Funny that she should . . . Good grief! Nora had said, "Proud as a paycock wid that watch Mr. Alec let her took." Butter! Watch! Mad Hatter! A horrible suspicion brought the girl up standing with a suddenness which overturned her chair. She struggled with an hysterical impulse to rush out of the room. Instead she mumbled;

"Betty! I must take her home. Time for . . ."

Her niece's high pitched voice interrupted from the doorway;

"Here I am, Nanny."

"Betty, come here."

The child obeyed promptly but avoided her aunt's eyes. A sure sign of guilt with her. What had she been doing? Uncomfortably conscious of the presence of Geoffrey Hilliard behind her, of Alec Pryde beside her, Nancy spoke as evenly as she could with that disconcerting suspicion hammering in her mind;

"Betty, return Mr. Pryde's watch. We must go. Thank him for letting you . . ." The sentence thinned into a gasp as she caught sight of the strap about her niece's chubby wrist. A greasy strap. An abominably greasy strap.

"Betty! What have you done to that watch?"

The child replied with difficulty through a food-clogged mouth.

"Nuffin' much, Nanny. I wus 'sper'mentin'. Daddy was al-*wus* 'sper'mentin', Muvver said. The Mad Hatter put butter in his watch an' . . ."

"Butter!" interrupted Nancy hoarsely.

"Butter!" roared Pryde as he snatched the greasy strap from the greasy little wrist.

"Butter!" chuckled Geoffrey.

The Hilliard sisters breathed hard and said nothing. Luke Small's black eyes were alight with diabolical satisfaction as he stroked his small mustache. For once Nora was stunned into silence. The culprit was the only one serenely unconscious of the extent of the catastrophe. Nancy Caswell threw an indignant glance at Geoffrey Hilliard who still chuckled behind her chair before she demanded;

"Betty! What possessed you to do such a naughty thing?"

The child struggled with the impediment in her mouth;

"But, Nanny, it was the best butter. Nora said it was."

Her aunt choked back a sound which was a blend of laughter and sob before she queried sternly;

"What are you eating?"

Pryde glared at the offender across the buttered works of the watch he held. He growled;

"She'd be eating ground glass if I had my way. If ever I get a chance at disciplining you, you mischiefmaker ..."

Geoffrey Hilliard swung the child up into his arms as he inquired curtly;

"Where do you get the big idea that you'll ever have that chance. Alec?"

Chapter IX

Geoffrey Hilliard looked thoughtfully about his father's
office at the paper mill. How completely the pattern of his
life had changed since the afternoon when Nancy Caswell
had crashed down into the road in front of him. Had
anyone told him then that he would slip into the harness
of business he would have laughed at them. Nancy didn't
believe it now. Her spicy inquiry over the tea-cups at
Valleyview.

"Can we tempt you to stay over for the festivity?"
proved that.

"She'll believe it after today," he vowed before he
returned to a contemplation of the office. Except for its
golden oak finish in place of a profusion of plate glass and
gum-wood it was the last word in equipment. His glance
lingered on the filing cabinets. Distant machinery
hummed and rumbled an accompaniment to his thoughts
as he speculated as to which one held the correspondence
relative to the newsprint contracts. Peter Hilliard, rumi-
native gaze on the tree branches beckoning flirtatiously outside the window, tilted back in his desk chair. He looked
keenly at his son as Geoffrey announced;

"I want a job, Squire. Got a place for me here?"

"Don't make up your mind in a hurry, Geoff."

"In a hurry! I've been at home almost a month. The
first night of my arrival I had a hunch that I should stay
but you warned me to Stop! Look! Listen! I did. I'm
sure."

"If you really mean it . . ."

"I do. I know nothing of the actual running of the mills
except what I learned when I hung round here as a boy.
Do you still clean, dust, boil, wash, bleach and reduce
your raw material to pulp? Beat, color, sheet or roll,
surface and cut as you did then? You're so up to date,
though, I suppose you've changed your method."

"The actual paper-making hasn't advanced so much as you'd think it might. Of course we've gone into wood pulp for newsprint, we weren't doing that when you were a boy. We've installed machines with a wider trim and a higher speed. It won't be necessary for you to know the mechanical end at first. I'd like you here in the office with me. Think you can stand the confinement?"

"Stand it! Don't make me feel like a fool, Squire. Why did I put in those years at Business College? Now I know that subconsciously I was preparing to come here. How are things going? The last time I heard you and Small talking you'd lost a big newsprint contract. Haven't asked how the matter came out because I've felt that Luke might resent my interest and I didn't want to stir up trouble for you. Have you ever found out why that purchasing agent turned down the Hilliard Mills without a hearing?"

"No. I went to his office twice but he was vacationing abroad. No one else either could or would give me information. Said I'd have to wait till he returned. I couldn't see myself following him up again. We've always dealt directly with the magazines, not through an agency. Luke has had the handling of the renewals."

"Renewals! Do your other contracts call for notice of renewal?"

"Yes. They're drawn for a period of one year—shows how business has changed, they used to be drawn for three—with option of renewal for one year more upon notice in writing at least one month before written expiration thereof."

"And your biggest customer refused to renew?"

"Yes. I'll be hanged if I understand why. We can make an excellent price to New York customers because we don't have to ship far."

Geoffrey started to speak, stopped, considered and then observed with a nice imitation of his father's tone;

"I'll be hanged if we can afford to lose any more contracts."

There was a suspicious huskiness in Peter Hilliard's voice as he answered;

"That 'we' warms my heart, Geoff. It has been the dream of my life that you should carry on the mills your great-great-great grandfather started back in the time when a skilled engineer received about three dollars per week without board. It seemed a crime to have this business pass to a stranger."

"Why haven't you said so?"

"Because I have seen the tragic results of forcing boys into a business, through sentiment, for which they were unfitted. You have an income from your mother's property, you are heir to all that your aunts and I have. You seemed absorbed in book-collecting. Why should I influence you?"

"You stayed in the business. You had a private fortune."

"I stayed because I liked it and because there are workers in the mills who have been on the payroll fifty years, many of them forty. A new employer would think them too old for their jobs, would make a clean sweep of everyone sixty or over, probably. I couldn't let them down. Besides, I like seeing things grow. To me the most interesting thing in life is trying to do what I have to do superlatively well. Get a tremendous kick out of it. When I was ordered to quit the office and take up golf I put all there was in me into the game."

"And you're a cracker-jack at it for a beginner, I hear."

Peter Hilliard laughed.

"I'm not too bad. Now I'm back on this job again, I suspect that the mills have been running on three cylinders instead of six while I've been playing. With you to help we'll get going in high again—if you stay."

"Doubting Thomas. I'll stay, all right. I'll gradually take over the office work and in time, well, I've picked up an idea or two on paper-making while I've been fooling round with old manuscripts and books. If I'm here Luke will be free to give all his time to the mechanical end and you'll be free to compete in golf tournaments, national and international."

"That listens well, meanwhile I'll stick to this desk for a time." Peter Hilliard's tone was grave as he added; "I don't care for the way the Upper Mill is encroaching on our trade."

"I thought that smashed for keeps when Luke's father

died. Didn't you keep it from pounding on the rocks for several years?"

"Yes. Sometimes I have a feeling—mere imagination of course—that Luke is resentful because I didn't keep on financing it. I couldn't and keep these mills going. About a year ago the buildings suddenly hummed into activity. A group of men had bought them. Couldn't find a name among the lot I knew, and competition was on. They're hot on our trail. I suspect that they got the contract for newsprint we lost."

Into Geoffrey's mind flashed the remembrance of his first meeting with Nancy Caswell. When he had asked her why Small hadn't nailed the contract for the Hilliard Mills she had answered;

"He has tried to—he says. But, he's had an advantageous offer to go with the Upper Mill."

Had she intimated that Luke would bear watching? Had she had distrust of him in mind when she had written that letter of reproach? If she had it would have been for the Squire's sake, he couldn't flatter himself that she had felt anything but contempt for the Squire's son. His pulses broke into double-quick as he relived the few tense moments when he had carried her across the brook. Again he looked down into wide startled brown eyes, crushed her slender body close as she flung her arms about his neck, smelt the faint fragrance of sandalwood. He had fought back a mad impulse to press his lips to the hollow of her throat. He had come off victor then. Later, when she had flouted him, his self-control hadn't been worth a darn. Would she ever forgive him? Of course he loved her, had loved her from the very moment he had looked down into her laughing, radiant eyes as she sat in a little hay-covered heap in the road. No use side-stepping the fact any longer. Would she ever care for him or was she already fluttering in Alec Pryde's net? He shouldn't have her!

"I'll call Luke. We'll take a look at the other newsprint contract although he says that it doesn't call for renewal for a couple of months. Great Scott, I'm just beginning to realize how completely I've left the running of this business to him."

It took Goeffrey an instant to switch his thoughts from

Nancy Caswell to his father's suggestion. He proposed hurriedly;

"Why ask him for that contract just yet, Squire? He'll think I've been snooping round before I've even landed a job. Tell him for a starter that I'm coming into the mills as secretary to you, to relieve him of office work."

Peter Hilliard's eyes under overhanging iron grey brows sharpened.

"Suspicious of Luke?"

"I won't say that. Perhaps my point of view is influenced by jealousy of your dependence on him. He makes no bones of broadcasting his opinion that I'm a flat tire."

"You're mistaken, Geoff. Luke admires you enormously. He's always referring, a trifle enviously it seems to me, to your skill in sports, your growing reputation as a connoisseur of old books."

Crafty Luke to feed the flame of the Squire's pride in his son's non-business achievements so that he would keep him out of the grind of the mills, Geoffrey thought. Aloud he admitted;

"Fair enough. I'll try to show him something to admire in the way of business administration. Call him and let's get his reaction to the joyful news."

Peter Hilliard spoke into the mill telephone on his desk. He hung up the receiver.

"Isn't in his office. They've sent for him." Irrelevantly he inquired; "How long is Pryde going to stay with us? I think it's in mighty poor taste for him to remain in this village next door to the Caswells."

"Then you know?"

"Of course I know. I haven't told your aunts how he touches the lives of our neighbors across the hedge. They like him. He is good company. Why spoil their pleasure in a visit which I supposed would last only a few days?"

"I could blow up the works when I remember that I was responsible for his coming."

"How could you know that he shouldn't come, Geoff? I had written you nothing about our neighbors' affairs. After he'd been at Valleyview a week I stumbled out an apology for his presence to Noah Caswell. There was a curious tinge in his voice as he answered;

" 'Don't let the situation trouble you, Squire. You're

not responsible whatever happens. If you want to help, encourage Pryde to stay until I ask you to turn him out. The Lord moves in a mysterious way his wonders to perform.' How that last observation can apply in this case I can't imagine."

"Perhaps his daughter wants Alec to stay. She seems to have fallen hard for him." Geoffrey walked to the window. Peter Hilliard tapped his desk reflectively.

"I can't believe that."

"Then why does she encourage him to be with her? Curious as to his reactions? Is she playing Pandora, in a green sports suit, knocking off the lid of the proscribed jar with a garden trowel, to let loose a plague of complications? It's a hideous picture."

"Too hideous to think of in connection with Nancy Caswell. She loves her brother. Your suggestion that she is seriously interested in Pryde, the man who has broken up his home, is absurd. You have been unjust to the girl every since you met her. I'm sorry. I had hoped that . . ."

Remembrance of Nancy's frank aversion to him hardened Geoffrey's voice;

"Don't hope. She told me what she thought of me the first time we met. The plot thickens with Sybyl Caswell in the village. Came to see Betty—she says."

"I should say that the plot had thickened. It's preparing to sweep up to a smashing climax, or I miss my guess. The ingredients for an explosion are assembling. Sybyl is following up Pryde, of course. She must have heard that he's mad over Nancy Caswell."

"Then you do agree with me?"

"That Nancy is encouraging him to be with her because she's in love with him? I don't. Not for a minute. Here's Luke."

As Small entered the room he glanced at Geoffrey perched on his father's desk. He stiffened as he suggested;

"Perhaps you'd rather I came later, Squire."

"No. I sent for you to tell you that Geoffrey is coming into the mill."

Small's color paled to sallow white. His black eyes snapped as he demanded;

"In what capacity? Office boy?"

Peter Hilliard's eyelids half closed. His already ruddy

face flushed. He bent an ivory paper-cutter back and
forth in his sensitive fingers as he explained courteously;

"No. Thanks to his business training he won't have to
begin by filling inkwells. He is coming as my secretary.
Gradually he will relieve you of office detail so that you
may devote all your time and thought to the manufactur-
ing end."

"But, suppose I don't care to give all my time and
thought to that end, Squire? Remember, I told you a year
ago that if your son came into the business I was through.
You were quite sure he wouldn't come, but—I've had a
hunch he would. He'll never let the Hilliard Mills revert
to me. I won't work under him or with him. If he comes
into the business—I go."

Geoffrey opened his lips to protest and as quickly
closed them. This was his father's affair to handle. Except
for the heightened color, a darkening of his grey eyes,
Peter Hilliard showed no consciousness of Small's insolence. His voice was clear and cool, the fingers gripping
the pliable bit of ivory steady as he inquired;

"Mean that, Luke?"

Small shifted his weight from one foot to the other and
reversed the process. His voice was suavely propitiatory
as he acknowledged;

"I mean that and more."

"That is quite enough. Why add more? You may in-
form your friends at the Upper Mill that you'll be free to
come to them as soon as may be possible. Why not the
first of the month? Short notice, but I suspect that thanks
to that 'hunch' the transfer will be easily arranged."

Small glared at Geoffrey before he demanded;

"Has your son been putting ideas into your head,
Squire?"

Hilliard the elder smiled serenely.

"The idea, as you call it, that you've been negotiating
with the Upper Mill isn't an idea, it's a conviction. That's
all. You may go."

Chapter X

Geoffrey was thinking of his father's curt dismissal of Luke Small as the next day he looked from the window on the twentieth floor of a New York office building. For how long had the Squire suspected his right-hand man of duplicity? He himself had seen Luke coming from the Upper Mill. He had thought at the time that there was something surreptitious in the constant twist of his head over his shoulder, now he was sure of it.

Hands hard in his pockets Geoffrey looked down upon innumerable city roofs. Chimneys smoked like hot springs in the Yellowstone. A flag or two fluttered. Innumerable radio towers flung afar network connections, frail as a spider's web, mysterious as a wizard's spell. Windows rose tier upon tier under a ragged sky-line. Far below in the canyon which was a street, midgets moved about like flies, automobiles crawled like prehistoric bugs. Faintly rose the sound of motor horns, the clang and rush of a fire engine.

Without, from building to building flashed wireless currents of thought, enterprise, achievement. Within, messenger boys rushed in and hurried out of doors letting out the click of typewriters. Men came and went to the same tune. Harassed men, confident men, aggressive men, but never shabby men.

Geoffrey glanced at the clock on the wall. He had left Sunnyfield at dawn. He had arrived at the building before the office force had begun to drift in. He hadn't stopped for coffee, even. He had been waiting an hour. He intended to wait hours more to see that purchasing agent, intended to stay until he had found out why the Hilliard Mills had lost the business of this big concern. He had told his father that he was running up to the city before he slipped into harness to make sure that Taka and his apartment hadn't blown off the top of the building where they were located.

"Boss'll see you," a voice interrupted his communing.

It emanated from an enormous head of a small body which seemed strung on wires. Geoffrey had the sense of being catapulted into the presence of a man behind a desk. He couldn't have described him except that he wore a bright red tie, had eyes opaque, colorless, in an impassive face. With a nice appreciation of the great-one's importance and the motto blatantly displayed above his desk;

THREE MINUTES IS A LONG TIME!

Geoffrey plunged into his subject;

"I'm the junior Hilliard of the Hilliard Paper Mills pinch-hitting for Hilliard senior, the Squire, we call him. We want to know why you didn't renew your contract for newsprint with us."

"Why I didn't renew!"?

The repetition was a cross between a roar and a growl. Geoffrey was reminded of the king-lion at feeding time. He wondered of just what brand of indigestion or disappointment it was the result. There was a bag of golf clubs in a corner. Perhaps the purchasing agent had been off his game yesterday. He persisted bluntly.

"We were told you wouldn't renew."

"You were! Were you also informed that this office wrote twice to your mill, telephoned to your mill, to get your best figure on a larger order?"

Geoffrey felt the color oozing from his face. His suspicion of Small had been right. He had double-crossed his employer. Gripping his rising anger he answered evenly;

"The Squire was told that you refused to renew."

"Who lied to him?"

"Our manager, Small."

"Why wasn't the old man on the job himself?"

Geoffrey shot a surreptitious glance at the bag of clubs in the corner before he answered;

"He had to cut out the office last spring. Doctor's orders. Prescription, golf. Boy, he's made good at the game. He's a bear at direction. After he really started he hasn't lost but one ball."

The opaque eyes of the man behind the desk showed a

faint glint, much as a pool of drab ice might reflect a stab of sunlight. He waved a thin, nervous hand in the direction of a chair;

"Sit down. Sit down. How long has the Squire, as you call him, been at the game?"

"About seven months."

"I'm fairly good myself. Off my game yesterday, though. Drove four balls into the woods. Got so mad I almost had a stroke. Man with me ..." He broke off abruptly as though conscious that he was departing from the suggestion of the other placard on the wall behind him;

BUSINESS FOR BUSINESS HOURS.

He growled;

"Never liked that man Small. Looks like dirty work to me."

Geoffrey remembered his father's suspicion.

"And yet you've given your contract to the Upper Mill to which he goes the first of the month, haven't you?"

"What's that? What's that?" The purchasing agent pressed a buzzer on his desk. A young woman in a henna bob and a matching jersey slithered into the room with the assurance of a novice entering a lion's cage. The man behind the desk commanded;

"Bring the correspondence on the Hilliard Mills renewal. See if you can get what I want this time." From which addenda Geoffrey deduced that it had been a hectic morning.

By the time the girl returned with the papers, the purchasing agent had warmed slightly. His anger flared again as he read the letters. It appeared from copy in his hand that his office had written twice to the Hilliard Mills. There had been no response. Aloud he read the clause in the contract relative to renewal. He flung down the papers and tilted back in his chair. The slight glow had faded from his eyes.

"Sorry. Nothing to be done. We've signed on the dotted line with the Upper Mill for one year."

Geoffrey rose.

"We're out of luck. I was after information. I have it.

Thank you. If ever you're in the neighborhood of Sunnyfield stop and have a game of golf with the Squire. The links are good. He's good in spite of the fact that he will hold his right thumb straight down the shaft of his club."

"I have difficulty keeping my right toe where it should be. Some day I'll come. Pity you didn't take hold of the Hilliard Mills before, boy," he growled and jammed the buzzer on his desk in token of dismissal.

In the outer office, Geoffrey all but collided with the girl in the henna bob and a purple rage. Her cheeks burned with resentment under their coating of powder. Her eyes sparkled with anger. She nodded in the direction of the door he had closed behind him;

"They're feeding him raw meat today, chunks of it," she sibilated between clenched teeth, as she flashed by to answer the summons.

Ten minutes later Geoffrey paused on the threshold of the living room of his apartment. The place seemed curiously empty. Like a shell from which life had departed. Yet the treasures which he had picked up on his travels were there. Rugs from Arabian bazaars, glowed like dusky jewels on the floor. There was a brass-bound chest from China, ivory carvings of unbelievable delicacy, a cabinet full. A mandarin coat of green, heavy with gold embroidery, was flung over the back of a deep couch. Originals of famous cartoons hung on the walls. Boxes, lacquer, enamel, crystal, gem-set, silver, glistened on tables. Books, no end of them, covered two sides of the room from ceiling to floor.

A sudden, nauseating aversion to those books swept their owner. The years he had spent acquiring them! Nancy Caswell's crisp criticism flashed through his mind;

"Collecting doesn't seem to me to be a full-sized job for a young man."

Perhaps it wasn't, but it had been mighty interesting. Geoffrey removed a book carefully from its cardboard case. He opened it as though it were fashioned of spun glass and held a page to the light. Plainly he could see the shadowy design of the arms of London, the water-mark of the first paper mill in the country operated under a grant of 1728.

"Why can't the Hilliard Mills make age-proof-worm-proof paper which will last through the years," he asked himself. "I'll get the Squire to let me experiment. If I should work out something, the time I've spent collecting old books might be justified, even in the unfriendly eyes of Nancy Caswell."

He replaced the volume tenderly and crossed to the window near which was a small table set for one. He had telephoned Taka to have a combination breakfast and lunch ready for him, he was eager to get back to the mill.

That table for one was what made the place seem like a shell, he decided as he looked down upon it. He had been living with people. He missed them. Suddenly he had the sense of shedding an outworn self. He had a blasting glimpse of the futility of the life he had been leading.

"What price freedom," he commented under his breath as he looked from the window. The city spread northward to a pinnacle crowned by a gigantic goldencock weathervane. A violet haze dimmed the towers of Manhatten, the long piers from which the great Atlantic liners set sail, ships, tugs, the silvery glint which was the harbor. The effect was that of a huge Claude Monet canvas.

He turned to greet the servant who entered with cat-like tread. The Oriental's denatured smile crackled the old ivory of his skin. His leanness was accentuated by his sleazy black house clothes. How old, how young was he, his employer wondered, as he had wondered the first time he had seen him. The man bowed and smiled, each movement tipping the lacquer tray he carried at a dangerous and breath-snatching angle.

"Excellency, I shed much smile at return."

"Everything all right here, Taka?"

"A'right. Make much study at night as suggest. Bring large quantity brain to work."

Geoffrey seated himself at the small table.

"I'll bet it does. You'll have to take care of the apartment for me this winter. I shan't be here except occasionally for week-ends."

"I shed much tear of disappointment."

"I'm sorry too, in a way. Keep on at night school. Anyone you know there?"

The Jap tenderly uncovered a silver platter and revealed a delicately browned breast of chicken lapped in

the luxury of broiled mushrooms; solicitously placed an
emerald crystal plate holding crisp, faintly green leaves of
lettuce, sprinkled with a delectably pink paprika dressing;
poured a clear, dark amber stream of coffee into a cup,
before he answered;

"The most strongest friend leave with considerable
quickness."

"Why? Fired?"

"Nogi burn? Not so you will take notice. He go to hon-
orably conduct place of eating under so glorious stars."

"What the dickens do you mean?"

"What the joyful Nogi respectful speak as Night Lunch."

"Oh, a night lunch car. Where is it?"

"On so honorable highway two delicious hours out of
city. He smother me with attentions to bend my joyful
flivver that way."

"Have you been?"

"The one time. It is of entire comfort. Many much
heated canine consume."

"You mean hot dogs? How's his business?"

"Office not too sinfully crowded. He put in telephone
so he talk much business orders. Nogi say, he make
garden in spring. Much plants. He get much trims from
Japan. Much people come. Reside under trees to joyfully
consume tea. I listen to how he say the world he'll tell
that he take disgusting much money from them. I feel
most considerable pity for drinkers of tea."

"You needn't. Have you unpacked the other books
yet?"

"Much piles in study room. Carpenter obligingly make
shelves. I think so continuously you come. I wait to know
where they repose."

"I'll show you before I go. Put that mandarin coat in
the chest, the boxes in the desk drawer. I don't like them
here. Did you get that costume for me?"

"Waiting in box. Made to last shining thread, like
honorable sketch you send."

"Then bring along your accounts."

Curious how stripping that room of detail seemed to
reduce it to masculine terms, Geoffrey thought as he
drove homeward. He'd been on the highroad to becoming
a finicky bachelor, immersed in artistic values. Since the

day Nancy Caswell had come into his life he hadn't given a thought to his books. Suppose, there were something in his idea of making paper for a fair price, which would be worm-proof, age-proof? It was worth trying.

He smiled as he passed the night lunch outfit with "Nogi" in electric bulbs along the side. It was an abandoned trolley car. He could see plants in the end which had been the motorman's headquarters. He hadn't a doubt but that the proprietor would take "disgusting much money" from his patrons. That seemed to be the easiest thing foreigners did. It wasn't only foreigners, he reminded himself, as he remembered Luke Small's treachery. The growl of the purchasing agent echoed through his mind;

"Pity you didn't take hold of the Hilliard Mills before, boy."

The words were still pricking as he entered his father's office in mid-afternoon. He had made record time from New York. The room throbbed with the whir of distant machinery. If he had come home when he left Business College would the mills have lost that big customer? Darned waste of time to regret! Better get busy following up the other newsprint contract. Luke had said renewal wasn't due for two months. If he would lie about one wouldn't he lie about the other?

"Curious, no sign of it here," he thought as later he slid the last compartment of the filing cabinet into place. Had Luke Small removed it? The Squire wouldn't have thought of it. He was absorbed in readjustment now that Luke was leaving. It wasn't a job on which he could help his father. He didn't know the personnel. How would he stand the strain? Serena had said;

"Land's sakes, work never kills nor ages. It keeps folks young. Worry is the murderer, not work."

Apparently Luke's defection was not worrying the Squire. He wished that he could say as much for himself. He had the sense of warily treading a thin crust above a volcanic fire. He wouldn't feel on firm ground until he had that other newsprint contract in his pocket signed by the magazine people. He turned from his absorbed, unseeing contemplation of the world outside as Peter Hilliard entered.

"Didn't expect you back here, Geoff. Thought you'd have a lot to do for the costume ball tonight. Find everything o.k. at your rooms? Taka on the job?"

"Yes. He shed much smile at my return. He's a faithful old scout. Tell him to do a thing and it's done. He never forgets, never flubs."

Peter Hilliard sighed.

"I wish I had a few like him about the mills."

"I also interviewed—I'd better say he interviewed me—the purchasing agent of the magazine company whose account we lost."

"Did he see you?"

"He did."

"Good boy! You are taking hold. What did he say?"

"That his office had written twice to us, had telephoned, not only in regard to renewal but to ask our figures on a larger order."

The ivory letter-opener which Peter Hilliard had been bending snapped. He flung the pieces on the desk. His face was dark with color as he commented:

"So-o. That is their version. I'll take a look at that other contract."

He started for the filing cabinet.

"No use, Squire. I've been through it. It isn't there."

"Where is it? I'll call Luke. He knows."

"Don't ask him yet. Better that he doesn't suspect that we are interested. Is he going tomorrow? It will be the first day of October."

"I haven't given him a chance to change his mind. I've readjusted everything."

"Has he helped?"

"He's made a bluff at it. I wonder what reason he's given the men for his abrupt departure?"

"It is abrupt."

"Can't help it, Geoff. Won't have a man round a minute who thinks he has a grievance. Bad influence. Yeasty. Spreads like the dickens. Luke said he was going. He goes. He'll get his salary to the first of the year but he gets out of this place tomorrow."

"Will the Upper Mill take on a man who's practically been fired?"

"It's a new concern. It will gobble him thinking to swallow our customers at the same time."

"You were right in your suspicion that the contract we lost went to them."

"I can't understand Luke's reasoning. What more can he get there than he could get here? Even if you came into the business I had planned to offer him a fair amount of stock in the company."

"It may be that always he has cherished an ambition to see his father's mill re-established."

"Why try to pull me down in the process?"

"You said that you had felt that he resented . . ."

Peter Hilliard indulged in a long, low whistle;

"Can it be possible that during these years when I have been helping him he . . ." He began to drum a five-finger exercise on the desk as Luke Small entered with a paper in his hand. He tapped it with the tips of his glistening-nail fingers. There was a tinge of bravado in his voice as he announced;

"I came to you before signing with the Upper Mill, Squire. Having grown up here I hate like the devil to leave."

"Why do it?"

"There is not room here for me and for your son."

"And you think yourself of more importance to the business?"

Small bristled like a hedgehog rattling into action.

"Of more importance! What does Geoff know but sports and old books? Haven't I learned the business from the basement up?"

"You have. From rag-picker to manager. A steady climb with every facility offered you to mount fast. Don't forget that."

Small shifted his weight from his right foot to his left and back again.

"I'm not ungrateful, Squire, but, I claim that I have the right to do as I like."

"The right. Curious term, that. Are you prepared to accept the obligations that 'right' to do as you like carries with it? Ever heard the word loyalty? There is such a quality. In quite common use, too. If you ignore it don't be surprised if things go wrong with you. Sign up with the

Upper Mill." As Small turned to leave the office he added;

"Just a moment, Luke. Where is the contract with the magazine people for newsprint? The one which you say will come up for renewal in a few weeks."

"Isn't it filed here?"

"You know that it isn't. Bring it to me."

"But, I'm sure that it is here." He took a step toward the cabinet. Geoffrey suggested equably;

"Don't waste your time going through that, Luke. I've examined every paper in it. No contract—for newsprint. You must have it. Of course we can get a duplicate from the magazine—they'd think we'd been asleep at the switch, all right—but we want our own. Dig it out."

"You mean to insinuate . . ."

Peter Hilliard broke into the furious question;

"Only that it must be in your possession, Luke. You had charge of all contracts, of all business while I was away. Who would have it if you haven't? You boys will both want to get away early to dress for the ball. Get a hustle on, Luke."

Small left the office with a growl of protest. Geoffrey marvelled at his father's patience. He knew that Luke had double-crossed him, yet his voice had been almost tender when he had said, "You boys." What move would Luke make now? Had he told the truth about the newsprint renewal? Suppose he were stalling so that it would expire by default too? Good Lord, were they too late? He bent over his father and confided in a low voice;

"I've a hunch we'd better 'phone the purchasing agent of that magazine company. Now. How do we know Luke isn't fooling us again?"

"I was thinking of that. Go to it. Geoff."

It seemed an incredibly short time before a nasal voice informed;

"Here's your party."

Geoffrey could hear the soft pad-pad of his father's fingers on the desk as he talked with the magazine company's representative. Questions and answers flew over the wire like shuttlecocks with an expertly handled battledore at either end.

"I'll have that signed renewal at your office at ten o'clock tomorrow morning. Anything else?" In the instant

Geoffrey waited for a reply he heard a faint click. His eyes narrowed. Someone listening in? At which end? "All right! Good-bye!" He hung up the receiver and answered his father's unspoken question;

"According to contract our consent to that renewal should be in their hands tomorrow morning. They've been 'phoning and writing too. A close shave as no mail goes out from here tonight. I can easily make it in my roadster. I'll pull the Cinderella stunt. Leave the ball at midnight for New York, have a shower and breakfast at my apartment and be sitting on the front steps when their office opens. When Luke brings the original along—by the way, was that line I used strictly private?"

"Except for Luke's office. Why?"

"Nothing. Just wondered. Let's get at that contract. Don't call your secretary. I'll type it. They'll take ten thousand tons more per year if we give them better terms. We will, won't we? You dictate." He unhooded a typewriter; "Let's go!"

As, ten minutes later, he slipped the signed paper into his pocket Geoffrey suggested;

"If Luke does appear with the old contract, we'll say nothing of this. No need for him to know it is to be delivered tomorrow morning, either. I'll wait a few minutes to see if he comes."

He crossed to the window and looked out. The sun had slipped behind the hills. Dusk, faint as purple malines, was floating above the tree-tops. How short the days were getting. Winter in the country! Br-r-r-r! Well, he'd decided. He wouldn't backslide. Eyes on the darkening world he visualized the glitter of Fifth Avenue at this hour, the tide of life and fashion sweeping on; automobiles in varying degrees of luxury, busses, taxis, crawling, halting, at the command of the lights in the towers, while rays from the setting sun fired bits of polished metal, sparkled on glass, dazzled bright eyes, touched carmined lips.

There, homegoing crowds and—that empty-feeling apartment. Here, seemingly illimitable space; trees waving uncannily against a blush of afterglow; the distant wail of an automobile horn, the gruesome screech of an owl and—people for whom he cared. He pulled out his watch.

"You'd better trot along, Geoff," Peter Hilliard suggested. "You must have things to do in preparation for the ball. I'll wait for Luke."

"Loads of time. The ball doesn't begin until nine. Before that I have a date 'wif my sweetie.' I promised Betty that I would take her to the buccaneers' stronghold in the brook, that we'd build a fire and have supper there. It has been our secret. Except for buttering Alec's watch she's been a pretty good little girl, so her aunt consented— with reluctance. I've cleared out the cave and bridged the brook with planks. We shan't be there but a short while, but, it seemed a pity for her not to have a little fun, when all the grown-ups are to play tonight. Even Phyllis is off with her mother to a party."

"The child adores you, Geoff. I don't wonder, you're so good to her."

"Good! Why shouldn't she have her fun? I haven't forgotten the thrills I had when a boy. I turn cold when I remember the stunts Mac Donovan and I used to get away with. I must have been a young savage."

"A young pirate. Great Scott, how you as Captain Kidd, Donovan as your understudy, and your buccaneers used to swarm up and down the river on rafts! I can hear you now storming Nora's kitchen and shouting;

" 'S'death woman! Hand over the cookies or you'll walk the plank.' "

Geoffrey laughed.

"Nora was always a good sport."

"She'd let you walk over her. You were a curious combination, Geoff. When you weren't playing pirate, you were one of King Arthur's shining knights. Does Betty ever speak of her mother?"

"Not to me. Phyllis has taken her to the Inn every afternoon since Mrs. Caswell arrived. Curious situation. I can't understand why Aunt Serena and Aunt Sally chucked overboard their life-long views and called upon her yesterday when they're so crazy about the Manse people."

"They went at Noah Caswell's request. He told them that he would appreciate any attention they might show

Betty's mother. Get that? I don't know what to make of his attitude toward Pryde. Sometimes I think that— Come in!" he answered a soft knock at the door.

He and his son sprang to their feet as a woman swung it wide. A small woman with a soft felt hat drawn low over eyes not quite blue, not quite violet. Her smart sports suit was of delicate beige color, a fox skin hung at precisely the fashionable angle over one shoulder. There were shadows—artificial—under her luminous eyes, a twist to her delicately rouged lips.

"Mrs. Caswell!" the two Hilliards exclaimed incredulously.

Chapter XI

Sybyl Caswell regarded the two men for a second before she apologized; "Forgive me for coming here. I have taken my courage in both hands to ask . . ." she hesitated.

Geoffrey sensed in the cool arrogance of her voice a note of wistfulness like the muted vibration of a fiddle-string when lightly touched. Was she after money, he wondered? He had met her in the village several times. To his surprise instead of disliking her he had been sincerely interested in her. She didn't belong to the ghastly hard-boiled smart class as he had expected. She was several shades too emotional for that.

The elder Hilliard's brows met in a troubled frown. His voice was grave as he reminded;

"Whatever you ask, remember that Noah Caswell and his daughter are my dear friends."

He drew a chair forward and resumed his as the woman sat down. Hands in his coat pockets Geoffrey stood by the window. Sybyl Caswell's eyes and voice were dashed with defiance as she explained;

"What I ask will be no disloyalty to them. I—I want you to insist that Alec Pryde terminate his visit in your house."

With difficulty Geoffrey suppressed a soft whistle. Jealous? What would his father answer? Noah Caswell had asked him to keep Pryde under his roof for the present. Peter Hilliard's voice was tinged with compassion as he protested;

"I can't do that. Alec is the guest of my sisters."

The woman nervously bit the lips which were the only color in her chalky face.

"If you and Mr. Caswell are friends, you should protect his daughter."

"His daughter!"

With the exclamation Geoffrey took a quick step for-

ward. His blood seemed to crawl back to his heart in an
icy tide. What did she mean? Why should Nancy Caswell
need protection from Pryde? He met his father's steady
eyes. He obeyed an almost imperceptible motion of his
hand and retreated to the desk. He leaned against it, arms
folded hard on his chest. Poor little fool, he thought as he
regarded Sybyl, poor little silly fool, trapped in the mesh
of Pryde's fascination. Her laugh was edged as she observed;

"Your son seems concerned if you are not, Squire
Hilliard. You see, I haven't forgotten your title."

"I am concerned about anything which threatens the
happiness of my neighbors," Peter Hilliard corrected
gravely. "I can't see Mr. Pryde as a menace—yet. He is
your friend, is he not?"

"Friend! You know he is the man whom I'm to marry.
Nancy Caswell knows it. She's deliberately trying to win
him away from me. And she poses as a model of virtue.
She won't smoke because she's a . . ."

"Don't go on, Mrs. Caswell. You'll be sorry if you do.
I suggest that you leave the village. Undoubtedly Alec
will follow. He may feel that you have come here to
check up on him, may be taking this way of showing his
resentment."

Sybyl Caswell colored under her powder as she protested vehemently;

"I didn't come to Sunnyfield because he was here. I
came to see Betty and to be near . . ." She caught back
the name as though frightened. "It is evident you won't
help me. Very well. I won't be relegated to Alec Pryde's
retired list without making him pay for it. Good-bye."

Geoffrey ceremoniously held the door open for her.
The two men listened to the tap-tap of her high heels
along the hall. A slam resounded through the building.
Outside the chug-chug of a taxicab waned to diminuendo.
Peter Hilliard shrugged as he resumed his seat;

"History repeats itself. Wouldn't you think that in time
—in time—women would learn that a man who would
encourage them to break a solemn convenant, would have
no respect for a promise he might make?"

"Same old spider and fly stuff."

"But, the modern woman or girl is such a wise fly—

except where her heart and a man are concerned. I wonder whom Mrs. Sybyl meant when she said that she had come to be near—and left the sentence suspended in air. She is correct in her suspicion that Alec Pryde is seriously interested, at present, in Nancy Caswell."

"I'll say he is. He is at the Manse every moment she'll permit."

"I still can't believe that she, who is so poised, so executive, so tender, can be hoodwinked into believing that he would be true to her more than to the girls on his retired list, as young Mrs. Caswell expressed it."

"Remember your sage observation, 'Except where her heart and a man are concerned.' " Geoffrey glanced at the clock. "What's keeping Luke? I ought to go for Betty. If he doesn't come across with that contract promise me you won't go after it."

"Go after it! Why should I? He'll bring it. Perhaps he's screwing up his courage to ask to stay with me. Luke has lots of good qualities, Geoff."

"Most people have. You're too easy with him, Squire. Sandy's coming to drive you home, isn't he? I'll leave my car at the Manse. Betty and I will take the short cut to the brook across the field. Great adventure for her to go picnicking at this time of day."

"I'd like to hear her comments. Go along. Don't worry about me."

But even Betty's excited chatter, as, buttoned up in a woolly coat of dark blue, she sat on a stone beside a small fire on the island, couldn't keep Geoffrey's thoughts from his father, from Luke's treachery to the man who had befriended him. The child's eyes were like lighted sapphires as she watched him toast bacon over the coals, heat water for cambric tea. The rush and splash of the brook couldn't quite drown the curious sounds of hidden life in the shrubs and moss. The air was cool and clear. Fireflies flashed and faded. The sky blossomed slowly with stars.

Geoffrey answered the child's torrent of questions automatically until the name "Nanny" registered sharply. He looked up at the eager little face and demanded;

"What's that?"

"I know what Nanny's goin' to wear at the costume ball tonight. She . . ."

"You mustn't tell, dear," Geoffrey hastily blocked the confidence.

"Mustn't I? Wouldn't Nanny like it? Phyl-*us* says she's awful touchy these days. Says she guesses it's 'cause Mr. Alec Pryde's gettin' round her an' Gran wif the ol' oil. What's the ol' oil?"

"Phyllis shouldn't talk about your aunt like that."

"Is Phyl-*us* naughty too? She says it knocks her for a loop the way Nanny's fallin' for Mr. Alec. I call him Mr. Cain. Makes him madder than the Hatter. What's knockin' her for a loop mean, Prod'gal Son?"

"Look out! Keep away from that fire! You'll fall in. Now we'll scatter the embers so it can't flare up."

"Wus that the way you an' the buc—buc'neers used to do it?"

Geoffrey put his arm about her:

"Yes. See the river? We used to pole our rafts to the mouth of this brook then up to the island. Hard going, edging by that cascade. When we'd had good marks at school all week we were allowed to camp here Saturday nights."

The child peered into the darkness of the field-stone cave and snuggled closer.

"Was that your str-strong'old? Where you hid?"

"Yes. We pirates stationed a guard at the shore and one at the bridge to give warning of the approach of the enemy. Come on. It's getting late. If we're not home on time we won't be allowed to come again."

He heard her catch her breath as, held close against his shoulder, he carried her across the plank bridge above the rushing stream. Safe on shore she looked back and called;

"Good-night, strong-old!"

As, hand in Geoffrey's she started up the meadow path which led to the gate of the Valleyview garden she inquired;

"Was Mr. Luke one of the buc-buc'neers? Phyl-*us* says it's a scream the way Mr. Alec's cuttin'-in on him wif Nanny. What's cuttin'-in mean, Prod'gal Son?"

"It means—stop talking, Betty. Look about you. If you're going to be a good woodsgirl you must watch the path so that you will know the way again."

As the child snuggled her hand closer in his, Geoffrey's

thoughts surged on, accusing, defending, magnifying. So, even Phyllis was noticing Nancy's absorption in Alec. If only he had slammed the door of Valleyview in his one-time friend's face! Nice mess things were getting into. Who would move next in the complicated game being played out in this country village?

Scooty pelted downstairs on his stomach to greet them as, hot, disheveled, slightly smudged with woodsoot, Geoffrey walked into the living room at the Manse with the child in his arms. He stopped in surprise as Nancy Caswell, Sybyl and Alec Pryde turned to regard him. What the dickens was going on? Too late for tea though the Georgian kettle was purring sociably on the table near the boisterous fire. Evidently they had just come in as Nancy wore her soft felt hat of a green to match her frock. Betty's arm tightened about his neck as she greeted;

"Hulloa!"

Sybyl Caswell's rouged lips twisted into the travesty of a smile. Pryde became absorbed in lighting a cigarette. Nancy's eyes registered dismay, her voice concern, as she held out her hand and inquired;

"Did you have a wonderful time, Betty? Come with Nanny, dear." As the little arm tightened about Hilliard's neck she reminded; "Remember, you promised that you'd go to bed promptly, when you came home from the buccaneers' cave."

"I'll carry her up."

"No, Mr. Hilliard. Betty must keep her promise and go herself."

It was "Alec" and "Luke" but never "Geoff," Geoffrey reminded himself savagely, before the child replied;

"Allrighty. Put me down, Prod'gal Son. I want to kiss my Muvver."

Geoffrey heard Sybyl's gasp of emotion as her little daughter flung arms about her neck. She caught her close. Betty wriggled free, poised for flight, hesitated. She patted her mother's cheek;

"Good-night, Beaut'fulest. That's what Daddy al-*wus* said. Now I'll come, Nanny. Good-night, Mr. Cain. Good-night, Prod'gal Son."

Clinging to her aunt's hand, chattering like an English

sparrow preparing to nest for the night she hopped and skipped out of the room. Her high little voice floated back from the stairs;

"Did you ever go campin' wif your bestes' boy frien', Nanny? Why's Muvver here? Not to take me away! I won't go wif her. Phyl-*us* says . . ."

The voice faded. The three left in the living room stood as immovable as the stone lions at Valleyview. The tall clock ticked monotonously. The fire snapped briskly. Sybyl's eyes were on the photograph of Bruce Caswell on the table. A door closed overhead. The sound broke the spell. She laughed. A sad, disillusioned little laugh.

"As neither you nor your father would help me, Mr. Hilliard . . ."

"As my father wouldn't," Geoffrey corrected gravely.

"Then, as your father wouldn't, I came to Nancy. I flung pride into the discard when I went to Reno. If Alec is pretending that he loves her as he swore he loved me . . ."

Pryde muttered a protest. She turned on him, eyes flames in her white face as she accused vehemently;

"You not only made me think you loved me but you tried—notice that I say tried—to make me believe last year that no one would be the wiser if I went week-ending with you occasionally.

"That's a lie! You know that's a lie!"

Sybyl shrugged thin shoulders at his furious denial. Geoffrey suggested curtly;

"Alec, it would be in better taste if you and your—Mrs. Caswell—fought out your differences in another house."

"You're right, Geoff. Sybyl, I'll drive you back to the Inn. My car's outside."

"I wonder—if I dare go with you? It would be so easy for you to run into a tree and dispose of me forever."

Alec Pryde's eyes were cruel as he retorted;

"In that case I might have to go with you to that far country where reckless motorists sojourn. Can't. I have a bet on with your lovely sister-in-law that I'll recognize her at the ball tonight. I'm bound to win. I shall be very careful of myself till she pays that debt. Better come."

Sybyl drew her fur close about her throat as she taunted;

"If this were a movie I'd fling vitriol at you and ruin 'your fatal beauty' forever. As it's life, real life—I'll marry you instead."

She flung the last words over her shoulder as she preceded him from the room. As the front door closed Nancy Caswell ran down the stairs. She stopped on the threshold and whispered;

"Have they gone?"

"Yes. Alec's driving her to the Inn."

"Is it safe? He seemed so furious with her."

"Of course it's safe." The intense embarrassment and fury he had experienced during the tragic dialogue of the last few moments roughened Geoffrey's voice.

"Don't growl about it. Oh, such a mess."

The girl dropped into the wing chair and leaned her head against its comfortable back. Her eyes were on the photograph of her brother. Arm on the mantel Geoffrey Hilliard faced her and demanded;

"Well?"

"Well what?" The query came back like the snap of a whip.

"Is it worth it?"

"Is what worth what? You have a conundrum complex, haven't you? It's a gift. What a help you must be to your hostess at dinner. I shan't try to guess the answer. I can see it trembling on your lips. I'll bite."

With difficulty Geoffrey controlled an urge to shake her. He forced his voice to coolness;

"I was inquiring if this affair you are carrying on with Pryde . . ."

"I carrying on!"

"Don't fence. You are deliberately making him think you care for him, encouraging him to love you, aren't you? Stepping between him and that poor, charming little woman."

"Poor! Charming! Little! Good grief! So you're in love with her too."

"I'm not in love with her."

Her laugh had the effect of a dash of cold water on his furious contradiction. She was only tormenting him, she couldn't believe it, he told himself. Her voice was maddeningly superior as she acknowledged;

"My mistake. You couldn't be in love, could you. You're a relic of the ice-age." Sudden color flaming in her face burned away her voice. Was she remembering that he had kissed her, Geoffrey wondered. He a relic of the ice-age with that hollow at the base of her throat always setting his blood on fire? He held her eyes with his as he inquired;

"Must I demonstrate again . . ."

She had taken refuge behind the wing chair before he could finish the sentence. She gripped the back of it with white knuckled hands.

"Don't dare come near me."

The struggle to refrain from crushing her in his arms till she begged for mercy roughened his voice;

"Come near you! Why should I want to? You thrust at me the first day we met, you've improved every chance you've had since. I've seen a good many girls and I've never seen one so disagreeable and unlovable."

With maddening deliberation she patted her hand over her lips to conceal a dainty yawn, before she inquired;

"Only one of my kind in your young life?"

The telephone on the table interrupted. The shrill call seemed to broadcast a curious portent of disaster. Nancy whitened as she furtively regarded the instrument. Was the same thought in both their minds, Goeffrey wondered. Her voice had lost all trace of the late unpleasantness as she whispered, as though fearful that the person calling might hear;

"Sybyl! Alec! Do you suppose anything's happened to them?" Her lips were colorless as she answered the ring;

"The Manse. Nancy Caswell speaking—Oh, yes! Yes, he is!" She held the receiver out to Geoffrey. Her voice was vibrant with relief; "It's for you. I thought—there was something about that ring . . ." the sentence rippled into a shiver as he took the instrument.

"Hilliard junior speaking—Yes, Squire—He has? When did you discover it?—I'll come at once." He snapped the receiver down upon the hook and started for the door. The girl caught his sleeve.

"Not bad news?"

He freed his arm.

"That depends."

There was a touch of wistfulness in her brown eyes as she queried a bit unsteadily;

"Am I the most disagreeable and unlovable girl you ever met?"

Geoffrey regarded her incredulously. That tone from her? What did it mean. He couldn't stay for an instant to find out. His father needed him. Just another of her moods probably. He answered evenly;

"I'll discuss the matter when I see you at the ball."

"You still think you'll recognize me?"

"I don't think. I know."

As he drove at law-breaking speed through the quiet village the wistfulness of the girl's eyes and voice kept intruding as he thought out the significance of the tele-phoned information. Luke Small had left the mill, had gone without returning to the office with the contract. His father's voice had been a mere whisper. He shouldn't have left him at the mill alone. Better to have disappoint-ed Betty. What would happen to the child if Nancy married Alec Pryde? She shouldn't marry him! Why had he lied to her? Why had he told her that she was unlovable, disagreeable? Unlovable! He seemed to be looking straight into wistful brown eyes as he brought his car up with a jerk in front of the administration build-ing of the mill. A moment later he was in his father's office.

Where was the Squire? What had happened? The re-ceiver of the telephone dangled by its cord as though dropped in a hurry. Geoffrey's heart congealed.

"Don't go off at half-cock! Keep your head," he ad-jured himself. He restored the receiver to its hook and looked about. His father's desk was in beautiful order. Perhaps he had heard a sound in Small's office and had rushed to investigate.

Geoffrey followed hard on the heels of the conjecture. He tiptoed down the hall, why, he couldn't have explained. Luke's office was dark. He listened. Someone moving? Static generated by his own excitement. He snapped on the light. The room appeared to be in order except that the safe door stood open. The wall over the desk was spattered with reminders in varying types and sizes.

DO IT NOW!
LIFE IS JUST ONE DARNED THING AFTER ANOTHER!

At the moment Geoffrey was in entire sympathy with that sentiment. The last twelve hours had proved it. He looked into the safe. Empty. Had Luke disposed of the papers? The Squire might be as charitable as he pleased but . . .

The Squire! For a moment he had forgotten him. Where was he? Had Luke made way with . . .

"Don't be a darn fool," he ridiculed himself as he sprinted back to his father's office. "You've been reading to many yellow headlines. Luke may be cagy but . . ." He sniffed.

Something burning? Paper? Had Luke set the building on fire? Orders would pour into the Upper Mill should the Hilliard supply of newsprint be put out of the running. He relaxed. The mill couldn't burn. Every ceiling was crossed with automatic sprinklers which would drench whatever was below and keep the fire from spreading. Sniffing he followed the scent of burning paper.

"Geoff! Geoff! Hul-lo-a!"

The hollow call rose from the basement. His father's voice! Why so faint? Was he exhausted from a struggle? Geoffrey plunged down the stairs.

Chapter XII

As the door closed upon Geoffrey Hilliard, Nancy glanced at the clock. Not so late as she had thought. It seemed as though she had lived years since Sybyl had burst into the living room where she and Alec Pryde were having tea by the fire. He had brought her home from the Town Hall where she had been helping with the decorations for the ball. She had driven with him every afternoon lately. It had become quite a matter of course for him to call for her wherever she was working and bring her home. It was the first time that she and her late sister-in-law had met since Sybyl had come to Sunnyfield. She had changed. Her beauty had lost a certain indefinable quality.

Nancy rested her foot on the fender, her head on her arms stretched along the mantel as she gazed unseeingly down into the red coals. Pryde impinged but remotely upon her thoughts. They were of her brother. He had adored his wife. What a mess! Why had Bruce rushed off to South America? He had made royally good at his profession of engineering. Why, why had he let Sybyl go so easily?

"Nancy!"

The girl turned in answer to the soft whisper. Sally Hilliard poised on the threshold as though just lighted from a flight. A fleecy pink scarf was thrown over her elaborately dressed white hair, it lay like a rosy cloud on her shoulders. Her arms clutched a huge bundle of the squashy proportions of a feather-bed. Nancy hastened to relieve her of her burden. She caught the contagion of the plump little woman's suppressed excitement and whispered in her turn;

"Let me take it. What's happened?"

A bit short of breath Sally Hilliard dropped into a chair. She leaned forward to inquire cautiously;

"My dear, where is Phyllis?"

110

"Gone with her mother to a family supper. They departed for the great open spaces an hour ago. Why?"

"Because that girl has the ears of a microphone and all its broadcasting facilities. I suspect that Alec knows what you're planning to wear tonight."

"How could he—good grief, I laid my costume out on my bed before I left to decorate the hall. Who would have told him about it though?"

"I may be wrong, but, there was a cat-and-canary cast to his grin when he said to me this afternoon;

" 'Fraid you won't share in that ten pound box of candy, Miss Sally.'

"It set me thinking. Sybyl said yesterday that she wasn't going to the ball, she had nothing to wear. I told her that I would loan her great-great grandmother Hilliard's gown which she wore to the reception given to Lafayette when he returned here after the revolution. I wore it once and had a white wig made to go with it. While I was pressing it for her—I was to send Sandy to the Inn with it in plenty of time for her to dress—I kept thinking of Alec's smirk, I had an inspiration. I'd bring the gown to you and send the one you were to wear to Sybyl. You're about the same size. Isn't that blindingly brilliant?"

"Yes—Miss Sally but . . ."

"But what, my dear? You don't mean that you have such hard feelings against Sybyl that you won't let her wear your gown?"

"Of course not—I was thinking that if Alec should mistake her for me . . ." Nancy paused. Why enlighten Miss Sally? Why not let her remain ignorant of the wretched entanglement?

"What if he should, my dear? The better joke we'd have on him. Be a good sport. Take that bundle up stairs and bring down your own costume wrapped in the sheet. Everything is there except the slippers. You'll have to wear your own. Feet were smaller in great-great grandmother's day."

Was she weakly letting Alec, Sybyl and herself in for miserable complications, Nancy wondered as she obediently tied up the witch costume that she had planned to wear and ran down the stairs with it.

"Good girl," Sally Hilliard approved. "We'll fool those boys. I snitched a package of Geoff's cigarettes. Take them."

"But those are not in character with great-great grandmother Hilliard's costume!"

"Blow the smoke through your hair and gown. If you don't you'll be the only girl in the room who won't smell of tobacco. The boys will notice it. Isn't that a Machiavellian touch?"

"It is. Your talents are wasted in Sunnyfield, Miss Sally. You should be in the Secret Service. Are you sure that Sybyl will like the change of costume?"

"I doubt if she realizes it. Her mind wasn't listening when I talked with her yesterday about the ball. She isn't happy. Of course it is her own fault, but that's the hardest kind of unhappiness to bear. Serena has no use for her but my heart aches for her. I told Geoff that I was loaning her the costume and he quite approved."

"When he sees it he will think that I am she!"

"So much the better! He was just as cocksure as Alec and Luke that he would know you. I wish that you appreciated that boy, Nancy. I've racked my brains to think of some way to make you."

"Don't worry about us, Miss Sally."

"I try not to. I must run along." Clutching her white bundle she paused on the veranda step to warn;

"If we are to get that box of candy and you're not crazy to pay that 'small favor' to be named by Alec—dodge the pirate!" She hissed the last three words.

Nancy's voice was a mere whisper as she repeated;

"A pirate! Alec a pirate?"

Miss Sally sniggered her excitement.

"Didn't Nora prophesy that a dark, foreign man would try to run away with you? Doesn't a pirate sound dark, foreign? I like Alec—but, he's not fine enough for you. In the bottom of my heart I don't trust him. Besides I have an uncomfortable convinction that a wave of excitement is vibrating our way. Nora's nonsense got under my skin, I suppose. But, I mustn't alarm you with my foolish suspicions. You ought to be dressing."

"Plenty of time. I promised Betty that I would come to her room when I was ready. She is so excited over the brook picnic that I doubt if she gets to sleep at all. You should have heard her prayers. Such a funny jumble. I shall wait until she quiets down before I go to the hall. Dad is to be nursemaid tonight."

"The Squire is coming over to keep him company. My dear, you don't know how flighty I feel to be dressing up in brocade. Even Serena is thrilled. We are to be in the receiving line so we don't mask. I wish that we did. It would be such fun."

Incorrigible youth. There was no age to Miss Sally's spirit, Nancy thought tenderly. She encouraged;

"You'll be two raving beauties."

"Don't be foolish, child. Better touch up your lips. The boys will recognize you if you don't and be careful about speaking."

Nancy spelled with her fingers;

"I won't talk."

"Good," Miss Sally approved, before she hurried down the steps and across the lawn. The girl watched her out of sight. She looked up at the sky. Gorgeous night! Too fine to spend in a hot ball-room. She'd like to ride to the end of the world and back in this glorious air. With whom? With Alec? In spite of all she knew to his discredit, in spite of the mess he had made of Bruce's life, she did enjoy being with him. Was it because his flattering manner was in such contrast to Geoffrey Hilliard's grim disapproval?

In some remote cell of her mind clanged a warning, insistent, muffled, like the far-off clamor of a grade-crossing bell. Alec's threat! Would he run away with Sybyl in revenge? Would Sybyl go with him? Forwarned was forearmed. She would avoid the pirate. Pity that Miss Sally hadn't been as communicative as to the costumes of her nephew and Luke. With a last look at the stars with their knowledgeable twinkle she closed the door.

"Nanny!"

She ran upstairs in answer. Betty called again from her little white bed where she lay with lids slightly droopy over her blue eyes. Scooty on the floor whacked his stub of a tail in greeting and regarded her solemnly with one beadlike eye. The child raised herself on a dimpled elbow to whisper;

"I'm keepin' awake to see you all dressed up for the party. Phyl-*us* says . . ."

"Betty! Does Phyllis know what I'm to wear? Did you tell her?"

"No, not her. I—I didn't tell anybody. She knows what Muvver's gown is though, Mr. Alec Pryde gave her a dollar to tell him."

So that was the way Alec had found out what she herself was to wear. He had bribed a maid! Clever Miss Sally to think of changing the costumes, Nancy approved before she demanded;

"Did Phyllis take the money?"

"That's what her Muvver asked her an' Phyl-*us* said;

" 'Did I take it! Gee, Ma! You ask that! An' you al-wus oratin' 'bout seizin' little ol' op'tunity! Ain't life hum'rous!' Who's little ol' op'tunity, Nanny?" She flopped back on her pillow. Without waiting for an answer to her question she admitted;

"I'm sleepy. If I close my eyes a teeny, weeny bit while you're dressin' will you wake me up when you're ready? Cross your froat an' hope to die?"

"I promise, dear."

Nancy snapped out the light and entered her own room, a room cool with orchid and yellow tints. All the detail in it was on the generous dressing table which filled the broad space between the windows. She looked down upon the amber toilet articles which Bruce had given her piece by piece. Bruce! Where was he? It had been a fortnight since she had received a letter from him. Usually not a week passed without a scribbled line. He might be ill. Ill and alone. The thought hurt unbearably.

For ten minutes she rested among the heaped up pillows on the chaise longue. She was tired now that she had stopped to rest. Her father was right. She did everything too hard. She had spent the hours before she went to the Town Hall superintending the preparation of lily beds on one of the large estates. Bulbs of Lilum Candidum had been planted. Holes for the later bulbs had been dug and covered with five inches of leaves. She closed her eyes and visualized the garden in bloom. There would be high white drifts of Auratum rayed with golden bands; rosy clouds of Speciosum Rubrum with their curved and recurved white petals shading to pink, spotted with crimson. It rested her merely to think of their beauty. Garden-making was a thrilling occupation providing one had vision and imagination. One wouldn't get far without.

Later, it had taken time to solve the intricacies of great-great grandmother Hilliard's ball gown, Nancy critically studied her reflection in the mirror. Remembering Miss Sally's suggestion she deepened the color of her lips.

"One touch of lipstick makes all women kin," she paraphrased aloud with a delicious little laugh.

A smile curved the corners of her mouth, excitement starred her eyes as she regarded the looking-glass girl. Two curls of the white wig drooped coquettishly to one of her shoulders. Shoulders, almost as creamy as the strands of synthetic pearls she had wound about her throat, were framed in an exquisite lace bertha. Flounces of the same cobwebby stuff on the delicate green brocade of the bouffant skirt were caught by little nosegays of pink roses. Long white lace mitts covered her arms to the elbows, narrow green ribbons were bowed about the wrists. The long skirt showed barely the tips of her own brilliantly buckled green satin slippers.

Not too grubby, she congratulated herself with a little laugh of pure excitement. She turned to pick up the myrtle green velvet cape with its enormous hood, lined with the faintest shell pink. On it lay the cigarettes. She remembered Miss Sally's warning. With the package in her hand she fairly flew down the stairs and into her father's study.

"Dad! Never mind your old sermon! Light one of these. Blow smoke through my hair."

"Your hair! Where did you get it?"

"Miss Sally! Quick! She says that they'll know me at the ball by the absence of tobacco scent."

"Where did you get that dress! I thought you were going as a witch."

"So did—others. Miss Sally brought it. Hurry, Dad! Light one!"

Her father chuckled;

"Haven't felt so devilish since I rolled my own of corn silk behind the barn.

" 'Sublime tobacco! which from east to west
   Cheers the tar's labour or the Turkman's rest.' "

He quoted Byron with theatrical fervor before he puffed
and blew smoke over her. He repeated the process till he
stopped from sheer exhaustion.

"Can't smoke any more. I'm dizzy now."

"Thanks lots!" his daughter called back as she flashed
across the threshold. She slipped on her black mask before at the door of the nursery she announced softly;

"I'm coming, Betty!"

A sleepy voice answered;

"Allrighty!"

Masked, slender, lovely in her green brocade and filmy
lace Nancy made a deep curtsy. Scooty sprang wide
awake to bark frantically at the strange figure. The child
gasped before she jumped from the bed to fling herself on
the dog. In her brief pale blue pajamas she looked like a
modern little boy angel as she clutched him in a strangle
hug.

"Keep s-still, S-scooty! I'll spank you an' I-I don't
mean maybe!" she threatened in a voice which seemed to
be giving her trouble. She apologized for her dog; "He
di-didn't mean it. Nanny. You s'prised him. If I hadn't
known it wus goin' to be y-you, I'd been s'prised too."

Nancy pulled off her mask.

"It's only Nanny. Jump back into bed." She tucked the
blankets about the little body. The child patted her bare
arm.

"You look pretty, but I fought you were going to be a
black witch. Phyl-*us* says the uvver girls'll be washouts
side of you. She says you're a snappy number."

Washouts! A snappy number! Nancy groaned in spirit.
Betty's vocabulary was growing with the luxuriant rapidi-
ty of Jack's beanstalk. Aloud she suggested;

"Shut your eyes. Remember, you had the nice picnic
and if you want to go again . . ." she hesitated sugges-
tively.

"I want to go again but every time I shut my eyes I see
the buc-buc'neers stealin' up the river an' . . ."

Before she could complete the sentence she had
dropped asleep. Nancy opened the windows and snapped

out the light. As she crossed the threshold she heard
Scooty's woof of relaxation, the child's soft breathing,
then, sharply, insistently the ring of the telephone.

She answered the call. Her brows crinkled in surprise
as she recognized Geoffrey Hilliard's voice.

"Nancy Caswell speaking. You Squire—Want me? To
come to the mill?—I'll be there in ten minutes. Good-
bye!"

Something serious must have happened for Geoffrey
Hilliard to appeal to her for help. Hadn't he told her in
this very room that never had he met a girl so disagreeable, so unlovable as she? She had recognized his voice at
once. What imp of contrariness had nudged her to pre-
tend that she thought the Squire was calling! She couldn't
stop to think that out. He had asked her to come to the
mill for him. She would better change to her own frock.
No knowing what she might have to do.

In her own room she pulled off the white wig, wriggled
out of the gown of brocade, slipped into one of green
jersey. She caught up a long coat and crushed a soft hat
over her hair. She stopped in the workroom to pick a
lone, late pansy from a plant she had brought in from the
garden. Her father looked up in amazement as she appeared at his door.

"Another costume! I shan't smoke you again, Nan. My
head has spun like a top since that last fumigation.

> " 'For thy sake tobacco, I
>   Would do anything but die. ''

he declaimed melodramatically.

"It isn't smoke this time. It's an—errand in the flivver.
Can't stop to explain. I'm leaving Betty in your care. No
one else in the house. I'll be back before I go to the ball.
Don't forget. You're here alone with Betty! I'll put this in
your buttonhole for remembrance.'

She fastened the pansy to the lapel of his shabby brown
velveteen coat. She left him protesting that she was libel-
ling him, that he never forgot. In the hall she caromed
into Luke Small. He caught her arm;

"What's the rush? I stopped on my way home to ask if
I might take you to the ball."

Nancy twisted free. She called back as she dashed out the door;

"Thanks, but I'm going alone."

Luke had looked queerly excited, she thought, as she started the flivver. Had the call from the Hilliard Mills been concerned with him? She stepped on the accelerator. Not until she had whirred far along on the road did she remember that she still wore the green satin slippers with their brilliant buckles.

Chapter XIII

The basement of the administration building of the mill was but dimly lighted when Geoffrey reached it. Uncannily still. His heart plunged like a cast horse. He listened. He called softly;

"Squire! Squire!"

"Here, Geoff!"

The sepulchral whisper came from the direction of the smaller of two massive heaters. Geoffrey's throat contracted with apprehension. What would he find? His father hurt? Perhaps mortally injured?

Relief surged in a quickly strangled laugh as he regarded his parent seated astride a galvanized ash-can rolled on its side. Was that the immaculate Peter Hilliard? The white patches in his black hair were smudged; perspiration had etched dusky channels down his face; his grey eyes glinted through lashes fringed with soot. Dirty but unharmed. Relief gave way to laughter. His father grinned in sympathy as he held up a blackened, warning hand;

"Sh-sh! He may not have gone."

"Who?" Geoffrey's stage-whisper was own twin to the Squire's.

"Luke."

The younger Hilliard soundlessly tipped an ash-can on its side and seated himself astride.

"What the dickens are you doing?"

Peter Hilliard held up the bunch of papers;

"The contract."

"With the magazine?"

"Yes. And some for the finer grades."

"He tried to burn them?"

"Yes."

"Well, I'll be darned! What a dirty trick! What's the use of talking about him. Come on up."

119

"Has Luke gone?"

"He's made his get-away all right. His office's stripped. Where's Mike, the watchman?"

"On his rounds. Roll these cans into place before we go. He mustn't suspect I've been down here. He'd think I'd gone crazy."

Noiselessly Geoffrey restored order. Remembering the smell of smoke which had greeted him when he entered the building, which might have come from something larger than those burning contracts, he investigated every corner of the basement. He snapped on the light in the great room filled with enormous rolls of newsprint. There were tons and tons of it ready for shipping. He sniffed. Nothing burning there. He regarded with satisfaction the sprinklers which striped the low ceiling. The heat from even a small fire would set them in action. Torrents of water would discourage the most husky flame. No fire could get a start there if Mike were on his job. He preceded his father up the basement stairs. If anyone were waiting to surprise them he'd take the brunt of the attack.

But no one was lying in wait. Their office was as calm and peaceful as a summer day when Father and son reached it. As Peter Hilliard removed the soot and grime from his face and hands he remarked jerkily, because of the force of his ablutions and shortness of breath;

"You—might have argued with me till—Doomsday, Geoff, and unless I had seen it with my own eyes you couldn't—have convinced me that Luke would have tried to double-cross me like this."

Geoffrey was examining the charred papers on the desk.

"Where did you get these? You haven't told me yet."

"Luke came into this room after you had gone out— almost seemed as though he had waited to hear your car start. He ambled on and on about that contract, not at all like himself. He's usually crisp and businesslike. Said he couldn't find the paper we wanted. Even then, in spite of your suspicions and my conviction of his connection with the Upper Mill interests, I wouldn't believe that the boy whom I had educated would be dishonest with me. Finally he exclaimed;

" 'I remember! I sent all of our contracts to the bank

for safe-keeping.' He added something about being so busy while I was away that he wanted to get them off his mind."

"Bunk!"

Peter Hilliard hung a grimy towel on its hook, regarded the blackened nails on his fine hands regretfully and dropped into the chair before his desk. He tapped the blotter thoughtfully as he admitted;

"That was too thin even for me to believe. But, I didn't let him know that. He talked on and on. I nodded occasionally. It's an old saw, Geoff, never write when you can talk, never talk when you can nod. Finally Luke suggested that there was nothing to be gained by my remaining at the office. As he was going to the ball he'd be up most of the night anyway, that he would report at the Upper Mill early, get excused and go to the bank for our contracts."

"Did you fall for that cagy arrangement?"

"No. I assured him blandly that I couldn't consent to having the first day in his new position shadowed by a problem of ours and requested the duplicate key to our safety deposit box."

"And he gave it to you?"

"Of course he gave it to me. I dropped it into my pocket and picked up my coat. I sensed Luke's relief as he assured;

" 'I'll stay and lock up, Squire. Have a few more papers to clear from my desk. I'm sorry you and I are parting but I guess it's best all round. I hope you're not walking.' "

"I like his nerve."

"You'll be crazy about it before I get through. I permitted him to assist me with my top-coat—normally I'm fit to tie if anyone attempts to show me that old-gentleman attention—assured him that I walked back and forth from the mill over the bridge road to retain my boyish figure and departed closing the outer door of the building with an echoing bang behind me. I even walked out between the lighted gateposts in case he were watching.

"I waited for what seemed to me an aeon or two before I crept back along the shadow of the hedge and sneaked to the side entrance. As I unlocked the door the world was so still that the jingle of my keys seemed to clank like a fire-alarm. I tiptoed to my office. As my senses became attuned to the stillness I thought I detected the rustle of paper. In Luke's office? No mouse in a grain bin in fear of detection could have been quieter than was I. I heard a step on the stairs to the basement."

"Was that when you called me?"

"Yes. I tried to get Valleyview first. Then remembering that you were to take Betty home I tried the Manse. Great Scott, but I was grateful when I heard your voice."

"What happened next? I found this receiver dangling by its cord."

"Did I leave that down? Not to be wondered at. Just as I was about to hang up, the heater door in the basement was pulled open.—I know every sound in this building. Was Luke burning papers? Of course, hadn't he said he was clearing out his desk? What papers? I answered myself by starting for the stairs. I broke the world's record at tiptoeing. As I reached the bottom step in the basement I heard the side door close. Softly. Very softly. I called."

"Crazy thing to do. He might have black-jacked you."

"I never think of consequences when I've made up my mind to go after a thing. I called again. 'Luke! Luke!' Running steps outside the window. Unnecessarily loud, it seemed to me. Too obvious. Luke expected me to chase him. Wanted me to. Why? I yanked open the heater door. Pulled out this bunch of papers he hadn't wholly pushed in. They had just begun to blacken at the edges. I pinched out the edge of fire before I locked the basement door. When you arrived I was taking account of stock. Help me sort them, Geoff."

The two men bent over the charred papers. Some were merely scorched. Two were burned half off. Geoffrey read what was left of them. One was a contract for fine paper. He laid the other for newsprint before his father.

"This is the one I 'phoned about. Luke was letting this lapse as he had the other. We've spiked his guns. I'll have that renewal in our customer's hands tomorrow morning as per contract." He tapped the breast pocket of his coat.

"Unless Luke stops you."

The remembrance of the click on the wire when he had

been talking with the magazine representative in New
York not so many hours ago, flashed through Geoffrey's
mind. Had Luke been listening in? No need to worry the
Squire by the suggestion. It was a problem for him to
work out himself. He answered lightly;

"How can he stop me, Squire? He doesn't know that
we suspect him. We—what was that?"

"Sounded like a blow-out. The air is so clear tonight
that sounds travel. There's another . . ."

Father and son stared at one another as a third report
reached them clearly. Geoffrey sprinted through the hall,
Peter Hilliard at his heels.

He switched on all the lights of his roadster parked
beside the building.

"I'll be darned!" he muttered as he walked around the
car. "Every tire flat. 'Ain't life humorous?' " He bent over
a wheel, straightened and stared at his father. "Every tire
slashed. That was the sound we heard. Blow-outs. Luke.
He thinks he's fixed it so that I can't get that contract to
New York."

Peter Hilliard joined in another tour about the machine. In the dim light the two men regarded one another
speechlessly. The early evening stillness was accentuated
by the "ch-chunk! ch-chunk!" of neighborhood frogs,
by the sustained undertone of flowing water, by the
distant wail of an automobile siren. The elder man whistled softly;

"Getting nightmarish, isn't it? Luke's gone savage. I
wonder what the College of Business Administration
would recommend in a case like this?"

"Four new tires, I suspect. Can't drive the car as it is
without ruining it. We'll go back to the office and 'phone
the village garage to send men with tires. Then we'll get
word to Sandy to come for us. Come in. No use standing
here doing incantations over those wheels."

It seemed an eternity before Geoffrey got Valleyview
on the wire. His Aunt Serena reported that Sandy had
gone to the Inn on an errand for Sally—that Alec had not
returned—that Nora was foaming at the mouth because
the pop-overs which she had baked especially for "the
boys" were toughening—and that—Geoffrey hung up the
receiver. It was the only way to stop his elder aunt when

she started on a tirade. He answered his father's unspoken question;

"Sandy isn't there, neither is Alec. He drove Sybyl Caswell to the Inn. I'll try to locate him there. He'll come for us."

In response to his query he was informed that Mr. Pryde had driven away sometime before. Every taxi was out. He hung up.

"Check. Any suggestion?"

"We'll walk—no, that will take too long. Try Nancy Caswell: She'll drive over for us in her flivver."

"She'll be dressing for the ball."

"Try her."

Geoffrey hesitated. He hated like the dickens to appeal for help to a girl who made no secret of her detestation of him. Did she detest him? He remembered the wistfulness of her brown eyes as she had inquired;

"Am I the most disagreeable, unlovable girl you ever met?"

He dialed. The voice which answered his call held a buoyant note. His tone was guarded as he answered;

"Hilliard speaking—Not the Squire. You know that. Don't fence now. We need your help."

The wires faithfully recorded her little gasp of surprise. As he spoke he visualized the tender lines of her mouth, the challenging lift of her head;

"Will you drive to the mill for us? At once. Alone. We'll be at the entrance gate."

He hung up the receiver.

"She'll be here in ten minutes. I take off my hat to her. She didn't waste a moment asking. 'Why?' "

"She wouldn't. She grew up in a family of men. In that environment a woman learns to cut out the interrogation point to a great extent."

"I'll call Mike. Warn him to keep an extra watch tonight. Luke might come back. No knowing how far he'll go now that he's picked up the microbe of destruction."

It took time to locate the watchman. It took more time to insert under his shock of red hair the necessity of redoubling his vigilance. Peter Hilliard refused to have Luke named in the warning.

"Honest but dumb. Because nothing ever has happened to the mills he won't believe that anything can happen," Geoffrey growled as he and his father hurried through the hall in answer to the muffled summons of an automobile horn. As he opened the door of the flivver awaiting them, he noted the glitter of a buckle on a green satin slipper. He noted also the haste with which Nancy Caswell tucked her foot under the robe. Part of her costume? She explained;

"I was dressing for the ball when you 'phoned, Squire."

"When I 'phoned," corrected Geoffrey. "Shall I drive?"

"Please." She slipped from behind the wheel. As the car started she continued;

"As I was saying, when so rudely interrupted, I was dressing for the ball when your ring came. I am so glad that I could help. Luke came in as I dashed out."

"Luke!" echoed the two Hilliards.

"Yes. He came ostensibly to offer to take me to the ball. I suspect that really he was snooping round for a line on my costume so that he might win that bet."

"Did you tell him that we had 'phoned you?" demanded Peter Hilliard.

"Tell Luke! Why should I tell him anything about your affairs, Squire? Hasn't he left your employ?"

Only two days since Luke Small had received his congé and already Nancy Caswell knew of it. Was Sally right? Was there an understanding between them? Had he for the second time given his heart to a girl who couldn't care for him? No. There was a note in her voice when she spoke of Luke that wouldn't be there if she loved him, Geoffrey monologued mentally, even as he listened to the affectionate badinage between the girl and his father.

Later, after his aunts had departed for the ball, he put in a telephone call for New York. The surreptitious click as of a receiver being hung up softly, which had startled him when he had been conferring with the magazine representative, prickled in his mind. It had been kept active no doubt by his father's warning;

"Unless Luke stops you."

Perhaps Luke had no intention of attempting to sidetrack the delivery of that renewal to the magazine company tomorrow morning, but, it was safer to proceed on the assumption that he had.

Geoffrey stopped his restless pacing to look out of the window. What a night! A middle-aged moon cocked one jovial eye at a world all silver sheen and purple shadows. Its light set the nickel on his roadster in the drive agleam. Re-tired, gassed and oiled the car was ready for the midnight journey. No hardship driving miles tonight. Pity to go alone. Alone! Why should he? An outrageous suggestion surged through his mind. A wave of recklessness swept along in its wake. He'd do it! How? He was still working on the answer when the telephone rang. He responded;

"Yes—That you, Taka? Get pad and pencil and take down what I tell you.—Get this right—Ready?"

Chapter XIV

Upon her return to the Manse after retrieving the Hilliards Nancy found Betty sobbing. Her distressed grandfather was rocking her. Scooty, hunched up on the rug, was the picture of dejection. The child had wakened from a frightened dream of "buc-buc'neers 'tacking the str-stron'old." She had cuddled her and sung to her. Twice she had tucked her into her little white bed only to have her rouse with a terrified cry. By the time she was quietly asleep, presumably for the rest of the night, the clock struck eleven.

No more twilight picnics for Betty for a year or two, Nancy decided as she stole softly into her own room. She regarded the green frock with its billows of lace which she had so hastily discarded when she had responded to Geoffrey Hilliard's call. Would it be worth while to go to the ball so late? Betty's nightmare had brushed the bloom from the festivity.

Of course she'd go. She wouldn't be a quitter. She slipped into the quaint frock, adjusted the wig, regarded the green satin slippers. Geoffrey Hilliard had noticed them when he had opened the door of the flivver. Would they betray her? There would be more than one pair of green slippers in the ballroom, besides Miss Sally had told him that Sybyl was to wear his great-great grandmother's gown. She'd take a chance.

She was glad she had come, she told herself, as through the slits afforded by her black mask, screened by a massive column, she glanced about the Town Hall. Its harsh unlovely lines were obscured by evergreens and autumn leaves, ruddy oak and flaming maple. Masses of potted chrysanthemums, tans, yellows, browns, contributed by summer residents from their hothouses, made a background for the musicians on the stage. The air was spicy with the scent of spruce and balsam, it tickled, and sparkled and boomed with the rhythm of brasses and strings.

Nancy tapped her foot in time to the syncopated beat of the drum. Gorgeous music to dance by. It thrummed through her veins, set her heart and brain and pulses achingly alive. And she almost hadn't come! Had Luke and Alec and the confident Geoffrey Hilliard been looking for her? Was Sybyl here in the witch costume? Where were they all? She had seen no one as yet even faintly resembling a pirate.

Still under the aegis of the friendly pillar she watched the dancers. Their colors shifted like the designs of a kaleidoscope. Glistening green richly patterned in gold; a gorgeous glint of pumpkin yellow; a wave of rose and silver; amethyst shadows; turquoise and sapphire blues. Powdered hair and jeweled heels. Cavaliers in silken hose, satin breeches, velvet coats, with dagger hilts and buckles gleaming in the light. Monks and cardinals. Harlequins and Columbines.

A witch. Sybyl. A witch *de luxe* with her gauzy black frock which just covered her knees, stockings sheer as dusky malines, red satin slippers with preposterously high heels. Pon-pons on her shining peaked hat matched in color the red of her shoes. A black cat perched on one shoulder. She was dancing as gaily as though she were a heart-free girl with no shadow of divorce stalking her. Perhaps she and Alec had made up their quarrel when he had taken her to the Inn in his car. Her partner was a knight in chain mail, a shining, mysterious figure. Who was he? One of the three men who had bet that they would know Nancy Caswell at once? She had been warned to avoid the pirate. Had he arrived?

Above the heads of the dancers she could see the Hilliard sisters on a dais. Miss Serena in a stand-alone purple brocade, Sally in ravishing peach-color satin. Their white hair was elaborately dressed in Colonial fashion. They were smiling, delicately flushed, lovely as old portraits.

Saxophones, strings, drums crashed into a theatric finale. The dancers drifted off through the doorways in whispering, laughing, pantomiming couples. Nancy took a step forward and stopped. Her heart thumped deafeningly. Leaning against the pillar not fifty feet from her was the pirate. And such a pirate. He might have stepped from a painting by Howard Pyle. Through her mind flashed the bit from Kingsley's Last Buccaneer which was her father's favorite bit of declamation when shaving;

> "There were forty craft in Avès that were both swift
>   and stout,
> All furnished well with small arms and cannons round
>   about;
> And a thousand men in Avès made laws so fair and
>   free
> To choose their valiant captains and obey them loy-
>   ally."

No doubt but what the sinister figure leaning against the pillar was a valiant captain, a pirate chief. A broad black hat was drawn low but not so low as to conceal the red bandana bound about his head. It seemed like a bloody gash between the hat and the ebony-hued mask which covered his face to the drooping mustache. Coarse hair hung almost to his shoulders, through its meshes glinted the gold of hoop earrings. On his chest, bared by the rolled-back collar of his white shirt, was tattooed a skull and crossbones. Into a broad red sash were thrust a brace of villainous pistols, beautifully damascened with silver arabesque, a sheathed knife of bloodcurdling proportions. Baggy blue trousers were tucked into high boots of red leather, the tops of which wrinkled in the most approved mousquetaire manner. The red cloak which swung from his shoulders almost touched the ground. Gauntleted gloves completed his costume. A wise masker to realize how betraying are hands, Nancy thought breathlessly.

Alec Pryde, of course. Hadn't Miss Sally warned her against a pirate? Why did he stand there staring at her? She could see the glint of his eyes between the slits of his mask. He thought that she was Sybyl. Hadn't he bribed Phyllis to find out how she would be costumed? Until the very last moment she had thought she was to wear great-great-grandmother Hilliard's gown. Could he have discov-

ered the change? He had a confident, biding-my-time air
which sent a little shiver over her.

In an effort to steady her pounding heart she drew a
long breath. Silly to be afraid of him. She threw back her
head with the little toss with which she defied obstacles.
Immediately the pirate started forward, as though accept-
ing the challenge. His eyes behind the black mask met
and held hers. Her spirit seemed to rush to meet him. Her
flamelike response terrified her. What did it mean?

"Am I falling in love with Alec? Am I?" she demanded
of her horrified self. The orchestra burst into a fanfaro-
nade of invitation. Through the doorways swept living
rainbows of color. Nancy stood as though hypnotized as
the pirate, still holding her fascinated by his eyes, approached. He caught her wrist and hissed between clenched
teeth;

"S'death woman! You'll dance with me!"

Delicious fooling, Nancy assured herself, to counteract
the icy little chills which the hoarse command had sent
chasing up and down her spine. In the moment in which
she resisted him someone tapped her on the shoulder. A
voice exulted;

"I told you I'd find you!"

She looked up into the black mask of a Sheik, a
jewel-turbaned Sheik, the last word in a motion-picture
Sheik. Luke Small! His habit of shifting his weight from
one foot to another would have betrayed him if his voice
hadn't. He made no effort to disguise it. His black eyes
exultantly regarded her through his mask. Before she
could think to reply with her fingers the pirate had swept
her into the maelstrom of color.

For an instant the lights, the dancers, the shifting hues,
even the rhythm of the music faded from Nancy's consciousness. Only the feel of a tightening arm, the compel-
ling touch of a gloved hand, the faint thud of a man's
heartbeats seemed real. Brasses and strings swung into a
request number. The musicians sang;

    " 'Why am I lonely and why am I blue
      And why am I thinking just thinking of you?
      Why should I care if you've broken your vow

> And why do I wonder who's kissing you now?
> Because I love you . . .' "

Voice after voice caught up the refrain;

> " 'Because I love you . . .' "

The caressing vibration through words and music was like a soft whisper against her heart.

So, this was what it meant to dance with Alec, she thought tensely. He was a different Alec from the one with whom she had driven and had tea. She couldn't tell just why. She fought an almost ungovernable desire to rest her face against his sleeve. Frightened, panic-stricken— even as her feet moved in perfect rhythm with his—she rushed up the heavy artillery of reason to her defence. This man with whom she was dancing had broken up her brother's home. Her father had warned;

"From long practice Pryde's technique with women had reached superb perfection."

She'd say that it had when he roused in her this aching, melting desire to be crushed in his arms, in her who had been so coolly self-sufficient. She had seen the same thing happen in the lives of others, why should she expect to escape? What would she get for all she gave? Love? Love as rootless as a mushroom. Moth and candle stuff. She was a silly moth and Alec a super-sophisticated candle.

The music stopped. In the midst of the tumultuous applause for an encore the pirate swung her through a doorway to the foyer where an electric fountain spouted its crystal spray through softly changing lights. Evergreen trees outlined alluring retreats. Two Pierrots had commandeered one, a whispering Franklin and Marie Antoinette occupied another, a Sheik and a witch in red satin slippers sat close together in a third. Luke Small and Sybyl! The combination stirred a curious sense of foreboding in Nancy's mind. The pirate drew her into an enclosure.

"Told you I'd recognize you," he reminded. The faint effervescence of laughter sparkled through the thick guttural whisper. The girl answered with mitted fingers;

"Meestake. I come from far countree."

"Od's blood! A French woman!"

"Oui. Canada."

"How'd you get here?"

Her arms flapped like the wings of a bird.

"Flew?"

She nodded her head with its soft white puffs and curls. In the hall beyond the orchestra had yielded to the demands for an encore. Drums were tapping, trombones sliding, saxophones whining, strings sighing;

" 'Because I love you . . .' "

The pirate resorted to the sign language. Clumsily with his gloved fingers he questioned;

"Flying back tonight?"

" 'I've tried so hard but can't forget . . .' "

The melody sang on in the girl's mind ever as she answered in the deaf mute language;

"Midnight."

He growled;

"Cinderella stuff! Stab me, woman! You go with me— when the clock strikes twelve. My ship's on the river."

Ship! River! Go with him! Did he—did Alec think that she was Sybyl? Of course he did. They had patched up their quarrel. Should she undeceive him? The tap-tap of drums, the chuckle of saxophones, the thrum of violins accompanied Nancy's thoughts as they swept on.

Why not go with the man whose nearness sent her heart skyrocketing to her throat? She pulled herself back as from the edge of precipice. To even consider it was disloyalty to Bruce now that she realized Alec's attraction for her. She was dishonorable to allow the temptation to send out even the tiniest root.

" 'Because I miss you I often wish we'd never met' "

If only the silly song would stop thrumming against her heart. She rebelled; "Oh, but I'd like to be gorgeously reckless! My whole life has been spent taking care of people. Why shouldn't I do as I want once?" She admonished herself sternly;

"Indulging in self-pity, are you? You'd better make your get-away, Miss Caswell, while the going's fairly good. Break the spell of this bluggy pirate."

He caught her with his gloved hand as she turned away. She threw the green cape with its ample hood over

her shoulder. She was going home. The lights, the
dancers, the perfumes, the cigarette smoke, the fight between her heart and her loyalty to Bruce had become
unbearable. No one would see her go. Thanks to the
syncopated thrum, thrum of the orchestra everyone was
dancing. As she reached the wide-open door of the building the village clock ponderously boomed the hour.

" 'The iron tongue of midnight hath told twelve,' " she
quoted under her breath in her father's most dramatic
manner. Her father! The thought of him was like a potent, soothing balm on the turmoil of her spirit. She could
hear his rich voice saying;

" 'I have set watchmen upon thy walls, O Jerusalem.' "

Watchmen upon the walls. The thought warmed her.
Her sense of humor came tripping back as she realized
the ludicrous surreptitiousness of her departure. She
laughed;

"Cinderella fleeing on the stroke of twelve."

She ran down the broad steps. At their foot she stopped
and looked back. Lot's wife brought up to date. The
laughter vanished from eyes and lips as a man appeared
in the doorway. The pirate! Was he following her? Silly
for her heart to pound. Why couldn't she remember that
this was part of the fun, part of the masquerade. If Alec
was too convincing an actor it was her fault for being so
credulous. But, he seemed so real. So savage. With inex-
plicable terror she began to run. She couldn't have done
anything more idiotic, she scolded herself as she heard
quick steps behind. Of course he'd chase her. Part of the
game. She'd stop and then—a hand caught her arm; a
rough voice reminded;

"Od's blood, woman! Did ye think to escape? You're
coming with me."

He threw his cape about her and held her in one arm
as he hurried her to a roadster in the shadow. She struggled as she was unceremoniously lifted into it. For an
instant she was terrified. Horrible stories flashed through
her mind. Hadn't Nora warned her that a dark, foreign
man would try to run away with her? Should she call for
help? Always she had wondered if she would be able to
make a sound in time of stress. Terror was so numbing.
Absurd. Of course the pirate was Alec. Hadn't Miss Sally

warned her to avoid him? Hadn't she sensed an undertone
of laughter through his voice even at its roughest? Why
couldn't she remember that she was at a masquerade ball?
Why didn't she play the game?

She forced herself to sit as quiet as the proverbial
mouse. She would be a sport. She would let Alec drive
her to the Manse. She wouldn't dare go further with this
aching awareness of him tugging at her heart. Would
Bruce despise her if he knew?

Was someone shouting behind them? With a sound
which was a cross between a growl and a highly seasoned
invective the pirate threw in the clutch. Nancy pushed
back the hood of her cape. It lay on her shoulders like a
soft pink shell as she turned. In a beam of light in the
doorway stood the Sheik. A wildly gesticulating Sheik.
Luke Small? He started down the steps.

With superb skill the masked man at the wheel backed
from between parked automobiles and reached the highway. Nancy saw a speeding car behind them. It kept in
the shadow. Was Luke driving it? Why should he be in
such furious pursuit? Had his smoldering hostility to Alec
Pryde burst into flame? The car stopped. A dusky figure
jumped out. A puncture? She hoped that there were four.
She forgot her distrust of the man beside her, forgot the
tragedy of her flaming response to his presence as she
exulted;

"To borrow from the vernacular of Phyl-*us*, the Sheik
is sunk, Alec."

"Alec!"

With the gruff repetition the pirate pulled off mask and
mustache. The gleam of white teeth in his bronzed face,
the smoldering brilliance of his dark eyes, were in character with his barbaric costume as Geoffrey Hilliard corrected;

"I'm not Alec! Sorry to disappoint you, but—you'll go
with me just the same. Stab me, if you won't, woman!"

Chapter XV

Nancy gazed incredulously at the clean-cut profile of the man beside her. Geoffrey Hilliard! It was Geoffrey Hilliard to whom her pulses had flamed response. How could she have mistaken him for Alec? But, Miss Sally had told her—Miss Sally! Had she deliberately misled them all?

Where was he taking her? She didn't care. She drew a long, ragged breath of relief. The pirate was not Alec Pryde. That was all that mattered for the moment. Why hadn't she known it? Love Alec! She couldn't. Entertaining and companionable as he might be her contempt for him was as impregnable as Gibraltar. Was the pirate really Geoffrey Hilliard or was she dreaming? She stole a glance at his stern face. No dream. Reality. In response to his eyes her heart had grown wings and flown straight into his arms. His photograph had had a curious fascination for her; she had written that letter hoping that it would bring him back to Sunnyfield—only for the sake of his people? Had she loved him subconsciously?

Her thoughts surged on in time to the fast moving wheels of the roadster. She had honestly believed that she disliked him, disapproved of him. She had been flourishing a wooden sword and now it lay in pieces at her feet, snapped like the toy it was by the glint of eyes behind a mask, by the touch of a man's arms. Thank heaven that her heart had kept her from disloyalty to Bruce and her ideals. The relief, the unutterable relief to be free of the nightmare of this last hour when she had thought she loved a man like Alec Pryde. Her spirit soared. She laughed.

"Glad you find the situation amusing." Geoffrey Hilliard commented icily.

Her buoyant mood chilled in response. He hadn't mentioned her name. She still wore her mask. Miss Sally had told him that Sybyl was to wear his great-great-great-grandmother's gown. He had spoken of her as that "poor,

135

charming, little woman." She was fascinating. Hadn't he declared Nancy Caswell to be the most disagreeable and unlovable girl he had ever met? Would he choose her for a companion this glorious night? Not a chance. Had he disliked her so much that day when he had kissed her? Memory caught at her breath.

"Better take off that mask and make yourself comfortable. You're going with me even if I'm not Pryde, Miss Caswell," the man beside her announced curtly.

Miss Caswell he had said, not Mrs. Nancy's heart spun into a merry-go-round of jubilation and steadied. He knew who she was. If he thought her disagreeable why had he asked her to come? Asked her? That was funny. There had been no invitation in his gruff;

"Od's blood, woman! Did ye think to escape? You're coming with me."

Why question? Why not enjoy the present? A sigh, soft as a bit of down, registered her content as she pulled off her mask. Heavenly air. The breeze flung back the hood of her cape till it billowed like a faint pink cloud on her shoulders, ruffled and tossed the curls of her white wig. Her heart threw over a few sandbags of discretion and mounted buoyantly into her voice as she inquired;

"How did you know me? Miss Sally had told you that Sybyl was to wear this costume."

"I begin to suspect that my aunt Sally is a deceiver of the deepest dye. I asked her for two brass portière rings of which to make these spectacular earrings I'm wearing. That was all the clue she needed as to my costume. Know you! I'd recognize you anywhere by the tilt of your chin—and in spite of the scent of cigarette smoke."

"Then you didn't think I was Sybyl when . . ."

"I kidnapped you? Not a chance. I wanted a companion on this midnight excursion. Sorry to disappoint you by being myself, not Alec, but, it's better for you. Little country girls shouldn't go night-riding with cavaliers from the gay city."

"Aren't you from the gay city?"

"No. I'm a sedate mid-state paper manufacturer. A domestic, feet-on-the-fender type."

"You! Domestic! Feet-on-the-fender! A new self fresh from the mint? You've been roving the world for years."

"I've changed all that. Old Sophocles was right when he said that no man can avoid his destiny. Looks as though it was up to me to keep the Hilliard Mills going. New methods are coming into the paper industry and we'll have to keep abreast of them or be relegated to the back-number class." He added irrelevantly, "I shan't forget your voice when you called me 'Alec' if I live a thousand years."

The clipped curtness of his words sent a stinging rush of tears to Nancy's eyes. Could she make him understand? She had thought that he was Alec, but, a new Alec, one whom never before had she realized. If only he would be a bit more approachable. Could she meet his indifference with indifference when she was so glowingly aware of him? She schooled her voice to lightness as she replied;

"Has my voice such a carrying quality? Think of its ringing down a thousand years. Would you mind telling me, Mr. Kidnapper, whither you are taking your struggling victim?"

"Good little sport to make the best of it. I can't spare the time to take you back even if I wanted to. I don't. Couldn't even stop to change this absurd costume. Business appointment. However, it will be safe to promise that I'll have you at the Manse long before the family is astir."

"Such a relief to know that I am to be returned," Nancy murmured. Her frivolous retort made no dent in his grave aloofness. She wondered if he had heard as with eyes intent on the road ahead he increased the speed of the car. It really didn't matter if she didn't get home until early morning. Her father knew that the ball would last until the wee hours. Phyllis and her mother must be at the Manse by now. The girl was alert to any sound from Betty's room at night. No one would be alarmed by her absence. No one need know of it until she appeared for breakfast. Why not slough off responsibilities and enjoy every moment of the swift motion through the crisp air?

Overhead the dark heavens were lighted by a broad boulevard of thickset stars. The moon, cosily cradled in a lone, fleecy cloud, kept vigil with one canny eye. Its light silvered a world set asparkle by the first frost of autumn. Faint perfumes drifted from walled gardens. Once the roadster swerved sharply to avoid a rabbit squatting in the road, its long ears rampant, its fascinated eyes like red sparks. Other cars swish-swished by. The World and his Wife seemed bent on enjoying the perfect night. An occasional state policeman on a snorting motorcycle would approach, pass with an appraising scowl at the roadster, and roar away.

"Comfortable?" Geoffrey Hilliard inquired.

"It's heavenly."

"That tone to me! Do you realize that this is the second time you've seemed really friendly since I came to Sunnyfield? I'll bet that tomorrow you'll blackball me again."

"I'm reversing that rule of the White Queen's, 'Jam yesterday, jam tomorrow but never jam today.' I'm being friendly today. I buried the hatchet, accepted the olive branch and waved a flag of truce in one fell swoop when instead of scrambling out of this car I remained in it," Nancy explained gaily.

"Then we'll make the most of the truce. You've been on the edge of the seat ever since we started. Lean back. That's better."

He glanced over his shoulder at the highway, which unrolled behind them like a strip of shining, dusky carpet, before he stopped the car. He tucked the rug more securely about her satin-shod feet and produced a silk muffler.

"Tie this over your head gypsy fashion, your hood keeps blowing back. No, tuck your hands under the run, I'll do it. Hold up your chin."

He kept his attention sedulously on his fingers. Nancy felt her heart coming flaming up into her eyes felt it beat its wings against his cool, grim detachment. More than anything she had ever wanted in her life she wanted him to kiss her, she whose spirit had fled into its inner temple and bolted the door whenever a man had attempted a caress. "Strangely potent this thing we call, for want of a better name, 'attraction,' " her father had said.

"All set?"

She nodded in answer to the curt question. The car slid forward smoothly. She had the sense of floating along on billows of happiness. Her anxiety for her father, her passionate rebellion against the smashing of her brother's

life, her disappointment—of which she had been horribly
ashamed—when obliged to give up her growing business
in New York, grew fainter and more like a misty troubled
dream with every mile through the stinging air with its
acrid scent of fallen leaves. On either side of the road
stiffened branches and twigs gave forth a fairy symphony
as they clashed softly one against the other making the
scraping sound of innumerable violins.

"Asleep?"

She shook her head in answer to the low question.

"In a comatose state of comfort shot through with
occasional flashes of wonder as to where and on what
mysterious business we are speeding. You aren't by any
chance in the Intelligence Department of the Govern-
ment?"

"You are getting warm." The gravity of his voice
quenched the laughter in her eyes. "I'm on a secret mission—of sorts. And all because your other admirer has
doublecrossed us."

"My other! Do you credit me with only two? If you
mean Luke what has he done now?"

"That query suggests that he has done something before. Were you warning me against him the day you
crashed into my life from the top of the hay-load? You
told me that that he had had an advantageous offer from
another paper mill."

"Not exactly warning."

"It took time for your meaning to penetrate but it sank
in finally. I've known, the boys with whom I grew up
knew, that Luke Small was infernally jealous of me. It
was excusable enough at the time. His father, his home,
the family mill were swept away. Apparently I had everything he'd lost. One of the reasons why I have kept away
from Sunnyfield these last years was to avoid embarrass-
ing the Squire. I knew that if I came there was bound to
be a show-down between his manager and his son. I
thought that Luke was invaluable to the business. Then
your letter came. There was no reference in it to complications at the mill but somehow it breathed a warning. I
came. I watched. I waited. When the Squire decided that
I could help him Luke blew up. Warm enough?"

Nancy nodded and moved the fraction of a degree

nearer. The feel of his arm against hers gave a heart-
warming sense of safety and well-being. The car swerved.
He righted it swiftly. A clear cold wind rushed by. The
frosty road crackled under the wheels. Trees and shrubs
sparkled like Christmas greens powdered with artificial
snow. A black cat with eyes as huge and green as a
Maharaja's emeralds scampered across the road with
brazen defiance of danger. From a long, low barn came
the scent of hay and warm animal bodies, the wavering
light of a lantern, the grotesquely distorted shadow of a
man, the bleat of a new born calf. Geoffrey Hilliard
slowed down the car.

"Hear the soft clash of a cow-bell? I love the sound. It
recalls so many happy memories of my life here as a
boy."

"I was brought up in a city. I'm a twentieth century
model except in respect to cows. I confess to mid-
Victorian terror of them at close range. Am I to know
what Luke Small has done to make this midnight trip
necessary?"

"That information is due you in return for your prompt
help in getting the Squire and me away from the mill.
You won't like it. Aunt Sally intimated that there was
a stronger bond than friendship between you and Luke."

"We owe him a great deal for recommending Dad to
your father for the mill parish and he is always patient
and dear with Betty. Miss Sally has a match-making
complex. If her suspicion had foundation the more reason
I should know the truth about Luke. We've had matrimo-
nial mistakes enough in our family."

"And yet you allow Pryde . . ."

"About Luke? You were saying?"

He laughed shortly before he began to relate the events
of the last twelve hours. Nancy listened incredulously.
Except for the absence of automatics and skulking accom-
plices the story was stout melodrama stuff. It seemed
unbelievable that a man whom she had known and liked—
with reservations—could be such a traitor. Should she tell
Geoffrey that the Sheik who had started to follow them
was Luke Small? He must know it else why had he driven
away from the Town Hall at breakneck speed? He closed
the recital with;

"That renewal must be in the hands of our customer by ten tomorrow—no, this morning."

"How can you deliver it and have me back at the Manse before the family is stirring? We'll be stopped as lunatics at large if we are seen in these clothes. What is that long lighted thing ahead? Are we near enough to the city for it to be a trolly car?"

Hilliard leaned forward.

"It is a car but—apparently it's being used as a night-lunch place. See the lights along the side? A name. N-O-G-I, isn't it? Want some hot coffee?"

"I'd love it, but I ought to tell you. I am sure that Luke Small started after us."

"Thought it was he. Had a blow-out, hadn't he? He'd have to stop to change a tire. His car can't begin to make the time of mine. We're safe enough. We need that coffee. Wasn't it Napoleon who said that an army fought better on a full stomach?"

"Are you looking for a fight?"

"Not here."

He stopped the roadster at the boardwalk approach to the lunch car. Nancy tingled with excitement as she confessed;

"One of the desires of my life is about to be gratified. Coffee at a night lunch emporium. I'm thrilled to death. What will the proprietor think when we burst in upon him in these costumes?"

"He must have all sorts of queer patrons on this highway to New York. He may suspect that we are . . ."

"An eloping couple?"

"One guess is as good as another—for him. Come on."

He caught her arm as the high heels of her green satin slippers skidded treacherously on the frosty planks, kept a tight hold as they mounted the tricky steps. As he pushed open the door the gamy wraiths of countless long-ago hot dogs, of gallons of strong coffee rushed to greet them. The white coated Japanese proprietor dozing behind the counter sprang to his feet. His black hair shone like lacquer, his white teeth glistened. He brushed his claw-like hand across his eyes as though to assure himself that he was awake as he stared at the man and girl who entered. His gaze riveted on the sinister skull and cross-bones on

Geoffrey Hilliard's chest as the pirate threw back his long red cloak.

From the realistic imitation of tattooing his eyes flashed to the bandana bound head, to the broad red sash, widened as they lingered on pistols and knife, traveled on down the baggy blue trousers and wrinkled-top boots. They shifted to the girl in her quaint green velvet cape, to the white curls which hung below the kerchief. His observation concluded, the Jap's face settled into calm inscrutability. He bowed as low as the counter behind which he stood permitted.

"Gladful overpowering. Lady and gent much come from movie-acting?"

Geoffrey Hilliard laughed.

"Of course. We're Doug and Mary." He lifted the cape from the girl's shoulders with disturbing care. "You'll be too warm with this. Sit here and decide what you'll have to eat."

Perched on the high seat Nancy crossed her slippered feet with their sparkling buckles in an effort to maintain her equilibrium. Hilliard indicated the hanging placard which presented the menu:

"What will you have?"

"Wheat cakes and coffee. The mere thought of them makes me ravenous."

The proprietor approved ingratiatingly;

"Wheat cakes most glorious special-ity. Excellency with pistols also partake of such deliciousness?"

"Yes. Do you cook this most glorious speciality yourself—or have you a helper, Nogi? You are Nogi, aren't you?" Geoffrey Hilliard inquired before he hung his red cloak on a peg, and crushed his black hat on another. He was even more convincingly a pirate without them, Nancy decided with a queer little shiver. She looked at the proprietor to note his reaction. A glint of expression like a faint light flashed over his mask of a face before he assured;

"I cook usual, most time. Last night esteemed relative from Tokio appear. He say, 'Nogi, I out of job. Give me most honorable position to cook hot dog.' An' he say, 'I cook. You try.' He cook. I eat. Hot dog most delectable, quite."

Why did Geoffrey allow the man to waste time talking, when every moment counted, Nancy wondered. Had he forgotten that Luke Small had started in pursuit of them? He wouldn't give up the chase if a dozen blow-outs retarded him. If only the Jap would hurry. The slight drawl which had been absent from Geoffrey Hilliard's voice these last few weeks was in evidence again as he debated;

"I haven't a doubt but what you think he's a cook, Nogi, but, I'll take a look at that relative before you serve his wheat cakes to the lady."

Nancy protested;

"Oh, don't stop for that. Of course he's all right."

The Japanese interposed with wounded dignity;

"Most honorable movie sir doubt Nogi? This way, then. Relative from Tokio be superbly honored."

He bowed and pulled aside the curtain which screened the end of the car, once the motorman's bailiwick, now the kitchenette, if the smells and sizzles emanating therefrom were to be believed.

Perched on the high stool Nancy looked after them. Curious that Geoffrey should be so fussy as to the cook. One would think that he had all the time in the world. Perhaps though, he knew better than she, perhaps he knew that Luke Small was not on their trail. She opened her hands clenched on her lap. How like her to get tense over the situation.

She looked about her. On the wall hung a calendar of mammoth proportions, augmented by the picture of a girl of incredible blondeness and unbelievable pink and whiteness. The long, marbleized counter was abundantly supplied with impregnable vinegar and oil cruets, robust mustard pots and adamantine salt-shakers. Standards of glass-shelves displayed a tempting assortment of pies and cakes. The rear end of the car was evidently devoted to living quarters. Against the broad glass was a shelf which held a varied and shining array of curious Japanese plant receptacles. There were struggling begonias, geraniums showing a scarlet tinge in their slightly open buds, an anaemic heliotrope, a fern or two, a stout-hearted ivy which already had begun to climb. A scrubby batch but to Nancy it represented a little garden-spot of color, a little garden-spot of growth.

The proprietor padded in with a heaped-up plate of sizzling hot wheat cakes, light as down, appetizingly brown. He deposited it before her, added a pat of the yellowest butter she had ever seen, drew forward a pressed glass jug full of a dark and mysterious looking liquid and vanished into the kitchenette. He reappeared in an instant with a mug of imperishable thickness full of what smelled to be delicious coffee. He answered the girl's glance toward the kitchen.

"Most Excellency say the lady not wait for himself. He make sure his wheat cakes be of particular brownness."

"Curious that Geoff doesn't hurry," Nancy thought, "But no more curious than other events of this dream-like night." She ate and drank, conscious of the bright bead-like eyes of the Japanese upon her. From the kitchenette came the rumble of voices. She drew a little breath of relief as Geoffrey Hilliard appeared and apologized;

"Forgive me for leaving you so long. Got interested in the esteemed relative from Tokio. I've spent months in that city. I ate my cakes while I listened to him. Weren't yours good?" He frowned down upon the portion remaining on the plate.

"Delicious but enough for an army. Did you think me the demon cake-eater? Oughtn't we to—a car stopped!" Geoffrey laid his hand over hers which had gripped his sleeve as they stood together listening. "It sounded like Alec's."

He withdrew his hand.

"You ought to know. It has stopped at your gate often enough. You . . ." he broke off to listen to the heavy footsteps crackling on the frosty boardwalk. They cautiously mounted the steps. He whispered, "I'll be back," and disappeared into the kitchenette.

Hands gripping the counter behind her, looking like a lady from a painted fan in her green brocade and filmy laces, Nancy faced the door. Why had Alec come, she wondered. Had he seen her leave the village? Had someone told him that— She stared unbelievingly as the door was pulled open and a Sheik appeared on the threshold. Luke! Had he borrowed Alec's car in which to follow Geoffrey Hilliard? The great jewel in the front of his turban blazed like a flame in the dingy place, his black eyes seemed to burn like coals as he stared back at her. The proprietor addressed him suavely;

"More bewildering movie actor? It becomes most delightful honor to . . ."

With a silencing wave of his hand Luke Small motioned him aside. He took a step forward as he announced roughly:

"Here's where I cut in on your joy-ride with that bounder, Pryde, Nancy."

Chapter XVI

If a sense of the swift on-coming of a crisis hadn't clutched at her heart Nancy could have laughed aloud in relief. Luke thought that she was with Alec! If only Geoffrey, on the other side of that hanging had heard, he could make his get-away and go on with the renewal. She raised her voice;

"Don't be silly, Luke. What business is it of yours what I do? Know of any reason why I shouldn't ride around the country at any old time I like? It's done by the best families now, you know." She strained her ears to listen. Had a door closed softly? Was there a slight crackle outside as of frosty earth? Luke mustn't hear. With an abrupt motion of her arm she swept plate and cup to the floor. The crash echoed and re-echoed. She smiled sweetly at the proprietor who hastened to pick up the débris.

"So sorry, Mr. Nogi. Careless of me."

Luke Small blustered;

"I feel responsible to Bruce for your safety, Nancy. When Mrs. Sybyl told me that you and Pryde had planned to elope tonight . . ."

"Sybyl told you that!"

"Said that Pryde had boasted of it to her when he took her home from the Manse."

Alec had said that? Fury set the blood ringing in Nancy's ears. She steadied her voice to demand;

"How did she know that the pirate was—was Alec?"

"Miss Sally told her. She intimated to me that you were going as a witch. But I knew you at once. I think the old lady mixed us up on purpose. When you and the pirate bolted into a roadster which looked like Geoff Hilliard's I noticed Pryde's parked near the Hall. I thought Mrs. Sybyl had been mistaken. Then I figured that he'd be cagy enough to borrow a car to throw people off the scent. I started after you in mine. Tire went on the blink so I hurried back and took Pryde's. All in a good cause. You'd better come home with me at once if you don't want a scandal."

"A scandal!"

"When Mrs. Sybyl confided her news as to the elopement she was so excited, begged me so hard to save you—that's what she said, 'Save Nancy,' that the couple near must have heard."

The girl returned to her perch on the stool. Nice mess Sybyl had stirred up. She patted her hand over her lips to stifle a pretended yawn. Had Geoffrey taken advantage of her tip and gone? He knew that she would be safe with Luke. The renewal must be delivered. Was that muffled sound a car starting! A smarting sense of disappointment stung her eyelids for a moment. She felt deserted. She shook herself out of the mood. Silly! Of course Geoffrey had to go.

"Where is Pryde?" Luke Small demanded.

She fenced for time.

"Luke, I won't have you following me about as though you were a watch-dog. How should I know where Alec Pryde is? Dancing his shoes thin, probably."

"No use stalling, Nancy. Whose pirate cloak is that on the peg? Whose black hat? Pryde's. I'll find him."

She caught his sleeve as he took a step toward the kitchenette.

"You'll do nothing of the sort. I'll not have you mixing into my affairs. What right have you . . ."

Her voice departed in a throaty gurgle. The entrance door directly behind Luke had opened a trifle! A hand on the key! Luke Small caught up her suspended sentence;

"I'll tell you on the way home why I've the right. I gave up a chance to checkmate Geoffrey Hilliard tonight when I came for you. Let Pryde sneak out of sight. Bounder! I've made it my business to find out one or two things which will end his career in this village. Put on your cape. You're going back with me."

He turned as the door behind him swung wide. Geoffrey Hilliard entered and closed it softly behind him. Below the red bandana headdress his eyes blazed with anger, the silver inlay in pistols and dagger-sheath glistened in the light. With bare arms, tattooed to the elbows,

crossed on the chest, red booted feet slightly apart he
leaned back against the door. There was no suggestion of
drawl in his curt voice as he contradicted;

"She's not going back with you, Luke. When I start
out on an expedition with a lady I see it through."

"Oh, but Geoff, you . . ." Nancy swallowed the remain-
der of the protest as she met his warning eyes. She bit her
lips to steady them. A moment more and she would have
betrayed the secret of his mission. She chilled to icy
immobility as she saw Luke Small's eyes. There was a
touch of fanaticism in their glare as he commented with
low-voiced fury;

"So, you're the pirate. She went joy-riding with you!
You've done me out of my job, now you're planning to
snitch my girl. You won't."

He caught Nancy by the wrist. She tried to wireless to
Geoffrey. He must go on. Would he understand? She
acquiesced lightly;

"Of course I'll go back with you, Luke. Why make a
scene about it. I love Alec's car. Let my wrist go. You're
hurting me."

She met Geoffrey Hilliard's eyes. Were they contemptuous? Didn't he realize that she was trying to help him by
getting Luke out of his way? He crushed his black hat
low on his head, flung the red cape across his shoulders,
opened the door with a flourish, as he agreed;

"Ladies choice, of course."

He kept his eyes lowered as she passed him. Small
radiated satisfaction;

"Glad to see that you know when you're licked, Geoff.
Hold on a minute, Nancy. I want a cup of coffee. I was so
keen to follow you that I didn't stop for supper at the
ball. I . . ."

The sentence was rudely interrupted by the sharp closing of the door with Geoffrey and herself on the outside.
He turned a key in the lock. Caught her arm. Steadied her
down the frosty steps. Hurried her to Pryde's Hispana
Torpedo. Where was the car in which they had come?
Stolen? Had that battered flivver been left in place of it?
No time to ask questions now with Luke shaking the door
as a dog might shake a rat. With one foot on the step she
looked back;

"Should we leave them? Luke may hurt the proprie-tor."

"Not a chance. Nogi is sitting on the back steps with the key to the kitchenette door in his hand waiting for us to make our get-away. I left the other in the lock."

He tucked the rug about her feet, slipped behind the wheel and turned the car.

"Aren't we going on?" the girl demanded.

"No."

"But, when I told Luke that I'd return with him it was to give you the chance to go on with the renewal without having him suspect your errand," she protested.

"Was that the reason you turned me down?"

"Of course. How will you get that paper to the maga-zine people in time now?"

"It has gone."

"Gone! To New York?"

"Yes. My man Taka was the esteemed relative from Tokio. I 'phoned him to meet me here. Concluded that he could deliver that signed paper as well as I. I suspected that Luke Small would try to stop me. It wouldn't take him long to find out that the tank he had slashed had been repaired."

Was that what Luke had meant when he had said that he had given up a chance to checkmate Geoffrey Hilliard tonight? She remembered the glint of fanaticism in Small's eyes.

"And Taka took the car we came in?"

"Yes. He can make better time in that. Luke will have the excitement of jogging home in the Jap's flivver. He seems to be looking for trouble. I wonder if Alec has yet discovered that his car is missing."

"When he leaves the ball and finds it gone he'll be furious."

"When he finds you gone he'll be furious. Who set Luke on our trail?"

"Sybyl. Miss Sally had told her that Alec was to be the pirate. He had told Sybyl that he and I were—were—"

"Were what?" Geoffrey prodded implacably.

"Were going to elope tonight."

"Were you?"

His cool insistence angered the girl. She replied flippantly;

"That is our secret." She felt him stiffen. If only she could know that he cared.

"And you intend to keep it."

Nancy's defiance crumpled. Why did he persist in misunderstanding her? If only she had the courage to tell him that she loved being with him. No. He had assured her that she was disagreeable, unlovable. The aching, passionate desire to feel his arms about her came sweeping back. She must overcome it. Valiantly she forced her thoughts into other channels.

An occasional automobile shot by like a ghostly shadow. The world seemed eerily still, as though it were breathlessly awaiting that poignant instant when the sun should fling aside the curtain of the night and set the vast machinery of life in motion. The coming of day would unleash joy and sorrow, passion and prejudice, war and peace, lust and greed, desire and despair. Nancy pulled her cape closer about her. The thought gave her a queer shivery feeling. Usually she loved the morning awakening to zest of new achievement, but today—what would the coming hours bring to her and to those she loved? Into her mind flashed the vision of three soldiers marching shoulder to shoulder through the woods. She could see their merciless, uncompromising eyes, their fingers ready on the triggers of their guns, could see them smile as they pressed forward, steadily forward, with gay courage.

An hour passed, she could tell by the faint boom of a distant clock. A meteor went skiing adown the milky way. One by one the stars blinked out. The dark, still east turned slowly to pale gold. Scattered farmhouses, their roofs glistening with frost, fused into villages, villages dwindled into scattered farmhouses. Except for an occasional inquiry as to her comfort Geoffrey Hilliard maintained an aloof silence, his eyes on the road, gloved hands on the wheel.

Of what was he thinking, Nancy wondered. His lips were set, his brows drawn. Quite a different face from that of the care-free debonair man whose car she had stopped by crashing into the road in front of it. He had shouldered some of his father's burdens. Luke had made his return as difficult as possible. Had Luke made his escape from the night lunch car? What instructions had Nogi received as to the length of his incarceration? Would he try to overtake them? Traitor! This was the day he was to begin work at the Upper Mill. If he didn't start home soon he would have to report to his new boss in the costume of a Sheik. She stifled a laugh at the thought.

"What's the joke?" demanded Geoffrey Hilliard gruffly.

" 'A little thing but mine own,' " she retorted crisply. She resented his tone. If he persisted in misunderstanding her, he could remain angry. He couldn't for one instant really believe that she had planned to run away with Alec Pryde, she argued to herself defiantly, even as she resisted an unsteadying impulse to rest her cheek against his arm and tell him all about it.

Sybyl had sent Luke in pursuit to "save Nancy," she had said. Poor girl. She was frantic now with fear that the man for whom she had given up husband, child and home would desert her. Was she, Nancy Caswell, to blame for his apparent defection? She might be the occasion but the real cause was his instability of character. Someone would have attracted him during the months Sybyl had been at Reno. Curious of what different temperaments humanity was fashioned. The silent man beside her had had no interest in women for years because one silly girl had disappointed him.

"Why should I care if you've broken your vow?"

The sentimental song began to hum its way through her thoughts again. Had Alec Pryde heard the clank of chains in his approaching marriage with Sybyl? Curious!—Was it time for lilies already—there they were—high white drifts of them—*"Why do I wonder who's kissing you now?"*—Betty was playing in a rosy cloud of blossoms—the knight in glistening armor seemed responsible for their magic growth—he was waving a mailed hand above them—he was drawing closer and closer to the child, stealing up on her like a malevolent foe—*"Because I love you."*—was the knight singing?—he raised his mask. Alec Pryde. He was smiling. A cruel smile—he must not touch Betty; he hated her—she must save her—must call a warning—could she make a sound—she'd always wondered if in a moment of terror she could cry out for help—terror was so numbing—she'd try—

What had happened? The field of lilies had vanished! Something had stopped with a jerk. She felt an arm about her shoulders, the pressure of a cheek against hers, heard a man's voice amused, shaken comforting;

"Darling! Darling girl, you're dreaming."

She looked through dazed eyes at a bronzed face with a red bandana bound about the forehead, caught the gleam of white teeth, noted the laughing concern of grey eyes. For an instant she rested in utter content, then she remembered. Of course Geoffrey Hilliard hadn't called her "Darling!" The word had been part of her fantastic dream. He thought her disagreeable, unlovable. She shook off his tightening arm with a twist of her shoulders, adjusted her gypsy headdress as she inquired airily;

"Did I speak?"

He put his hand back on the wheel.

"Speak! You let out such a blood-curdling yell for help it's a wonder you didn't bring one of the state police down upon us. The highways are alive with them scouting to make sure that the new regulations are obeyed. Good Lord, here comes one now!"

Chapter XVII

A motorcycle with side-car which had swept around the
curve ahead pulled up beside the roadster. A state policeman in o.d. uniform, with bits of gold glistening in the
light of the lamps, automatic in hand, jumped on the
running board.

"What's going on here?" The lower jaw of his keen,
acquisitive face, sagged in astonishment as his flash-light
illumined the fantastically attired couple. Geoffrey Hilliard laughed.

"Nothing going on, Sergeant. We're on our way home
from a costume ball. I'll admit we look like escaped
lunatics."

"Lunatics! Yeah, that's a good line. If that's so why'd the
girl yell for help? Say—" he paused to inspect the car with
amazed eyes. He grunted. "Now what do you know about
that! You kinder messed things when you made the girl
scream, didn't you? When you're joy-riding in a stolen car
. . ."

"A stolen car! What do you mean?" demanded Hilliard
furiously. In his excitement he flung back his scarlet cape.
The silver inlay on pistols and dagger hilt thrust into his
broad red sash glittered bravely. Nancy's heart stood still
as she remembered. They were in Alec's car which Luke
Small had appropriated without leave. Of course the owner believed it had been stolen, of course he would have a
description broadcast at once. With persuasive charm she
hastened to prop up Geoffrey's explanation;

"I screamed because I dropped asleep and was having
a horrible night-mare—Captain. I dreamed that I was
being pursued and tried to call for help."

"Tried! I'll say you succeeded all right. I'm not a
captain, an' you know it. Tryin' the old oil, aren't you?
You can tell your story to the Chief when I land you at
the county jail. Start up that stolen car you—pirate."

"Don't be a crab, officer. This car belongs to a friend of mine and he . . ."

"Is zat so! Knows you got it, don't he? So he just rings up headquarters an' says for the force to be on the lookout for it. An' just to make things int'restin' offers a big reward to the man who finds it. Try another. Start her up!" His eyes narrowed in suspicion as Geoffrey spoke in a low tone to the girl. "On second thoughts I'll take your lady friend along in my car. Step out!"

Nancy protested;

"Step out! How do I know that you're not a bandit holding us up? It has been done."

The shocked amazement of the officer's face was proof enough of the genuineness of his authority. She choked back a nervous giggle as he glared at her and demanded;

"Say, can't you see that my outfit is real?"

"I haven't had much experience in being held up by the state police."

"Yeah, you haven't. Do I look like a bandit?"

"Does he look like a real pirate?"

"I'll say he does. Are you going to step into this car, quick, or have I got to put you in?"

Geoffrey's voice was ingratiating as he suggested;

"Let her remain with me and I give you my word of honor that we'll follow you." He reached into the pocket of his cape and produced a bill-fold. "Here's my license to prove . . ."

"Your license won't do no good. That honor stuff is a great line, an' you in a stolen car. Did you suppose I'd let you follow me with those pistols an' that knife in your belt? I wasn't born yesterday." He leveled his automatic at Hilliard's chest as he commanded, "Let the girl pull 'em out and hand 'em over. Quick now, you know what you get for resisting an officer."

Geoffrey Hilliard's tone was light though his eyes were black with fury.

"Take the pistols—Nan— The sooner we obey orders the sooner we'll be out of this mess. Get into his car. I'll keep alongside. No motorcycle can out-distance this roadster."

As she followed instructions Nancy coughed to camouflage a gurgle of laughter. Always she had wanted

to ride in a side-car. All her wishes seemed to be in the
way of being realized at once. First the night lunch, now
this. As they shot forward she observed the set face of the
young officer. No deviating from the Chief's orders for
him. Spade's a spade type. As the motorcycle roared
along the wind tugged at the gay kerchief about her head
and flung it back on her shoulders. The white curls of her
wig blew straight out behind. Side by side the roadster
kept pace.

With a snort of gas and a belch of smoke the motorcycle stopped in front of a building which Nancy recognized as the combination Town Hall, jail and court house
of a county. The main street in front of it was cluttered
with automobiles mostly in an advanced stage of dilapida-
tion. Thank heaven that Sunnyfield wasn't far distant, she
rejoiced as she and Geoffrey Hilliard preceded their captor up the broad steps. Had he an automatic at their
backs? She wriggled her shoulders uneasily. She looked
up at her companion in crime to voice her suspicion.
There was a touch of savage outlawry in his stalk. His
broad hat was pulled low. She could see only the grim
line of his mouth. She didn't wonder that the motor-cop
had felt it incumbent to remove arms from such a fierce
looking captive.

Even at this early hour a crowd of men had gathered to
watch and make merry over the offenders the police net
had landed. Nancy was uncomfortably conscious of eyes,
millions of them. Hard eyes. Sympathetic eyes. Serves-
her-right eyes. She heard a hoarse whisper;

"Ain't she handsome?"

A counter whisper;

"Hmp! Handsome is as handsome does. I guess them
two've ben joy-ridin', all right. Rich swells. Get on to the
car they come in? Caught with the goods."

Red spots in the girl's cheeks burned like coals. Instinctively she caught Hilliard's arm. He seized her hand and
held it tight.

"Don't mind. Don't mind anything till we get out of
this infernally ridiculous mess," he pleaded in a low tone.

A clock in the Town Hall tower struck. Nancy
counted. She had expected to be at the Manse by this
time. Her father would be wild with anxiety if he came

down stairs and found that she hadn't returned from the ball.

"Make them hurry! Please make them hurry," she whispered to Geoffrey as they stepped into a large smoky room full of people. The motorcycle Vigilantes had harvested a bumper-crop of law-breakers. With one foot in its green satin slipper rigidly beside its twin on the concrete floor she looked about. In spite of the presence of the stern-lipped pirate beside her she felt like a very small fly in the web of a very large spider.

"Don't be silly," she told herself. "You've done nothing wrong, unless at your age you should have known better than to go night-riding." She tried to submerge her uneasiness in observation of her surroundings. This was all the police stations she had seen on the silver sheet—plus. Behind the desk on a raised platform was a chair. Where was the Chief who, according to cinema formula, should be occupying it? Underlings hurried in and out. The law machine was grinding to capacity. Telephone bells shrilled. A clock ticked ponderously. The air was a heavy blend of tobacco, humanity and hectic perfume. She traced the scent to a stylish stout in tight crimson and brown clothing. The woman had achieved the sartorial effect of a baked apple threatening to burst its skin. A girl with bleached hair and hollow, rouged cheeks, suggesting a past and present as twisted as her lips, nudged Nancy with a sharp elbow, winked and giggled. Sordid. Tragic.

A door clanged. Men and women stiffened to attention. A man stepped to the platform. A ruddy faced young man with twinkling eyes, not at all the hoary headed type of the celluloid screen. His glance roved over the faces. A high-voltage exclamation from Geoffrey Hilliard. The Chief stared at him as though disbelieving his eyes. He shouted with laughter. He bent forward to hiss;

"Od's blood! Straight into 'em before they recover their wits! Prepare to board!"

Geoffrey swooped forward thundering;

"The grapnels! Pass the word to the gunners! Mac!"

"Geoff!"

The two men shook hands as though they never would stop while officials and apprehended motorists looked on in a comatose state of wonder. The Chief sensed the situation first. He glanced in a boyish, shame-faced way at the men in uniform on either side of him. He beckoned to them and whispered. They grinned in sympathetic understanding. He included Geoffrey in the low-voiced colloquy. He nodded and chuckled as he listened to his explanation. Once or twice he interrupted with an eager question. Then it seemed but an instant to Nancy before she was stepping into Alec's car, before Geoffrey was beside her his hand on the wheel, before the young state policeman who had brought them there was presenting the damascened pistols and dagger. His face was a lively red as he apologized;

"Sorry for the mistake, sir, but the young lady did let out a yell to set your hair on end, didn't she?"

"She did."

"I hope you explained to the Chief. You seem to be a friend of his. I don't want to get in wrong with him."

"He understands. I suggest that the next time you confiscate firearms you examine them. These pistols have no triggers. Good-morning."

The car shot ahead leaving a crestfallen officer of the law behind it. The east was brightly pink. Day stalked over the hilltops. With breath-snatching splendor came the sun. Mauve and purple spirals of smoke rose from farmhouse chimneys. Cows stopped nubbing the greenish brown stubble in pastures to solemnly regard the roadster as it flashed by. Flivvers filled with workmen passed. Nancy drew a long breath of relief. The nightmare of that courtroom was behind them. She quickened to the beauty of the morning.

"That young state policeman must feel like the King of France in command of his forty thousand men. He marched us in then marched us out again. What miracle did you work?"

She smiled in sympathy with Geoffrey Hilliard's laugh.

"That Chief was Mac Donovan. His father was fore-man of our paper mills when we were boys. He was my most loyal, bloodthirsty understudy when he was a wick-ed buccaneer and I was a pirate chief. Haven't seen him since I went to prep school. His family moved away from Sunnyfield. Have always intended to look him up. He's made steadily good and is now in a position of authority.

Remembering how keen he was to make our prisoners
walk the plank I'll bet he eats up his present job. He said
that when he saw me before him in this regalia he thought
he'd died and followed me to heaven—or the other place.
I told him that I'd introduced Betty to the island stronghold. It didn't take long to exlain to him how I came to
be in Alec's car—good Lord, how he hated Luke Small—
and your bloodcurdling call for help."

"I'm sorry."

"Because you dreamed—against my shoulder? I'm not,
but, we won't go into that now. I was furious with myself
for having dragged you into such a mix-up. There was
nothing to do but obey the officer's orders. No use buck-
ing the fellows. They're Tzars when on the job. I'd rather
have them exceed their authority than have them lax. If it
hadn't been that you were sharing it I'd go through much
more annoyance for the joy of finding Mac again. He was
a great pal. I loved him, loved his rosy, buxom mother—I
lost mine just when I had begun to appreciate what a
mother meant—loved her shining kitchen and above all,
her molasses cookies."

His thoughts trailed off into the land of memory where
Nancy could not follow. His lips and eyes smiled, his
face, under the rakish hat and bandana was young, boyish. How he must have loved Mac Donovan and his
family, the girl thought with a twinge of jealousy. The
faint strokes of a village clock stole through the crisp air.
She counted;

One! Two! Three! Four! Five! Six! Seven! Eight!

Eight o'clock! The household at the Manse had been
astir long before. Was her father terribly anxious about
her? Geoffrey Hilliard divined her thought.

"Eight, and I was confident that I'd have you back
before daylight. My fault. I shouldn't have carried you
off, but—it's done. I'll explain to your father."

"Thank you, but I'll make my own explanations. I
could have protested against being kidnapped, you
know."

Good grief, how her voice had shaken. Would he understand that she meant that she had loved being with
him, Nancy wondered. But he only answered curtly;

"I haven't forgotten that you thought you were going with Alec."

Under a sky intensely blue the roadster sped between rows of standardized houses, their commonplaceness transformed to beauty in the lovely light of morning; passed wide lawns shaded with maples flaming with color deepening toward the trunks, vistas of gardens lightly frost-touched, sheltering hedges, green shadows, the warm red of bricks. And then the Manse, snuggling close to the ground much as might a downy yellow and white chick who regards the passing show from the sanctuary of the soft feathers of its mother's back. Geoffrey Hilliard stopped the car;

"Well, here we are!"

The door of the house opened as by magic. Noah Caswell stood on the threshold. Behind him Nancy glimpsed Sybyl's white face. Sybyl here! Why? Was this the last curious twist to the adventure of the night?

"Sybyl has stirred up Dad," she whispered. "Better not come in. The weather-spy perched aloft in my brain warns;

" 'Watch out for storms!' "

"I rather enjoy storms," Geoffrey assured gravely and followed her along the silvery pattern of stepping-stones which gave to the porch. Her father caught her hands and drew her into the living-room. The canary in its gilded cage rendered an ecstatic *aria* of welcome. The burning logs on the hearth rocketed a shower of sparks. After an incredulous stare at the pirate, Sybyl, in the witch costume, sank into the wing chair. She bit her carmined lips to steady their quiver.

Nancy saw the color flood her father's white face, heard his unmistakable sigh of relief as he recognized her companion. Had he thought she had eloped with Alec Pryde? Of course. Otherwise why was Sybyl here? Why did Geoffrey Hilliard stand by the mantel as though he were a prisoner before his judge? If only he would go home and leave the situation to her to manage. It wouldn't be his idea of chivalry. Noah Caswell cleared his throat before he inquired with a brave attempt at lightness;

"Going to tell your old Dad all about it, Nan?"

Emotion caught at the girl's throat. She might have known that he would take it like that. The affair would have been nothing but a humorous adventure if Sybyl hadn't turned it to melodrama. Had Alec lied to her or from suspicion had she fabricated the yarn about the elopement? How much could be told of the night's ride without betraying confidence? As though he divined her question Geoffrey Hilliard prompted;

"Go as far as you like."

Evidently Luke's treachery was not to be kept a secret. Sorry, she had liked him—to a degree. Her father laid his hand on her shoulder.

"Sybyl came here in great anxiety for you, Nan. She knew that you left the ball early. She had been told that you were going with Pryde."

"I thought that the pirate was he when we started. I had been given the wrong tip as to his costume. Crafty Miss Sally."

"Where did you think you were going with—Pryde?" Noah Caswell brought out the name with bitter contempt. Sybyl leaned forward as though holding her breath to listen. It was an effort for Nancy to keep her voice from traitorous unsteadiness as she answered;

"I didn't think. The moon was too beautiful, the air and the car too enticing. For once I threw my convictions as to the proper behavior of a clergyman's daughter overboard. I held them under water until they sank. When I discovered that the pirate driver wasn't Alec—I went just the same."

"But Alec told me . . ."

"Alec has told you many things, Sybyl, which are not true." Nancy was conscious of the lash in her words. Her sister-in-law colored hotly as she probed eagerly;

"Then if you've been driving all night with Mr. Hilliard of course you're engaged to him?"

The hope in her voice sent a wave of fury burning to Nancy's hair. Geoffrey Hilliard straightened, tossed the cigarette he had been smoking into the fire. Was he preparing to resent having the most disagreeable, unlovable girl he had ever met stuffed down his throat? She'd save him the trouble, she vowed to herself. Her laugh was edged as she derided;

"Conventions from you, Sybyl? Where do you get that engagement stuff? One would think you'd stepped out of the Victorian age. Just because I . . ."

Surprise stampeded her voice as Alec Pryde appeared on the threshold. Immaculate, perfectly groomed, faultlessly apparelled in grey sports clothes he radiated self-approval. A prodigal with charm to beguile the heart, a niggard with honor, Nancy thought contemptuously. In comparison Geoffrey Hilliard in his pirate costume, a smudgy shade of beard on his inscrutable face, looked tawdry to a degree. Pryde caught her hands in his as he reproached with caressing fervor;

"You've given me the fright of my life. It's all over town that you've eloped with a pirate. With *me*. Sweltering in chain mail, I was dangling after a black witch—I'll get even with that Phyllis girl—while you were joy-riding with another man. If I'd suspected it was you, Geoff, I shouldn't have worried. You're as safe as the Marble Arch."

"Alec, you told me that she was going with you!"

With the shocked, strained whisper, Sybyl sprang from the depths of the chair into which she had huddled at Pryde's entrance. Though white with surprise he was jauntily equal to the occasion. The cold cruelty of his eyes chilled Nancy's heart. but his voice registered only condescending forbearance as he evaded;

"You have a deplorable way of misunderstanding me, Mrs. Caswell. So glad to see you again in the home of your husband's people. Now I know that the story going the rounds that you have divorced Bruce is but malicious gossip. Congratulations."

Chapter XVIII

Sybyl put hand to throat as though she were choking;

"Alec! How can you be so beastly!"

Pryde shrugged and pulled his cigarette case from his pocket. Nancy noted the unsteadiness of his fingers. He was not as indifferent to Sybyl's reproach as he tried to appear. Her eyes met her father's. His said quite plainly;

"This has gone far enough!"

It hadn't, she told herself stubbornly, not until Sybyl realized what a cad Alec Pryde was. How expertly he had twisted her accusation. He had acknowledged nothing which could not be explained away to a woman who wanted terribly to believe him. Nancy remembered how plausibly he had lied to her that day by the tennis court, remembered his threat to run away with Sybyl if she refused to marry him.

She had the unreal sense of standing outside herself, observing her own reactions. She wouldn't waken out of this nightmare. She could smell the pungent fragrance of the lemon verbena by the window, could hear Sybyl's hoarse voice accuse;

"You know that I have my divorce, Alec Pryde! You know that you asked me to marry you! And now you . . ."

"Don't! Don't! Here comes Betty," Nancy whispered. Through the silence which followed her warning came the sound of little feet running down the stairs. The child dashed into the room, soft golden curls agog, light blue sweater pulled down over her short skirts. Fresh from her morning bath her skin was as soft and clear and pink as rose petals, her eyes as blue as cornflowers. Scooty barked and nipped at her heels. She flung herself on her aunt.

"Nanny, you're back! Where you been? Phyl-*us* said you'd 'loped." She caught sight of Hilliard in his pirate

162

costume, stopped, stared for an instant before she ran to him. "You look funny, Prod'gal Son. Where you been?"

Geoffrey caught her up and perched her on the back of the wing chair behind which he had retreated at Pryde's entrance. Her mother regarded her with strained, lustreless eyes. Scooty jumped to the seat. With forepaws on her lap, short tail wagging furiously, he licked her dimpled knees with his rough, red tongue. Geoffrey bent his head to hers and suggested in a low tone;

"Let's sneak off to Valleyview for breakfast. Honey and waffles."

The child wavered, shook her head in refusal. Every curl was in motion, her eyes big with bewilderment as she suggested;

"You stay here wif Nanny, Prod'gal Son. Phyl-*us*' muvver said, when Mr. Alec's car stopped at the gate;

" 'The Lord luv us! Here she is now! Well, I hope the Pryde man's made an hon'st woman of her. I guess 'twill stop his phil—philandr'rin for a while.' What's an hon'st woman, Prod'gal Son?"

For one horrible moment Nancy battled with hysterics. The child's inimitable imitation of the "cooklady's" voice and vernacular was irresistibly funny, its content infuriated her. Her voice shook from the conflict of emotions as she reminded;

"Betty, I have told you and told you not to repeat what Phyllis says."

"But this wus Phyl-*us*' muvver an' she . . ."

"Nancy, don't scold her. She has shown me my duty— and pleasure. You were out in my car—you'd have saved a lot of trouble for us both, Geoff, if you'd asked to borrow it—in a way I'm responsible for the gossip. Mrs. Caswell misunderstood me. Will you marry me?"

Alec Pryde's slightly ironical, slightly shaken voice cast a spell for a brief instant. Each occupant of the room seemed turned to stone. Noah Caswell stood by the window, his fine profile in cameo-like relief against the hanging. The pansy which Nancy had placed in his coat the night before, hung limp and wilted. Betty's head rested against Geoffrey Hilliard's shoulder, her blue eyes wonderingly regarded her mother. He was looking down at the child, his fine hand with its curious seal ring closed tight about her arm.

Sybyl was the first to move. She acknowledged bitterly; "You've won, Nancy. I've sensed you battling for Alec. Revenging your brother? I—I—" she dropped into a chair by the table and buried her face on one outflung arm. Her hand overturned the photograph of Bruce Caswell. Long, racking sobs shook her slim body.

Sympathetic tears blinded Nancy. Terrified, defeated, young, what thoughts, doubts, regrets must have been turmoiling in Sybyl's heart. Now they had broken through the crust of self-indulgence and recklessness to the surface. Betty wriggled down from her perch. She ran to her mother and smoothed the soft, wavy hair so like her own. Her voice was little more than a whisper as she comforted;

"Don't cry, Muvver. Daddy never 'lowed you to cry. He said you were too dear to be hurted."

With a strangled sob Sybyl caught the child close and hid her face against her hair. Awkwardly, a little frightened, Betty patted her shoulder.

"Don't cry, Beaut'fullest!" She pulled up her blue skirt in an attempt to dry her mother's eyes. Sybyl gripped the little hand and rose. Her face was livid, her eyes hard as she relinquished scornfully;

"Don't let me stand in the way of your marrying Alec—if you want him—Nancy. I wouldn't take him now if he were to beg me on his knees. Take care however, to keep a tight rein until you have him safely at the altar."

"Sybyl!" reminded Noah Caswell sharply as he looked down at the child who was staring up with frightened eyes. She dropped her mother's hand and ran back to the big chair. Finger between her red lips she watched and listened, forgotten except by her dog who crouched close to her little feet. Nancy clenched her hands tight behind her as she protested vehemently;

"All this commotion because I motored at midnight. I should think we were back in the 'eighties' with this talk of an—an . . ."

" 'Hon'st woman,' " supplied Noah Caswell whimsically. His daughter flashed him a smile of gratitude. "Sybyl, come with me." He laid a tender hand on the woman's shoulder. As his study door closed behind them Nancy rejoiced;

"Thank heaven I can always count upon Dad's understanding. Nothing mid-Victorian about him. Good grief! Here's Luke! Enter the Sheik! How did you get here?" she demanded as Small appeared at the door. She disciplined a nervous ripple of laughter. His jeweled turban was tilted at a ribald angle. His white garment was streaked, his hands were grimy, his black eyes sparked with red lights of anger as he evaded;

"Never mind how I got here. I'll settle that with him— later."

The jerk of his head toward Geoffrey Hilliard, resting folded arms on the back of the wing chair, unseated the turban. He caught it as it fell.

"I followed you to ask you to marry me, Nancy. Even you can't ride around the country all night in this region, without getting talked about."

"Another county heard from. You all seem bitten with the convention mania," the girl countered flippantly to camouflage her hurt astonishment. Had the sincerity of her life, her character, her ideals, made so little impression on these men that they felt in duty bound to shield her from malicious tongues? As though night-riding during and after balls wasn't one of the favorite outdoor sports of the postwar generation. Why didn't Geoffrey Hilliard say something?

"Aren't you coming to the rescue of my frail, Venetian glass reputation, Mr. Hilliard?" she demanded lightly.

He straightened, regarded her with disconcertingly direct eyes, untouched by the fleeting whimsical smile on his lips which seemed to push her miles away from him, as he declined;

"I wouldn't so insult you."

How agilely he had side-stepped, the girl thought bitterly. Anger, fanned by the burning smart of his rebuff burst into flame;

"I deeply appreciate the honor you all have paid me, but . . ." she remembered Alec Pryde's threat to run away with Sybyl if she refused him and temporized;

"I won't be rushed into a decision. Please go. All of

you! I'm hungry. I'm tired. This wig is hot. I feel terribly grubby. Please go!"

Pryde started at once, paused at the threshold to remark jauntily;

"Your procrastination is a degree better than nothing and—several degrees worse than what I want. We'll drive at four this afternoon as usual, Nancy." With a laugh of superb confidence he departed.

As the outer door closed Luke Small crossed his arms on his chest and announced arrogantly;

"You won't get rid of me as easily as you shook Pryde, Nancy. I insist upon an answer to my proposal."

In two strides Geoffrey Hilliard was between the man and girl. The veins stood out on his forehead as he commanded;

"Fade out, Luke!"

"And leave you here? Your mistake! You were asked to go, weren't you? Why are you staying?"

"I'll show you!"

With promptitude and decision Geoffrey Hilliard caught Small under the arms, rushed him through the hall. To the porch. Down the steps, Nancy heard him declare curtly;

"That's why I'm staying!"

The front door banged. Betty ran to him as he entered the living room dusting off his hands.

"Why'd you push Nanny's boy frien' out like that, Prod'gal Son?"

"He was annoying your aunt. We won't permit her to be annoyed, will we, Betty?"

"No, an' we don't mean maybe. Phyl-us says she'll be sore as a crab if you don't marry Nanny. What's marry mean, Prod'gal Son?"

Geoffrey caught the child up in his arms;

"To some it means beauty, heaven, to some . . ." he cleared the huskiness from his voice to question lightly;

"Coming to breakfast with me? If we don't hurry the waffles will be cold. You know you don't like cold waffles. Come on."

The child laughed and threw her arm about his neck. He whistled to the dog. He lingered on the threshold to observe with a tinge of laughter and a slight drawl;

"Hope you appreciated my superhuman self-control in the face of horrible temptation, a few moments back—Miss Caswell."

His voice, his eyes, sent the longing for his touch, his arms, rippling through the girl's veins. What had he meant? To condone his brusque refusal? How could she have suggested that he propose to her? She must have been still in the grip of that horrid nightmare.

At the window she followed him with her eyes as he jog-trotted across the lawn. His long red cloak fluttered and flapped grotesquely. Betty was laughing and clutching at his shoulder as they vanished behind the hedge. Nancy put her hands to her burning cheeks. Her head seemed as light as her heart was heavy. Had her plan to give Sybyl a chance to think things through wrought havoc? The solid ground of everyday living seemed in elemental tumult under her feet. She must go forward. What awaited her around the next turn?

As she left the window she caught a glimpse of herself in the mirror. She regarded her reflection anxiously. She hoped that she hadn't harmed the priceless costume of great-great-grandmother Hilliard's. No, the delicate lace of the bertha which framed her bare shoulders, the green brocade, the little nosegays on the filmy flounces of the skirt were not even rumpled. Only her own green satin slippers showed the stain of contact with frosty planks. She pulled off the white wig. Her hair with its coppery glints was matted close to her head. She made an adorable little face at herself as she approved;

"It's a wonder to me, my dear, you look as well as you do."

"When you get through admiring yourself, Nan, perhaps you'll tell me all about it," Noah Caswell suggested from the doorway. As he pulled forward the wing chair his daughter perched on the arm. She leaned her bare rounded shoulder, as softly tinted as the strings of pearls about her neck, against its broad back as she exclaimed;

"Such a night! Where is Sybyl?"

"Gone to the Inn. Caught Luke Small just as he was leaving in a dilapidated Flivver and asked him to take her. He growled but he did it. What has Sybyl been doing to him?"

"She sent him after me last night."

"She sent him? Why? Perhaps though you'd better wait until you've had your breakfast and changed into normal clothing before you explain."

"But, I'd much rather tell you now. I'd like to get it off my conscience. Do you know that you're a dear," Nancy queried irrelevantly. She bowed the dangling ends of his tie. With eyes on the sputtering fire, interrupted at intervals by the trilling of the canary, she related the events of the night, all except the realization of her feeling for Geoffrey Hilliard. Noah Caswell maintained a thoughtful silence. She concluded;

"That brings the story of my young life up to the moment I saw you waiting at the door, Dad."

"Slightly deleted, Nan?"

Nancy felt the color stealing to her hair. What had he meant? He went on gravely;

"Knowing your sentiments in regard to Alec Pryde—thinking that I know your sentiments—I don't understand why you didn't turn down his offer of marriage and turn it down hard."

Chin in palms, elbows on her knees the girl stared at the shadows cast by flickering flames on the shining brass andirons.

"I didn't dare. Not so long ago he threatened to run away with Sybyl if I refused him. I'll hold him till I'm sure she sees him as he is. Am I taking too much responsibility? Am I interfering unwarrantably in her life?"

In his turn her father regarded the glowing fire. After a moment he encouraged;

"I'm sure not. Neither you nor I have uttered a word of protest, a word of advice to her. She asked to come into this neighborhood. You are showing the man in his true colors. I agree with you that if we can help her get a perspective on her life, we owe it to her, to Bruce, to Betty. If, realizing what Alec Pryde is, she still loves him enough to marry him, we shall have done what we could—hurting only his self-love."

"He'll make her horribly unhappy."

"Inevitably. I suspect that she knows that. Poor child! *Facilis descensus Averno.*"

"No letter from Bruce this morning?"

Anxiety shadowed Noah Caswell's eyes.

"No."

"I can't understand it. He is so faithful about writing. I hope he isn't ill. Oh, what a mess it all is. Because of her shallowness Sybyl has forced his life into new channels at the cost of his happiness, his profession, perhaps his health."

" 'Alas the love of women! It is known to be a lovely and a fearful thing,' " quoted Noah Caswell gravely.

His daughter rose.

"I'm off to change and sleep—if I can. I rather dread to face Phyllis and her moon eyes. From the excerpt with which Betty favored us—did you ever know anyone who could inject embarrassment into a situation as can that child—I can imagine how her tongue and her mother's wagged over my midnight adventure. That's the trouble with being a sedate person. One deviation and you set the world agog with conjecture."

"You have neglected to tell me what happened after I left this room with Sybyl. What did Luke say when he appeared?"

"He joined the ranks of defenders of my reputation. He was decidedly upstage about it but he gallantly proposed marriage."

"And Geoffrey Hilliard?"

Nancy felt her face warm with color. She answered flippantly;

"When I suggested that he was slow in coming to the rescue . . ."

"When you suggested?"

"Don't worry. He didn't. As he had previously told me that I was disagreeable and unlovable, I—I—oh, I just wanted to hear what he'd say."

"What did he say?"

" 'I wouldn't so insult you.' "

"Good boy!" Noah Caswell approved softly.

Chapter XIX

Geoffrey Hilliard deposited Betty in the chair reserved for her at the Valleyview breakfast table. His aunts hovered about the child like fussy maternal hens over a lone, downy yellow chick. Miss Serena settled herself behind the purring coffee urn as she suggested;

"If you intend to change before your breakfast, Geoff, please start. Nora makes such a fuss if you're late."

"I'm going." He fixed the younger Miss Hilliard with a stern eye as he accused;

"Aunt Sally, isn't your conscience on the rampage after the fibs you told yesterday?"

Sally Hilliard's blue eyes twinkled. She shook with poorly suppressed mirth as she paraphrased airily;

"All's fair in love and a masquerade, Geoff. In the language of the immortal Buttercup, 'I mixed those children up and not a creature knew it.' "

"Why?"

"You were all so cocksure you would know Nancy."

"But why mislead her too?"

"It helped complicate the situation."

"I'll say it did. I'm going, Aunt Serena. Be good, Betty."

The child's lips, already honey-wreathed, smiled back at him.

"I'm al-*wus* good here, aren't I, Miss Sally? Phyl-*us* says it makes her sore as a crab the way I mind you. Why's a crab sore?"

Miss Serena registered a protest;

"Phyllis is a slangy, ill-bred little girl. You shouldn't repeat what she says, Betty."

"But Phyl-*us* must be nice, she's somebody's sweetie. Are you somebody's sweetie, Miss S'rena?"

Sally Hilliard sent a chuckle scurrying back into her throat. Soft, dark color slowly spread to her sister's hair.

Came the sound as of a ton or two of bricks being dumped in the hall.

"What the dickens is that racket?" Geoffrey demanded.

Miss Serena sighed exasperation.

"Nora stumbling over Alec's riding boots. He's taken to riding before breakfast, to keep himself thin, I suppose. He says he eats too much here. For a few times he set them outside his door for Sandy to polish. Rebellion. Now he brings them down and puts them in the hall. I believe that Nora stumbles over them on purpose as a protest against his expecting to have them cleaned."

Above the rim of a glass of milk Betty's large round eyes interrogated her.

"Doesn't Nora like to clean boots, Miss S'rena?" she inquired between swallows.

"She doesn't like . . ."

Geoffrey fled from the recital of the maid's peccadillos which the child's question had precipitated. Curious, he thought, as he mounted the stairs two at a time, how Betty reacted to the temperaments of his aunts. Apparently she adored Sally, rather feared Serena. From the first she had shown an intense dislike of Alec Pryde. Instinct? Did the little thing sense the havoc he'd wrought in her life? Alec reciprocated. His eyes had narrowed in distaste, he had made an excuse and left the table, when she had ridden into the dining room on the shoulder of her Prod'gal Son. After the events of the morning she wouldn't be likely to acquire him for a stepfather. No woman of spirit—Sybyl had plenty—would marry a man who had humiliated her as had Alec—he might be her uncle—if he married Nancy—

"Not a chance!" Geoffrey answered the eyes of the stern-lipped man who faced him in the mirror. If he served as long as Jacob for his Rachel he meant to make her love him, his thoughts surged on. Her voice last night when she had called him, "Alec" had been like music. Why? She disliked him cordially now.

She'd probably hate him after his answer to her flippant question in the Manse living room this morning. Had he asked her to marry him it would have been paramount to a confession that her reputation had been jeopardized by the all night ride. Who would think such

a fool thing in this age? There were several who would
and could in the village. Small town stuff, of course, but it
had a nasty way of registering.

Would she had drifted off to sleep with her head against
his shoulder had she really hated him? When he had
kissed her throat that afternoon—He swore softly under
his breath as he nicked his cheek with the safety razor—it
seemed that it could cut if properly mishandled. Even
after that she had spoken to him. This morning she had
said;

"I could have protested against being kidnapped you
know."

What had she meant by that? The old clock in the hall
struck the hour. So late! He had intended to be at the mill
early this morning. He hadn't liked his father's labored
breathing the night before. He broke his own speed record down the stairs. Nora was clearing the table in the
dining room.

"Where's everybody?" he demanded.

The Irish maid's tightly drawn back hair derricked her
eyebrows into sharp curves.

"All about their businesses, sure. Sandy druv Himself
to the mill, early. Mr. Alec wint off in his schnappy car.
Miss Serena's givin' thim village gurls a lesson in bed-
makin', they don't turn the corners to suit, an' Miss
Sally's a-feedin' thim goldfish twins in the parlor. Here's
some pipin' hot toast fer you. I'll pour yer coffee."

"Where's Betty?"

Nora flung up her hands regardless of the fact that she
held a cup in one. The bit of china crashed to the floor.

"Ain't that me luck! Did you hear it went?" She picked
up the pieces before she filled another cup. "Where's
Betty, ye're askin'? Shure that child's too bright to be long
fer this worrld. Says she to me;

" 'Get out my little wash-tub, Nora. I've got to be doin'
some laundry.'

" 'Laundry!' says I. 'An' what washin' has you got to
do?' She looks at me wid her head sidewise, fer all the
worrld like thet white an' black dog a-squattin' beside her
an' she says;

" 'The blankets Miss Sally keeps here for Scooty to
sleep on are dirty. I've got to wash 'em.'

" 'You have?' says I, an' looks at her hard. She looked as innercent as an angel from heaven, but somehow she made me think of our black cat whin I ketch him in the pantry a-lickin' his whiskers. But she held up the blankets. Sure enough, they were pot-black. So I took the tub out to the barn where she'd get plenty of water an' could slop all she wanted, give her a big bar of soap, tied a rubber apron on her an' there she is a scrubbin' an' splashin', bless her heart. Miss Sally 'phoned to the Manse to ask if she could keep her till she wint to see her mother this afternoon. The Hilliard gurls sure are crazy over the child."

"Be careful that Betty doesn't get wet through."

"Wurrah, Master Geoff! The likes of you tellin' me how to take care of the bairn! One'd think you were the father of a family. I guess Miss Nancy'd—the Saints luv us! I forgot. Sandy wus tellin' me as how 'twas all over town that she'd eloped wid somebody last night."

"You tell Sandy that she didn't. She was with me."

"Wid you, was she? Well, don't git so mad about it. An' that Phyllis gurl tellin' the cock-eyed worrld that Miss Nancy was goin' to marry Luke Small! An' all the time it's you."

Geoffrey rose and flung down his napkin.

"You and Phyllis talk too much, Nora."

From the threshold he looked back with contrition. The red-haired woman in her crackling, immaculate dress of dotted print was staring at him with open mouth. Had he hurt her brutally? He qualified;

"I know that your interest in me comes from affection, Nora, but . . ."

"Affection, is it? Hear the boy talkin' about affection whin he's crazy wid love an' don't know it!"

Know it! He'd say he knew it, Geoffrey told himself grimly as he took the short-cut road to the mill. He stopped his car for a moment on the bridge. The brook was high. The water boiled and eddied around the island. It splashed over the planks he had laid across the stream. The vines on the buccaneer stronghold had turned to brilliant scarlet. Sumachs on the banks burned like flames. The stream was higher than it had been the day he had carried Nancy across. Suppose he had told her then that he loved her? Suppose——he started the car with a jerk. Great helper, to be dreaming here when the Squire needed him!

The sight of Luke Small in his father's office wiped Geoffrey's mind clear of personal concerns with the thoroughness with which a wet rag sweeps chalk marks from a slate. Peter Hilliard was at his desk. His head was high. His face deeply flushed. As his son entered he spoke;

"Luke appears to be concerned as to that contract he can't locate."

Geoffrey glanced at the clock. Darned careless of him to be so late. Taka must have delivered the renewal by this time. He was as dependable, as unstampedable as the sun. He might telephone at any moment. He met Luke Small's smoldering eyes. "Nothing will ever cure him of the belief that I'm against him," he thought, before Small accused;

"The Squire insists that a lot of trash I burned last night was of importance to his mills. Would I be here if that were true?"

Geoffrey, perched on the corner of his father's desk took his knee into his embrace and demanded curtly;

"Why are you staying? If I remember right you asked me that same question a short time ago."

Luke Small's face turned a dull grey. His hands clenched. With an attempt to control his rising fury he answered hoarsely;

"Sometime I'll answer you as you answered me. I'll put you out of the running."

The bell of the telephone on Peter Hilliard's desk rang stridently. Geoffrey picked up the instrument.

"Hilliard Mills—At the 'phone—Yes—Yes—Got it?— Bring it over this morning. Come in my car. Yours is here. Yes. Good-bye."

Geoffrey hung up the receiver.

"The renewal is signed, Squire."

"What renewal?" Luke Small demanded.

"The renewal you were forgetting to renew, Luke. In spite of the slashed gas tank, in spite of being followed by you last night, it reached its destination." Geoffrey looked casually at the clock;

"Won't you be late for your new job? Before you go,

park that flivver you borrowed this morning at the door of the mill."

"I don't need your suggestion about my job."

Peter Hilliard held up his hand.

"That will do, Luke. After your forgetfulness—you see, I mean to be charitable—in regard to renewal of contract with our most important customer—you needn't speak, I haven't forgotten that you insisted that they refused to renew, we know differently—we looked up the other contract for newsprint. We discovered that unless renewed it lapsed today. The contract is signed, sealed and delivered. You won't have that to carry to your new boss."

Livid, with a suggestion of froth about his lips, Luke Small turned on Geoffrey and accused roughly;

"I have you to thank for this! I'd made myself indispensable to your father, to Nancy Caswell before you came. You drop down into this village with your drawl and your English clothes and upset everything. I'll get back at you! I'll give you a chance to show what the College of Business Administration has done for you. Watch me! Just watch me!" He slammed the office door behind him.

Geoffrey drew a cigarette case from his pocket. He struck a match before he remarked equably;

"I take it that the College of Business Administration is a thorn in Luke's flesh. Made himself indispensable! He's a great little self-advertiser, isn't he? He swats the tom-tom in front of his own booth indefatigably. He got a set-back this time."

"Can he 'get back at you,' Geoff?"

"I don't know how, if he comes out into the daylight and fights fair. No skeletons in my past whose bones he can rattle. I doubt if even he can hurt me with the girl I love, that's all that matters."

"Then you do love a girl, Geoffrey?"

"Mad about her. Guess who?"

Peter Hilliard laughed.

"Nancy, of course. How could you keep from loving her? She's such a glowing sort of person. And when the beauty of soul which lies behind her physical beauty shines in her eyes she's—well, she's irresistible."

"You're a poet!"

"I'm only a man who appreciates spiritual beauty when he sees it. I congratulate you. To think of my having a daughter—a grandson to carry on the mills."

There was a tinge of *vibrato* in Geoffrey's boyish laugh.

"Whoa, Squire! Not so fast. I haven't told you that she loves me. At present she accords me the same respectful attention she gives the dirt under her feet." He picked up the telephone in answer to an imperative ring.

"Hilliard Mills—Right here— You're wanted, Squire."

Arms folded across his chest, Geoffrey listened.

"This is Hilliard Senior . . ." Peter Hilliard's face flashed into a smile. He looked up at his son for an instant before he answered the voice at the other end of the wire;

"Glad you think so. So do I.—With the greatest pleasure.—Wish that we might do business together again. The Country Club here at—better make it three so that we'll have a chance to play eighteen holes.—At three. Good-bye."

He hung up the receiver and leaned back in his chair.

"That was the purchasing agent you interviewed. Wanted to talk with me. Wants to resume business relations if possible. He had to come in this direction so he called up to make a golf date with me this afternoon. How the dickens did he know that I play?"

"A bit of diplomacy on my part. When I went into his office he roared like a lion, looked ready to tear me leg from leg. I saw a bag of clubs. Introduced the subject of golf and—figuratively speaking—he lay down like a lamb."

"He said he thought you were a live wire. I agreed."

"I hope that I'll live up to your expectations, Squire," Geoffrey answered gravely. "Will he stay for dinner at the Club?"

"No, he has a date. I'd like to have you go round the course with us."

"I'll get there as soon as I can after Taka reports. Now, I'm going over the plant. This 'live wire' would better get on the job if we're to keep a lap ahead of the Upper Mill."

Geoffrey devoted the hours before the arrival of Taka

to acquainting himself with the working of the mill. He was warm, grimy, tired from the unaccustomed concentration over noisy machinery when the Japanese shuffled into the office. The renewal had been delivered. The little man with the ivory mask of a face produced the signed and sealed duplicate. As he departed in his 'joyful flivver' Geoffrey looked at the clock. He'd go home to Valleyview, take a shower and change before he met his father and the purchasing agent at the Country Club.

Later in his own room he looked from the window. A few late perennials were nodding encouragement to Betty Caswell as she dug in the garden. She was digging up the bulbs which only last week she had planted in the plot of ground Miss Sally had marked off for her. He watched the little blue clad figure settle back on her heels, solicitously regard a brown thing she held, painstakingly reinter it. Scooty on his haunches beside her cocked his head in bright-eyed approval.

Ten minutes later as he stepped from under the shower Geoffrey heard an angry voice outside. He flung a lounge robe over his wet shoulders. Hurried to the window. He shouted with laughter as he sensed the meaning of the tableau below. Livid with fury Alec Pryde brandished aloft his once immaculate riding boot, now streaked and lathered with dried soap. Betty Caswell, the gold rings of her hair stirred by the slight breeze, finger between her lips, stared up at him in fascinated silence as he accused furiously;

"You did that! Why?"

" 'Cause—'cause Miss S'rena said you wanted it cleaned and I—I wus washin' an' . . ." Her voice caught in a frightened gulp.

"Washing! I'll teach you to touch my things!"

With incredible swiftness Pryde slashed at the child's shoulders with the riding crop he had held out of sight. She gave one terrified cry. Geoffrey made a mad dash for his clothing. Anything! Anything to cover him! Sockless, Shoeless. Knotting the silk cord of his lounge robe about his waist he flew down the stairs. He shot by the living room door. Swept through the hall like a brown silk typhoon. His aunts called;

"Geoff! Geoff! What's happened?"

Through the kitchen. Nora flung up her hands. A tray of kitchen utensils fell with a deafening crash.

"The Lord luv us, Masther Geoff . . ."

The garden! At last! He stopped. Looked from side to side. Still, russet tinged, fragrant, it basked in the afternoon sun as peacefully as though no storm of anger had recently disturbed its enchanted calm. A car starting? Had Alec gone?

"Betty! Betty!" he called.

A sparrow hopping from twig to twig on a leafless branch twittered an answer.

"Betty! Betty!"

Nora ran out of the house.

"Master Geoff, have ye lost yer senses? Out here in yer bare feet a-hollerin' to that child. Ye'll ketch yer death a-cold. What you want her for in such a hurry?"

"Where is she?"

"Shure an' I see her run through the hedge not a minute before you come a-tearin' down the stairs as though the divil himself was afther you. It's this time a day she goes to see her mother. I guess she heard Phyllis a-callin' her."

Geoffrey relaxed. Phyllis was a horrible warning of what might happen to one's vocabulary if not kept on leash, but she was devoted to the child. She would comfort her. His old-time liking for Alec Pryde had reached the vanishing point before he saw him strike Betty. Now he was beneath contempt. It was quite time to intimate that he had outstayed his welcome. The Misses Hilliard met Geoffrey on the threshold as he entered the house. Miss Serena demanded severely;

"Why are you running round the garden undressed?"

He glanced down at his silk lounge robe, at his bare feet and laughed. He really ought to introduce her to the bathing hour at Palm Beach and points south. She needed broadening. He'd better not explain the cause of his tornado rush through the house. Betty was safe now. It would shock his aunts unbearably to know that Alec had struck her. He answered Miss Serena's question lightly;

"Wanted to catch Pryde before he left. Was Betty here all the morning?"

"Yes. She was in the garden only a few moments ago. I suppose now she has gone to see her mother with Phyllis. Sybyl is really a sweet little woman," Miss Sally defended. "Betty was the happiest thing this morning washing at her little tub in the barn."

Even while he followed his father and the purchasing agent round the golf course the picture of Alec striking at the child haunted Geoffrey. The blow had been like a lash across his own heart. Was it photographed indelibly on his mind, he wondered as later he drove his father home. The Squire was in a jubilant mood.

"Interesting man, Geoff. I gave him all the advantages due a player on a strange course, but I made a better score. He'll renew with us after this year. Said he never had trusted Small. Curious that I should have been so blind. Apparently this last year while Luke had seemed so absorbed in the Hilliard Mills he has been undermining our business. It may be my fault. I left too much to him. Why didn't he tell me that he wanted to re-establish the family mill? I would have understood."

"He has always been tricky, Squire. Why! What . . ." Geoffrey leaned forward to look at the Manse which they were approaching. "What the dickens is going on here? Every window lighted? Front door wide open!"

"Stop, Geoff! Something's wrong. Bad news from the brother, perhaps."

As the roadster pulled up at the gate Phyllis rushed down the path. She gasped as she jumped on the running board of the car;

"Oh! Oh, it's you, Squire Hilliard! Have you seen Betty?"

"Betty!"

"She—she left your house sometime this afternoon. They thought she was with me. The old ladies are sore as a crab because I went to the village—but her mother was coming for her and—after I'd gone . . . she 'phoned she couldn't come and . . . and . . ."

"Stop sniffling! And what?" thundered Peter Hilliard.

"No—nobody knows where she is! I'm sunk!"

Geoffrey administered a steadying shake as he demanded;

"Where is her aunt?"

"Mother says Miss Nancy went riding with Mr. Pryde hours ago. She—she hasn't come back yet."

Chapter XX

Nancy Caswell looked up in surprise as Alec Pryde bolted into the living room of the Manse. His face was white. His eyes glinted curiously. His voice was rough, as he commanded;

"Come on! I want to talk to you."

The girl studied him with oblique intentness behind the screen of her bronze-tipped lashes as she crushed her felt hat down over her hair. What had happened, she wondered as she slipped into her beige coat with its soft fur collar. Except on the afternoon when Betty had buttered his watch she had never before seen him angry. He had been icily brutal with Sybyl but now he was seething with fury. She had a disagreeable half hour coming sometime. Better get it behind her as soon as possible. When she was sure that he wouldn't take his anger at herself out on Sybyl she would draw a long breath of relief. She hated being untrue. Feeling as she did about him she was untrue to herself every moment she endured his companionship, entertaining as he so well knew how to be. It eased her conscience a little to remember that she was doing it for Betty. Mighty nice of the Hilliards to keep the child with them for the day. She herself, had slept like a log all morning regardless of the fact that lily beds galore awaited planting.

As she stepped into the luxurious roadster she inquired;

"Where are we going? To the Club for tea?"

"No. There would be a crowd hanging round you there as usual. I want to talk to you without interruption."

"Don't go too far. I must be back in time to read to Betty. I've been neglecting her of late."

The car shot ahead. Nancy settled back. The air was delicious. A rim of sun crowned the top of a distant hill with a flaming ruby tiara. Its light tipped the trees, trans-

formed them into golden spires pointing the way to a
mauve and rose tinted heaven. How smoothly Alec drove.
She glanced at the speedometer. Sixty! There must be
something wrong with it. The car couldn't be going more
than thirty miles an hour. It swerved with vicious intent.
Had the driver tried to run down the black cat which had
scampered across the road? She warned;

"You almost hit that lovely cat."

"Pity I didn't. I hate 'em."

"Do you attempt to run down everything you don't
like? You dislike children and cats. What else?"

"I didn't bring you out to talk about cats and children.
I brought you to hear you say that you will marry me."

"I? Marry you? What about Sybyl?"

"I have no responsibility there. She encouraged a desperate flirtation. If she took me seriously she's out of
luck."

"You weren't serious—ever?"

"Not after I met you. She's getting about what she
deserves, isn't she? A woman who will chuck over a
perfectly good husband and a—perfectly damnable
child," he added with vicious bitterness.

"Alec!"

"If you'd suffered at that kid's hands as I have you'd
hate her."

"What has she done now? She was horribly naughty
about the watch, I know."

"Never mind what she's done now. Forget it. I won't
marry a woman who has contracted the divorce habit, no
matter what Sybyl expected. That's that."

"So, even you have an ideal?"

"Cut out the sarcasm. It doesn't suit you. I know what
I want and I intend to get it. I want you."

It seemed to Nancy that all the blood in her body was
drumming in her ears. Dared she tell him what she
thought of him? He had expressed contempt for Sybyl.
Surely he wouldn't carry out his threat to run away with
her after that. Was Sybyl sufficiently disillusioned? This
morning she had declared;

"I wouldn't take him now if he were to beg me on his
knees."

Had she meant it? Whether she had or not an end must

be put to Alec's devotion to herself. They would better be headed for home when she told him. She suggested;

"It is growing dark. Turn around."

"We don't turn back until you've said you'll marry me."

"Then we'll go on forever."

"Suits me."

He stepped on the accelerator. The wind rushed by them. Nancy's eyelashes felt as though they were being yanked out by the roots. Every speed-law in the world was being broken. If only that zealous state policeman who had held up Geoffrey and herself this morning would overtake them, she wished fervently. She tried to protest. The wind snatched at her voice. Swept the words over her shoulder. She touched Pryde's arm. Put her mouth close to his ear as she parleyed;

"Stop Alec! How can I say 'Yes,' or anything else, when I can't hear myself speak?"

The jerky sentence reached its mark. The car slowed to an amble. The driver smiled indulgently as he brought it to a standstill in the shadow of a tree, a tree all drooping branches and purple shadows which fairly crooned an invitation to lovers. A divinely designed "love-lot" for a motion picture close-up, Nancy thought. With adeptness acquired by long practice he caught her in his arms and exulted;

"I knew you loved me!"

With expertness, also acquired by practice, she dodged his lips. Within her surged a tide of physical disgust such as she had never known before. How many such scenes had the old tree witnessed she wondered irrelevantly before she protested;

"Let me go! You ought to know me well enough to know that I won't permit this petting stuff!"

In his surprise his hold loosened.

"Petting stuff! Don't you believe that I mean to marry you?"

Nancy dexterously opened the car door. Before he realized that she was out she had slammed it and stepped back.

"I believe that you think that you mean to, but the

really important fact is, that I don't want to marry you. I shan't even go back with you. Drive on."

"You're a good many miles from home. Think of walking?"

"If necessary."

"I'll give you one more chance to ride. Will you marry me?"

She consulted her wrist watch.

"You'd better go. You know how Nora fusses if the family or guests are late at meals."

He started the engine. Even in her excitement the girl regarded him wonderingly. His veneer of courtesy had cracked off like a brittle shell. Was this the first time in his life that he had been crossed in a love-affair? Had he been invincible before? He didn't seem quite human, more like a soulless, malignant spirit as he sneered;

"Thanks for reminding me. Before I return to Valleyview I'll stop at the Inn. There's a boat for France on Saturday. Sybyl and I will sail on that. As you are walking home we shall have left the village before you get there." His eyes glinted maliciously as he added slowly, "I think after all, we'll take Betty with us. It will be the making of the kid. She needs discipline. You're too soft with her."

He laughed in the instant before his car shot into the dusk. Nancy stared after it until the red tail-light was but a bright cinder. Had he meant that. Would they take Betty? They couldn't. Bruce had made sure of that. Sybyl wouldn't go with him. Wouldn't she? She was like a fluttering bird caught in the snare of the man's fascination. Fascination! If only the women whom he had made care could have seen him a few moments ago! But he was too crafty to show them his real self until he was tired of them. He would give Sybyl a dozen explanations of his avoidance of her since she came to Sunnyfield. Plausible ones, that he had been testing her affection and so forth and so on. And Sybyl would listen. She herself knew how convincing he could be. He had almost won her sympathy and confidence by his pathetic story of a lonely, neglected boyhood. Suppose Sybyl listened and believed and went with him and took Betty?

"She needs discipline. You're too soft with her," he had said.

Alec disciplining that adorable baby! Never! She'd stop him! How? He was speeding to Sunnyfield. And she was miles and miles from home.

She crushed back a frenzied sense of futility and began to run. How slowly she moved! Her feet seemed leaden weights. Her coat weighed tons. Her heart pounded unbearably. Her throat dried to a crisp. Could she make it? Someone must come along soon who would give her a lift. A lonely road! Faint, stealthy sounds in the underbrush. Sinister, shifting shadows on the stone walls. A black shape skulking across a field. A dog's howl rising mournfully. She was not conscious of a fear of the supernatural but that distant sound set her spine to prickling. Was this what Nora had meant by her prophecy;

"Looks as though ye was goin' to be ketched in something"?

Curious that no car had passed. She stopped. Looked about. She was not on a highway. An old road. Where did it lead? She had been so engrossed combatting Alec that she hadn't realized that they had left the main thoroughfare. Coward! To desert her like this! Railing at him wouldn't get her anywhere. She must go on. In which direction?

"Get your grip," she scolded herself. Her breath panted in her throat as she took her bearings. The sun had striped the west with crimson. A hill loomed against it. Sunnyfield must lie to the east. She could tell by the glow of incandescents reflected in the sky. If she cut across fields she would be sure to reach a highway. Someone would give her a ride. How long would it take? Would Betty be gone? Resolutely she thrust the thought of the child from her mind. She must keep her imagination at heel if she were to get anywhere. She would walk slowly till the intolerable pain in her side subsided. After this she would run a mile a day to keep in training.

She followed a stone wall till the clamor of her strained heart quieted, till her mouth grew moist again. There must be bars somewhere which would indicate a crossable field. Was that the faint clash of a bell? Cows? Ooech! Cows on the loose! How she hated them. It wouldn't help

Betty much if she were gored and trampled. Cows or no
cows, she must go on.

She climbed to the top of a barred gate. She listened.
No suggestion of a bell. She dropped nimbly to the
ground and began to run in the direction of the copper
glow in the sky. She skirted a mammoth boulder;
scratched through a shield of weeping willows; bogged a
foot in the mud; caught her toe in a root, stumbled.
Plunged. Down! Down! Down! The force with which she
crashed to a stop upset her mental balance for an instant.
Coolness, dampness seeping through her clothing restored
it in a flash. Prone. Breathless. She listened. Water? Water
purling over pebbles! Faintly splashing, gently rippling,
softly lapping, an infinitude of tones.

A brook! From the smart of her knees she'd wager
that the skin of them was now incorporated in the silk of
her stockings. She lifted herself gingerly on her scraped
palms. What was that soft pad, pad, pad? Stealthy as the
approach of Destiny. Someone coming? She flattened out.
Lay motionless. Something snuffled over her ears, nozzled
her hair. Where was her hat? A rough tongue touched her
cheek. She smelt a rich, sickly sweet, heavy breath. A
cow! Good grief! A cow!

Just why should the creature be projected into the plan
of her hectic afternoon, she wondered. Nora would say
that it meant something. What should she do? Do, she
mocked. Stand up! Quite time she cured herself of
childish fear. She turned her head cautiously. Against the
copper-hued horizon the horns of the animal ruminatively
regarding her reared like twin petards on which she envis-
aged herself impaled. She shut her teeth hard. Dripping
with coolness arose from the brook. She waved her arms
with bravado she was far from feeling.

"Shoo! Shoo!"

The cow stood not upon the order of her going but
went at once. Nancy's fright evaporated in ripples of
laughter—each one a note more unrestrained then the last
till they mounted dangerously near the hysteria mark—as
she watched the creature shake its four legs, clap its
wicked hoofs together and scramper across the pasture. A
slap-stick comedy cow. She wiped tears of laughter from

her eyes. Her smile stiffened. It had stopped to watch her!
Other blurry shapes were closing in! A herd!

She took to her heels without stopping to compute the
strength of the enemy. She flew across the stubby pasture.
Squeezed her slim self between cedar bars. Breathless,
disheveled, safe, she looked back. The cows had lost
interest in her. They were ambling toward the dark bulk
of a shelter under trees. Bare braches above it spread like
a lacy black fan against the afterglow. She turned. Before
her curved the highway.

She walked slowly in the direction of what she was sure
was Sunnyfield. Automobiles passed her. One slowed
down. The driver smiled at her ingratiatingly.

"Ride?"

She shook her head. He lingered for an instant. Drove
slowly, very slowly on. She saw the car stop in the shadow of a tree. Was he waiting for her? She would go back.
She turned abruptly, almost into a motorcycle with side
car which seemed to spring from nowhere. A state policeman? She hailed the man eagerly.

"Oh, will you please— You!" she exclaimed incredulously as she recognized the officer who had dragged
Geoffrey Hilliard and herself before the magistrate not so
many hours ago. She regarded him hopefully, as though
he were an invincible guard against more frustration;
gravely as she wondered if his code would permit him to
deviate a foot from his schedule; grimly as she determined
that he should. He stared at her in return.

"It's the pirate's girl! Say, is that him down the road?"
He nodded in the direction of a blotch in the shadow of a
large tree.

"No! No! I don't know who that is. I turned back when
I saw him stop. You're a direct answer to a maiden's
prayer."

He grinned in response.

"I've been following him for a mile. Terrible anxious to
get someone to ride with him, he is. Where you going?"

"I must get to Sunnyfield. Matter of life and death.
I—Something happened to the car I was in."

"Where is it?"

"The driver took it on and . . ."

"And left you forty miles from home? Say, you're a glutton for trouble, aren't you?"

Nancy borrowed from Phyllis' vocabulary;

"I'll say I am. I'm sunk."

The smile faded from her eyes and lips. She pleaded;

"Could you possibly take me home? I'm the daughter of the clergyman of the mill parish at Sunnyfield. My little niece—I must get back to her." Her breath caught in a gasp as the remembrance of what she feared swept over her in a terrifying tide.

The officer scowled in the direction of the blotch under the tree.

"Jump in. It's a little off my route but the Chief was sore with me last night for draggin' you and his old chum in. Perhaps if you let him know I helped you this time it will square me with him."

"I'll let him know with interest," Nancy assured as she stepped into the side car. "Now I know why the cow horned into the plan."

"You know what?" With one foot on the ground, one leg thrown over the motorcycle he stared at her.

"Why the cow came in. If I hadn't fallen into the brook, if I hadn't waited a minute to get courage I should have missed you. See?"

He shook his head as with a rattle and snort the motorcycle shot forward. The sound had a magical effect upon the dark blotch ahead. It also shot forward. Had the driver sniffed the law? Too bad, she had hoped to sweep disdainfully by.

Nancy opened her lips to express appreciation of the speed at which they were proceeding. She felt as though she had swallowed a boisterous sliver of the North Wind. She counted the strokes of the village clock as they entered Sunnyfield. She would be too late to read to Betty. Betty! Alec must have reached the Inn some time ago. Would Sybyl already have taken the child? Breathless from the rush through the crisp air, knees stiff with bruises, she tumbled out of the side car the instant the officer halted at the Manse. Her lips were unsteady as she acknowledged;

"Never can I thank you enough. Mr. Hilliard will tell your Chief ..." she was running up the walk with the sentence unfinished. Why, why was the house illuminated from top to bottom? What had happened? She collided with Phyllis at the door. Her lips were red and swollen. Her button nose glowed like a red scabiosa. She sobbed;

"Betty's lost! We can't find her. I lighted every room so she'd see the house from a long way off. It didn't do no good. We can't find her mother! I'm sunk!"

Chapter XXI

Nancy clutched the girl's shoulder.

"Did you go to the Inn for Mrs. Caswell?"

"I'll tell the cock-eyed world I did. Just as I was goin' up the front walk I see her step into a car that was waitin' an' ..."

"What kind of a car?"

"Gee, Miss Nancy! Don't grab my arm like that! It hurts. I couldn't tell then. I saw her run up to it and then she kinder gave a scream and said;

" 'You've come! You ...' I guess the fella, it was a man behind the wheel, pulled her in 'cause I didn't hear any more. I called and ran toward the car. Then I saw that it was Mr. Pryde's. I guess they heard me all right but they beat me to it and drove off like as though they had the law after them an' me shoutin' to Mrs. Caswell that Betty was lost. Ain't life humorous!"

Heart cold with apprehension Nancy walked into the warm, cheery, fragrant living room and flung off her coat. The canary burst into a song of welcome. Missing the girl's usual response he subsided into a sleepy twitter. She dropped into the wing chair. She must pull herself together and think. Sybyl was with Alec undoubtedly. That didn't necessarily mean that they had Betty. Because of the brake she was jamming on her own emotions she commanded sharply;

"Stop sniffling, Phyllis, and think. When did you see Betty last?"

"This morning when I dressed her. She went over to the Hilliards' for breakfast an' they kept her. Yesterday Mrs. Caswell told me she'd come for Betty this afternoon so's I could go to the Girl Scout meeting in the village. When I got back at 'bout five, I begun to wonder where the kid was. The old ladies across the hedge didn't know. Nora said that 'bout three Mr. Geoffrey was lookin' for

her an' they thought she'd come home. He was here half
an hour ago an' was sore as a crab with me. Just as
though I could help her running off."

"Where is he now?"

"Shot off in his car to look for her."

"Where is my father? Does he know?"

"Now Miss Nancy, haven't you told me a thousand
times never to disturb him when he's writing?"

Nancy started for the study door.

"Good grief, Phyllis! Haven't you any judgment? You
should have told him at once."

"But he ain't there."

With her hand gripping the knob of the door Nancy
stared at the girl;

"Isn't there! You said—Where is he?"

"Search me! I was prowling round the bushes outside
his windows thinking Betty might be hidin' to fool us—
she's done it before—when I heard a car stop at the gate.
A man hurried up to the study door. 'Someone's dying or
gettin' spliced in a hurry,' thinks I, an' went on hunting.
Then I heard a kind of shout inside an' the next thing I
saw was two men a-hurrying back to the car by the gate.
One was your father. Gee, I'd know his white mop anywhere. The other kinder bundled him into the auto and
off it went." Bundled him into the auto! Nancy's heart
stopped. Had her father been kidnapped to prevent his
finding Betty? Alec Pryde was behind it all of course.
What should she do next? If only Geoffrey were here. The
thought of him sent her blood coursing back through her
veins. He would find Betty. He loved her. But she
couldn't stay at home doing nothing. She'd talk with the
Squire. He would tell her where to look. She reached for
the telephone. Before she could unhook the receiver a
high, strained voice called;

"Nancy!"

"Sybyl! Alec!" she whispered incredulously.

Except for the delicately rouged lips the face of the
woman standing in the doorway was colorless. Pryde,
behind her, was livid. Nancy brushed her hand over her
eyes. They were real. She wasn't just seeing them. To her
excited fancy the old clock in the corner seemed to tick
indignantly;

"You here? You here? You here?"

The fire sputtered a protest, the canary lifted its head from under its wing with a faint peep and retired. The man's eyes in his white face were alight with malice, the woman's were inscrutable. Was she dressed for her wedding. Nancy wondered as she noted the smart costume of delicate beige. Quite appropriate for a second marriage. Sybyl had a nice sense of dramatic values. Phyllis' voice outside frantically calling brought remembrance of the lost child hurtling back. She took an impetuous step forward. "Betty?" she demanded unsteadily. "Where is Betty?"

"We'll talk of her later. Now . . ."

"But, . . ."

"Listen to me!" It was evident that Sybyl's endurance had reached the snapping-point. "Alec insists that I go away with him at once, insists that we take Betty. I won't until you hear him ask me to marry him."

In spite of her contempt, in spite of the fact that the woman fiercely demanding a hearing had sent her brother's life on the rocks, Nancy's heart ached for her. She was desperate, frightened, swept along on the tide of her own faithlessness, clutching at Alec, who would prove as helpful for salvage purposes as a painted life preserver on a painted back-drop. Pryde's protest lashed;

"What's the big idea? I'm here. With you. That's enough."

"It is not. Ask me."

Nancy felt her face go scarlet with embarrassment. How like Sybyl to stage this denouement. Pryde's eyes were burning, merciless, as he parroted;

"Will you marry me?"

For an instant Sybyl seemed to shrivel under his look, then she straightened. Her voice was piercingly low as she responded;

"Alec, what I thought was love for you—I wonder if it was—has turned to loathing. I repeat what I said in this very room this morning. I wouldn't marry you if you were to beg me on your knees."

Did she mean it? Nancy's heart, which had been befogged in doubt and unhappiness, beat its way into the sunshine of hope. Her contempt was real. It was not acting. Impulsively she held out her hand. With a sob which seemed to tear its way up Sybyl caught it. She shook uncontrollably. Nancy put a steadying arm about her. Her eyes were hard as she suggested;

"Alec, if you have nothing more to say . . ."

"But I, as the missing side of this right-angle triangle, have something to say," protested a stern voice.

Bruce! Nancy pressed her hand over her lips to stifle a cry of joy. Was she dreaming? That seemed to be the best thing she did lately. No, it was Bruce blocking the doorway. Bruce, tall, bronzed, with deep lines between nose and lips, with eyes burning like coals. For an instant the room went green. Then she felt her father's hand on her shoulder, heard his voice saying tenderly;

"Nan, dear! Nan!"

Lips trembling, body shaking as with a chill, she smiled up at him and patted his fingers reassuringly. Had he come with Bruce? Sybyl broke into low, agonizing sobbing. As an arrow from a bow she flew to the man who had been her husband. She flung her arms about his neck and hid her face against his breast. His hands hanging straight at his sides clenched till the nails showed white. His lips were colorless, his eyes flames as he looked levelly at Alec Pryde and suggested;

"This is your cue for an exit."

With an inarticulate mutter Pryde strode by him. The outer door banged. Nancy drew a long, sobbing breath. That was ended. Why had Bruce come back? How long had he been at the door? Had he heard Sybyl's dismissal of her one-time lover? Just to look at him was a joy. As though he sensed her thought his eyes met hers. Eyes turned to ashes now. Why didn't he speak? Say something to Sybyl? Why didn't he put his arms about her? His clenched hands still hung at his sides. If only he had held them out for a moment to his sister. Selfish! Why think of herself when the tangle in his life was straightening out. Nancy blinked away tears as Sybyl implored frantically;

"Bruce! Bruce! You seem like stone! You heard me tell him, didn't you? Before I knew that you were here I told Alec that I despised him. I meant it Bruce. Really. After I went to—out there—I felt as though I were emerging from a sombre cloud—I—oh, how I wanted you! Wanted

your arms about me. I couldn't turn back. I had burned
my bridges. As the days went on I grew panicky. I didn't
know what to do. I wrote to your father—I felt that to be
near him was to be safe. It's a horrible feeling to be afloat
without a rudder. Horrible to know that you've made an
irreparable mistake, Bruce."

Through the turmoil of her emotions Nancy heard her
father say softly;

" 'And the fool hath said in his heart, "There is no
God!" ' "

She watched her brother through a mist of tears. His
face was like a grey mask. Why didn't he say something?
Had he been hurt beyond forgiveness? Sybyl's voice was
heartbreaking as she sobbed on;

"After the divorce I didn't know what else to do but
marry Alec. I came here. I realized that he was infatuated
with Nancy. I was frightened for her as well as myself. I
haven't slept nights thinking of the wrong I had done you
and Betty."

Betty! The name echoed through Nancy's absorption in
the drama before her. She caught Sybyl's arm and shook
it.

"Where is Betty? Wasn't she with you?"

Sybyl's face went a degree whiter. She swayed. Bruce
caught her close in one arm. Her violet eyes were enormous in her white face as she demanded harshly;

"What do you mean, 'Where is she?' "

"We can't find her. She hasn't been seen since three
o'clock. Phyllis said that you were to come for her."

"I phoned the Manse and told the maid's mother that I
couldn't come. Bruce! Bruce! Where can she be?"

"Sit down, Sybyl." As she sank into a chair Bruce
Caswell turned to his father. "You know better than I
where to look."

"I didn't know the child was missing. When you appeared at my study door I forgot there was anyone else in
the world. Tell us what happened, Nan."

With her breath catching queerly the girl told of her
return to the house, of Phyllis' terrified greeting, of the
arrival, as she started to telephone the Squire, of Sybyl
and—and—she couldn't make herself mention Pryde's
name.

"What shall we do now?" she concluded tensely.

With her beige frock tinged to soft rose by the firelight Sybyl leaned forward, hands clenched on her knees. Bruce Caswell's face was livid as he talked in a low tone with his father. Nancy felt her self-control slipping. "Why—why didn't someone do something? Betty might be lying somewhere hurt, perhaps ..." she jerked the bit of her imagination. It was running away with her. She bit her lips till she sensed the sickish taste of blood. She demanded shakenly;

"Why do we stand here talking, endlessly talking. Isn't anyone going to do anything?"

Sybyl held up a trembling hand.

"Listen! A car stopped at the gate!"

Chapter XXII

Geoffrey Hilliard drove slowly, peering into bushes, pulling up short at every rustle.

A brilliant afterglow tinted the roadsides palely pink. A star, blinking as though not yet quite awake to the night's watch, seemed to keep sympathetic pace as it moved higher in the heavens. He had stopped at Valleyview to leave his father and to question his tearful aunts and Nora as to the last moment they had seen Betty. Nothing new. Of course the cruelty of Alec Pryde lay behind her disappearance. The little thing couldn't run far, she must be near, he kept assuring himself. She might have been carried off in an automobile.

Who would abduct her? For what reason? Ransom? The Caswells had no money. Revenge? Alec? He had been furious when he struck the child but why should he want her? He had made it a condition that if he married Sybyl she must give up Betty. Anyone else disgruntled with the clergyman and his daughter?

Luke Small? But what would it gain him to spirit away the child? Wrong wave-length. Better go on to the mill. Mike, the night watchman, might have seen her on the road when he came from home. Geoffrey's thoughts spun on to the accompaniment of the rhythm of wheels. Betty might be with her mother. No, according to Phyllis, Mrs. Caswell had 'phoned that she couldn't come for her. Why? Because of Alec Pryde? If they had finally departed good riddance to them. Passion and surrender. Old as time. At least she was walking into unhappiness without blinders. Had they picked Betty up somewhere? Sybyl had relinquished all claim to the child. Would she keep that promise if she had broken the pledge of constancy she gave when she married Bruce Caswell?

But Phyllis had said that Nancy was with Alec. That disposed of the theory that Sybyl had run away with him.

Nancy must be at the Manse by now, must have been told that the child had disappeared. She would know what to do. Thought of her set his pulses hammering. The challenging lift of her lovely chin was before his eyes, the pressure of her head against his arm as she slept was in his heart, the feel of her soft throat was on his lips for all his life—and after.

Had he a chance with her? If he had would she consent to a home in this country village? Sometimes she felt as though she must break away, as though she were caught in a backwater, she had said. He would keep his apartment in New York. "We could spend more or less time there after I get the work at the mill systematized. We wouldn't be chained to Sunnyfield," he thought. We. Wonderful word.

He dragged his imagination back from a glamorous future to the consideration of the tangled present. Nancy would give no thought to him while Betty was missing. If only he could shield her from this unbearable anxiety. He stopped at the entrance to the mill. There was a chance that Mike had seen the child. A light in his office. Lucky to catch him before he had started on his rounds.

Geoffrey tapped at the window. The man's grotesque shadow shuffled forward in answer. He opened the door a crack. Something glistened in his hand. Armed? What had happened?

"It's Geoffrey Hilliard. Put up that automatic!"

The red-headed watchman flung the door wide. His grin disclosed a set of white teeth which had seen better days. He flourished a dripping tin cup as he explained;

"Automatic, it ain't! Come in! Come in! I came here to get a drink. The wife put six kippered herrin'—whoppers—in my supper box an' like a durned fool I et 'em all. Seems though I could drink up the river."

Six kippered herrings! Geoffrey's mouth and throat dried in sympathy. Mike took a long draught before he demanded;

"What's goin' on with you young fellas comin' here this time o' day? Small came in a few minutes ago."

"Luke Small! What did he want? He's gone with the Upper Mill. Owns a lot of stock, Mac Donovan told me. You shouldn't have let him in."

Mike scratched his bushy red head.

"Perhaps I shouldn't oughta, Mr. Geoff, but the poor bozo looked about all in, kinder wild like. Said he'd come back fer something' he'd forgotten. Thought it couldn't do any harm to let him get it. Said he'd left some instructions in the basement. You know he got yer Pa to put in this new sprinkler system. I thought might be about that. He's a smart fella. Tried to explain the workin' of it to me when 'twas installed, but I've no head fer mechanics, I ain't. I heard him slam the door. Gone, I guess. Curious you didn't run into him. How long you goin' to be 'round?"

"Only a few moments. On your way here did you see Betty Caswell or her white dog?"

"Nor hair nor hide of them. Missing?"

"She's been gone since soon after three."

"Say, that's kinder bad. Hev you 'phoned Mac Donovan at the county seat? His men'll locate her if anybody can."

"Just thought of him. I'll telephone from the Squire's office."

"Want I should wait?"

"No. I'll be off again as soon as I've talked with the Squire and Mac."

The watchman shuffled away. Geoffrey forgot him, forgot Small's visit to the mill as his father answered his questions.

"No. No news. Her description is being broadcast."

"Has Nancy returned?"

"Not yet."

"Is her father anxious?"

"He isn't at home— Don't shout in my ear like that, Geoff— Someone called for him in an automobile, Phyllis said. Think I'd better 'phone round for him among the sick he visits?"

"Yes. Quick. He ought to know about Betty. I'll 'phone Mac Donovan to start his men hunting for her. Goodbye!"

There was an outrageous amount of red tape to be cut before Geoffrey succeeded in getting the Chief on the wire. Hurriedly he told his story. Crisply Mac Donovan snapped back;

"Had she been frightened?"

"Yes."

A pause which seemed aeons long. Then,

"Didn't you tell me that you took her to our old pirate stronghold on the island?"

"Yes! What of it?"

"Looked there?"

"Good Lord, no. I will."

As he snapped the receiver on the hook Geoffrey remembered Betty's question;

"Was that your str-strong'old? Where you hid?"

Mac's suggestion was worth following up. As he reached to turn out the office light he heard the sound of running water. In spite of his anxiety he laughed. Mike filling his tin cup again. Six kippered herrings! Big ones. Made him dry to think of them.

A gong clanged through the silent building. The signal that the automatic sprinklers had burst into action. That was the sound of water he had heard! Not Mike drawing it. Fire? Where? He listened for the infinitesimal part of a second. He fairly slid down the stairs to the basement. Dimly lighted it shook with clamor. He shot past the two heaters. Snapped on the light in the newsprint storeroom. Instinctively turned up the collar of his coat. From a dozen sprinkler heads water deluged the floor.

Where was the fire? Must be in this room. He poked among the enormous rolls of newsprint. Not a spark. Cracker-jack sprinkler system to get the upper hand so quickly. Time to stop the downpour. Where the dickens was the gate-valve? Must be one in each room. It took him several minutes to locate it. Check! The wheel which shut off the water was gone. Had it been blown off by heavy pressure? Darned poor system, if that were so. On his knees he searched for the missing part. He glared up from under a drenched lock of hair as Mike burst into the room;

"Holy Saints! Where's the fire?"

"No sign of it. Gate-valve's blown out. Looking for the parts."

"Then how we goin' to stop that water? I know how to turn thet wheel but, if it's gone—plumber I ain't. Luke Small's the only man knows much about this."

Geoffrey stood up.

"But, Small isn't here and the water must be stopped.
I'm going for a monkey-wrench. Don't stand there gawk-
ing. 'Phone for a plumber, the mill mechanic, anybody
who might have an idea what to do."

He wrecked the orderly arrangement of the tool room as
he rummaged for wrenches, wire, pieces of tin, anything
which suggested usefulness in stopping the flow. Laden
with makeshifts he dashed back. He crashed into Mike.
Shaking as with ague the watchman caught his arm;

"Hold on! Git the Squire. The water's soaking down in
the sheet room same's 'tis here. Shut-off's on the blink.
Tons of paper there ready fer shippin'. There ain't been
no fire. Them little glass valves which set the sprinklers
goin' weren't busted by heat as they'd oughta be. Someone smashed 'em. I see the pieces. 'Phone fer the Squire.
He'll know what to do. You ain't any more use than I
am. I'll try to git the mechanic on the other line."

Geoffrey took the stairs three at a time. Soaked to the
skin, water rivuleting from his clothing to make puddles
on the floor, he dialed for Valleyview. Suppose the Squire
were not there? He might be at the Manse if Betty—
Betty! He'd forgotten her. At his father's first word he cut
in;

"It's Geoff! Mill's being deluged by the sprinklers—No
fire. Busted by hand, Mike says. Can't stop water. Gate-
valves out of commission. Tried everything. Wrenches
won't grip.—What?—Migosh! Shut off water at post indi-
cator? Where's that?—Main riser outside—Good-bye!"

He dropped the receiver and shouted;

"Mike! Mike!"

From down the hall the watchman's voice answered;
"What you want?"

"Shut off the water from the main riser—you dumb-
bell!"

A distant whoop. A distant shuffle. Three seconds later
at the door of the newsprint room Geoffrey watched
tensely. Some of the water struck the deflectors of the
sprinkler heads, shot toward the ceiling to drench that,
before it joined the descending showers. He'd give the
system a reference for thoroughness, he thought grimly.
The flow decreased to tiny rivulets. Diminished to drops.

Stopped. His face burned with chagrin. Darn fool not to
think himself of shutting off the main supply. He investigated the damage. The great rolls of paper, tons and tons
of it ready for shipping, were soaked, soggy, ruined. The
sheet room was the same, Mike had said. The mill would
have to run overtime to fill orders. Curious that the acci-
dent should have happened just as Luke Small left, when
they would need him more than ever.

Luke! Geoffrey's lids half closed over his kindling eyes.
Luke had entered the mill just ahead of him. Luke had
threatened to give him a chance to demonstrate what the
College of Business Administration had taught him! Luke
had smashed those sprinkler heads! Luke had put a crimp
in the Squire's "live wire"! It was clear to him now. And
he had risen to the emergency with as little intelligence as
Luke had expected. He visualized himself dripping,
disheveled, rummaging in the tool room for something,
any old thing with which to check the downpour, when
with a twist of his hand he could have shut the water off
the buildings. Well, Luke hadn't been any too thorough
himself or he would have put that strategic point out of
commission. As Mike slunk into sight Geoffrey observed
grimly, the while he choked back a desire to laugh:

"You and I make corking guardians of a mill, Mike."

The watchman shakily did something with a huge jack-
knife to a dark brown cake in his hand before he answered:

"I've been workin' round this place these ten years
back an' I never had occasion to shut the water off these
buildin's afore. When I come tearin' to answer that
alarum an' see you a huddlin' on the floor like a wet hen
an' the water rushin' down, I lost my head. How come
you to think of turnin' it off outside?"

"The Squire told me."

"Then you weren't so durned smart yerself, was you?"
He scratched his red head as he morosely regarded the
mush of wet paper. "It beats me who could have smashed
them sprinklers."

Geoffrey opened his lips to accuse Luke Small. Closed
them. It was the Squire's business. He had no right to
broadcast his suspicion until his father had been consulted.

"Any use to try to dry out these rolls?" he inquired.

"Divil a bit. It's gone. Tons and tons of it. I'll get some
of the boys here an' we'll mop up. No use your hangin'
round. Wasn't you lookin' for the Caswell kid?"

Betty! He had forgotten her. With a warning to the
watchman to leave the paper in both rooms undisturbed
for the insurance adjustment, he hurried to his roadster.
With wet clothing under his top-coat sticking uncomfortably to his body, hatless, he sent the car swiftly
toward the bridge. Mac's suggestion that the child might
have taken refuge on the island seemed improbable but
he'd look there. Long before he reached it, above the purr
of the roadster he heard the murmurous rush of the
brook.

In the balsam-scented dimness he stopped on the
bridge. The lights of his car illumined a roadster parked
close to the shrubs ahead. Luke Small's! What was he
doing here? He peered downstream. The island was a
dark bulk set in an unearthly whiteness of swift water.
How still the world was. Almost as though for a moment
it had laid down its tools to listen to the oratorio of the
flowing stream. Tones and overtones. Trees, ravaged by
the early frost, dropped their leaves lingeringly, softly, as
though loath to lay away their gay loveliness. Branches
trembled in the shaken mirror of a star-lit pool; shadows
lengthened, deepened; sounded the far, faint hoot of a
lonely owl; the near-by answering yelp of a dog.

Scooty! Scooty on the island. That meant Betty. He
swung his car till its powerful lamps illuminated the stream,
the island, quickened the cascade to fluid silver. As clearly as though it were day he saw the child, the white dog, a
man stooping over a flickering flame. The man turned.
Luke Small. Luke Small and Betty!

Luke was "dear" with Betty, Nancy had said, Geoffrey
remembered, as he ran down the brookside path. He
wouldn't hurt her—unless—he must have been a little
mad when he wrecked those sprinkler heads. A shout. A
fanatical laugh. A rip of planks. Luke had flung the
makeshift crossing between island and mainland into the
stream. The current caught it. Spun it. Shook it. Plunged
it. Shot it over the cascade.

Chapter XXIII

Speechless with fury Geoffrey glared across the swift water at the man staring back at him with malicious exultation. He jammed the brake on his temper. Diplomacy, not anger, was his line till he had Betty safe in his arms. He tried to keep his voice even as he reminded;

"The Caswells are your friends. Don't drag them into your feud with me, Luke. Bring the child across."

Small's laugh was blood-chilling.

"Not on your life. I found her. I was on my way to see Nancy when I heard the dog bark. I'll return her. Her aunt will be mighty nice to the person who brings her back. Get me? You've come from the mill, haven't you? You'd like our old friend Mac Donovan to get his talons into me, wouldn't you? He won't. I'll keep Betty here till I get devilish ready to take her home. Try—and—stop me!"

His voice was rough, his eyes in the glare of the roadster glittered uncannily. Envy and hatred had twisted his reason for the moment. He must get the child away from him, Geoffrey decided as he splashed into the stream. Finger between her lips Betty stared up at the man looming over her, her eyes wide with wonder. Scooty, close at her feet, growled a warning as Luke put his hand on her shoulder. She twisted away from him. Her breath caught in a sob before she refused passionately;

"I won't stay here, Mr. Luke, an' I don't mean maybe! I'm goin' wif my Prod'gal Son." She dashed into the water. With a joyous yelp the white dog followed.

Geoffrey plunged for her. Small grabbed futilely at her skirt. She slipped. The current caught her. Tossed her like a chip. Swept her on. Scooty snapped valiantly at her heels.

Geoffrey's heart seemed to go dead as he splashed and

slipped and struggled after her. The cascade! The caldron below! Daring as the boy buccaneers had been they had given that a wide berth as they had poled their rafts upstream. Could this be the gay, chatty, friendly brook of his boyhood, this clutching, twisting, sucking, bloodthirsty horror which seemed to be muttering in ghoulish triumph?

Up to his hips in water he caught the hem of the little skirt. It slipped through his fingers. Was Luke shouting? Why didn't he come on and help? With both hands he grabbed a foot. Caught it tight. He had a confused sense of a white furry thing sweeping by as he pulled the child up into his arms. He cradled her wet head tenderly against his shoulder as he slipped and swashed his way to the bank. He looked down at the little white face. How still she was. Terrified he pleaded;

"Betty! Open your eyes."

Her lids lifted. Her lips quivered;

"I waited an' waited for you to come to the str-strong'-old, Prod'gal Son."

She was safe. Unharmed. She had been in the water only a short while. He had lived through an eternity of apprehension in but a moment of time. He pressed his lips to her tight wet curls in thanksgiving.

"All right dear? Not hurt anywhere?"

"Only my back. Mr. Cain—Mr. Alec—hitted me when I cleaned his boots. He said;

" 'I'll teach you to touch my things!' Are boots things, Prod'gal Son?"

In spite of the fury which surged through him at thought of Alec Pryde, Geoffrey laughed in relief. Betty was her funny, questioning self again, and she might have been—he hugged her impulsively before he started on the path to the bridge. Luke return her to her aunt? Not a chance. Luke! Where was he? He looked back. Good Lord, what had happened?

In the very middle of the rays of light from the road-ster lamps lay Luke Small, face down, across a boulder in midstream. One leg and foot swayed with the current, the other was knee deep in water. Foot wedged? Geoffrey knew from experience the treachery of the brook bed. He ought to get Betty home at once. He couldn't leave Luke like this. He set the child on her feet. She leaned against him as he explained;

"Mr. Luke has fallen, dear. Will you stay here quietly while I help him?"

"I'd like to see Nanny, Prod'gal Son."

Geoffrey steeled his heart against the quiver of the little chin, the sob in the child's voice;

"It won't take me but a minute. Be a good child—and—and—we'll ask Nanny to let me take you to the Zoo." He used the first inducement that came to mind.

"The big Zoo in New York?"

"The biggest we can find."

"All righty."

With a backward glance to make sure she was not following he waded into the stream. In water to his thighs he tried to free Small's foot wedged between two rocks. The icy water numbed his hands. Fortunately Luke had fainted. He would have been in torture else. In the struggle to liberate himself he had broken his ankle, Geoffrey surmised.

The thought of Nancy waiting for news of the missing child gave him superhuman strength. He tugged at the rock. It moved. The foot which had been held as in a vise came slowly to the surface. He straightened and drew a long breath. That was that. Now to get him out of the stream. Jaws set hard, muscles straining, veins in neck and forehead corded, he lifted Luke to his shoulders. In a flash came the remembrance of the dark night he had carried a comrade out of range of fire on the Front of the Front. He slipped. Went half down. Regained his footing. Swished on.

Carefully he swung Luke to the ground and bent over him. Faint only. His face hadn't touched the water. Small opened his eyes. Blinked in the glare of the lamps. Dazedly regarded the child looking curiously down at him. Closed them. Geoffrey touched his arm.

"Luke! I must take Betty home. Nancy thinks she's lost. Do you hear me?"

Small's eyes opened. He tried to move. Groaned. He flung his arm over his face as a shield from the glaring light. He muttered hoarsely;

"Broken my ankle. Go on with her, Geoff. You've

won. You always won. Sorry about the mill. I lived a lifetime trapped out there. A little mad, I guess . . ." His voice trailed off. His eyes closed.

"Keep your grip, Luke. I'll have someone here for you within ten minutes. Hate to leave you like this."

Luke Small struggled to his elbow.

"Go on! Get the child home. The brook got me—hot irons jabbing my ankle— Od's blood! Straight into them before they recover their wits! You're chief, Geoff! Prepare to . . ."

He fell back, mumbling brokenly, arms outstretched.

Geoffrey swallowed an uncomfortable lump in his throat. He mustn't stand here like a graven image pitying him. As he caught the child up in his arms she inquired;

"What's recover veir wits mean, Prod'gal Son?"

He tucked her into his roadster without answering. With the rug from Small's car he ran down the path.

"Luke! Luke!" he called softly as he covered him warmly.

The white-faced man on the ground opened feverishly bright eyes.

"Listen, Luke. I can't get you to the bridge without nearly killing you. Keep still here . . ."

A glint of irony twisted the man's lips;

"Can you see me running far on this foot?"

"I'm going to the mill for help. The men are there. They'll bring a stretcher, have you out of this in a jiffy. Understand what I'm saying?"

It was evident that Small was holding his mind to attention with all his strength as he answered;

"Yes. And why the men are there. Go on!" he mumbled incoherently as he covered his eyes with his arm.

Betty was asleep when Geoffrey returned to the roadster. With her warm little body snuggled against him he drove to the mill. It took but a moment to start Mike and his helpers to the aid of the injured man, to telephone his father. As the car shot off in the direction of the Manse Betty stirred and opened her eyes;

"Where's Scooty, Pro'gal Son?"

Scooty! He had forgotten Scooty. Had the white dog been swept and tossed along by the current at the moment he had rescued the child? The cascade? The caldron? Scooty gone? The far, faint hoot of a lonely owl drifted through the trees. There was no answering yelp this time. If he hadn't caught Betty—impulsively he drew the child closer as he comforted;

"Scooty must have taken the—the short way home, dear."

"What's the short way home mean, Prod'gal Son?" the child inquired drowsily.

She was asleep when he carried her into the Manse bundled in a rug, her wet head against his shoulder. He stopped on the threshold as a bronzed faced man stepped forward with an inarticulate cry. Bruce Caswell! Had he never seen his photograph he would have known him by his resemblance to his sister. The child's lids flew wide. She held out her arms;

"Daddy! Daddy! You've comed!"

Speechless from emotion her father caught her close. Sybyl flew to them;

"Don't shut me out, Bruce! I love her too! I'm her mother. Don't shut me out," she sobbed.

With an uncomfortable tightness in his throat Geoffrey slipped away. Sybyl had not gone with Alec. From her voice and eyes one might suspect a resurge of love for her husband, he thought, as in his room at Valleyview he changed to dry clothing. He had had but a glimpse of Nancy, white, shaken. She had been with Alec Pryde, Phyllis had said. Where was he? What was that curious whining outside? He followed the sound. Where the path from the brook stopped at the garden gate he found a mop of exhausted, wet dog. Scooty! He must have fought against the current to the shore. Good boy! He picked him up in his arms. The dog rubbed his wet head against his sleeve and licked his hand. He'd give him a rub before he took him to Betty.

He returned to the house. As he entered men were carrying Luke Small upstairs. His voice faint, appealing drifted back. Eyebrows rearing, green eyes snapping Nora watched till the stretcher was out of sight. She sniffed her exasperation;

"Ain't that just like the Squire to have him brought here 'cause he lives in a boardin' house, Masther Geoff? Did ye hear the sweetness of his voice? Huh! Whin the

Divil is sick the Divil a saint wud be; whin the Divil is
well, divil a saint is he. That's Luke Small." She hurried
upstairs, her print dress crackling with every move.

As Geoffrey entered the hall at the Manse with Scooty
fluffy and dry in his arms he saw Nancy Caswell on the
stairs. He sent the dog scampering up before he joined
her. Her eyes were big with excitement, her face was
white as she demanded in a strained whisper;

"What happened? Betty says that Alec stuck her, that
Luke lay down in the water and went to sleep."

"She fell into the brook; she had been hiding in the
buccaneers' stronghold. Luke plunged after her, caught
his foot, broke his ankle. Don't look like that. The child's
all right, isn't she?"

"Yes, except that she is terribly excited. I didn't dare
question her. I can't make out much from the jumble of
sentences." The soft color stole from her throat to her
hair. Had his eyes brought it there? Her whiteness, her
concern for the child had thrown him off guard. With an
evident attempt at gaiety she went on;

"I was going down to 'phone you. Betty is demanding
your attendance at her prayers with all the assurance of a
Pasha's favorite. Will you come?"

He took the stairs two at a time. Betty greeted him with
a crow of exultation. The dog, already asleep, was clasped
tight in her arms.

"Nanny said you wouldn't come, Prod'gal Son. You
did, didn't you? Have you asked her if we may go to the
big Zoo?"

He pulled up a chair, loosened her arms and gave the
dog to Nancy. He took the child's hands in his as he
reminded;

"Poor old Scooty must have taken the long way home
instead of the short way. He's about all in. Nanny'll put
him on his own blanket. Lie down. We'd better not ask
her to let us go to the Zoo until you've shown her what a
good little girl you can be by going to sleep."

She dropped back on the pillow and regarded him with
troubled eyes;

"I'll try but I guess I'm sunk. Phyl-*us* says she's 'scouraged 'bout me bein' good."

She folded her hands on her breast, screwed up her

eyes and began her prayers. Nancy on her knees rested
her head against the little white bed. The child's petition
drowsed to a close;

"Please make me a good girl so's the Prod'gal Son will
take me to the big Zoo. Don't be 'scouraged like Phyl-*us*.
Try harder, God. Try harder. Amen!"

Fringed lids curtained her blue eyes. On the floor exhausted Scooty tapped his tail feebly and drew a long
sigh. Gently Nancy smoothed the covers. She motioned
Geoffrey to the door before she opened the window and
snapped off the light. In the hall he caught her hands in
his.

"Where's Alec!"

Her tense whisper wiped the light from his face. She
wanted Alec. Stonily he answered;

"If I knew I wouldn't tell you."

She gave his arm a little shake as she implored;

"Don't misunderstand me, please! Alec struck Betty.
Bruce must not know. He would be wild with anger." She
put her hand to her heart as she added unsteadily;

"How life hurts!"

All his love for her, his tenderness for her, surged in
his voice and eyes as he comforted;

"It does, dear. But not so much if someone who adores
you holds you close in his heart. Going to love me?"

Dazed by the suddenness of his question she looked up
dumbly. He laughed unsteadily as he pleaded;

"Try harder, Nan! Try harder."

"Nancy!" Noah Caswell called from the hall below.

The girl twisted her hands free. Geoffrey was close
behind her when she entered the living room where her
father, brother, Sybyl and the Squire seemed to be waiting—for what? As Noah Caswell looked up from the
book in his hand she announced;

"Here I am, Dad."

He smiled whimsically;

"So I observe. Bruce and Sybyl wish to be married
here. He sails for South America tomorrow."

She checked a startled protest. Her brother put his arm
about her shoulders as he explained;

"I'm in honor bound to return as soon as possible. Nan.
I came back for Sybyl. I had let her go too easily, I

realized as the days went by. When I arrived here I found father in his study, rushed him off to vouch for me when I applied for a marriage license. I was determined to take my wife back with me. We are going to New York tonight. You and father are to bring Betty on in time for the sailing of the ship."

"You are not taking Betty away from us!"

Her face went white at thought of losing the child she loved, then she smiled at her brother with radiant tenderness. How like her, Geoffrey thought with fervent sympathy. Always she would go forward unvanquished by life, her weapon of defense gay courage. Bruce Caswell answered her protest.

"Her mother and I need her, Nan."

Geoffrey's attention strayed from the words as the clergyman read the marriage service for his son and the woman who not so long ago had deserted him. What thoughts lay behind the inscrutable eyes of Bruce Caswell? Had his return been prompted by the cold process of reasoning or had he felt a warm passionate belief that the woman who had fallen from the pedestal in his heart could be patched into the semblance of the woman he had loved? As the years went on would doubt of her loyalty flit, wraith-like though the haunted corridors of his memory? Would Sybyl's present disillusionment challenge her to higher, more unselfish living? From time to time she might hear the call of flirtation but never again would she be lured into the maelstrom of passion of that he was sure. How wonderful Noah Caswell was with his imperishable belief that humanity is capable of dwelling on the mountaintops of high thinking, noble, unselfish living. Erect. Lean. His features were those of a Greek god. But no Greek god's face radiated such spiritual beauty, no Greek god's head ever was crowned with soft waves of silver hair, no Greek god would wear that shabby velveteen coat, nor a broad tie with one end dangling. Was ever a voice so rich, so stern, so significant as his as, with deep, dark eyes on the man and woman before him, he commanded;

" 'Those whom God hath joined together let no man put asunder.' "

Chapter XXIV

Bells rang. Men shouted. A belated passenger barely cleared the gang-plank to the deck before it was drawn up. The narrow strip of oily green water between dock and ship widened. Lights in staterooms flashed on. Flower-laden voyagers waved farewell to friends frantically wig-wagging in reply. Near the stern stood Bruce Caswell holding Betty with Sybyl close beside him.

In spite of feeling as though her heart were being pulled out by the roots as the face of the child she loved grew dimmer, Nancy, standing between her father and Geoffrey Hilliard on the dock, silently gave thanks as the ship glided majestically oceanward. Her brother and Alec Pryde would not meet now for years, perhaps never again. If Bruce had known that Alec had struck Betty— he hadn't, so why let her imagination run away with her? As she strained her eyes for a last glimpse of the group by the stern she saw the child throw one arm about her mother's neck and draw her close. Then she heard Noah Caswell beside her say softly;

" 'If a house be divided against itself it cannot stand.' That house of Caswell will stand, Nan."

When Nancy's vision cleared the group was but a blur against a darker background. Betty had sailed out of her life. She turned abruptly away.

"Let's go. I'm not constituted to see people off. I'm glad that Miss Serena and Miss Sally didn't come. I shall never forget their faces nor their white hair in the sunlight as they waved to Betty from the steps of the Manse. Smiles and tears. Phyllis and her mother sobbed an accompaniment in the background. Poor Scooty! Did you note his expression as he was dragged below? Dad, that chapter of our lives is finished. What next?"

Her father slipped his hand under her arm as they manoeuvered their way through the lingering crowd to the

Hilliard sisters' limousine in which Geoffrey had transported Betty, her entourage and her luggage to the dock. Noah Caswell belatedly answered his daughter's question;

"Next we'll have dinner. Geoffrey suggests the theatre after."

"No theatre for me. Acting would be but pale paprika after the biting cayenne reality of the last forty-eight hours. Where are we dining?"

Geoffrey opened the door of the car.

"At my apartment. Coming?"

The unsteadines of his voice, the unguarded ardor of his eyes sent her heart to her throat. She started to protest, remembered her father's words;

"Going straight on is the only situation in which I can see you, Nan."

A smiling Oriental opened the door when they left the hotel lift at what seemed the very top of the world. Was this Taka, "the esteemed relative from Tokio"? His parchment skin crinkled alarmingly as he welcomed;

"Gladful overpowering. This way to remove most delectable hat."

As in a dream Nancy followed him through a book-lined hall to a room, charming in coloring, restful in the absence of detail. She removed hat and coat and sank into a chair. This was the first moment she had had to herself since Alec and Sybyl had walked together into the living room the evening before. Every member of the household, the Hilliard sisters across the hedge, had been caught up in a whirlwind of preparation for Betty's long journey.

There had been unpleasant interludes, two of them. First Alec Pryde had materialized out of the everywhere, to pledge eternal constancy if she would marry him, to accuse her of wrecking his life when she declined. She had run across to Valleyview to see Luke in answer to his urgent request. Miss Serena, Miss Sally, even antagonistic Nora, who had been hovering over him, vanished like wraiths as she entered the room. His white face was heavily lined. In a voice weakened by pain he had informed her that he was the largest stockholder in the Upper Mill, that his treachery to the Squire—for which he was sorry now—had really been go-getter stuff. It had

been for her. She had made him think she cared. If she
didn't marry him she would wreck his life.

She had indignantly refuted his charge. She had never
encouraged him to love her, she had reminded. She
hadn't told him that last summer she had begun to distrust him. She had left him glowering at the wall. He had
refused to say good-bye.

The faint music of a Japanese gong chimed through the
room. A reminder to her? Before the mirror she frowned
appraisingly at her reflection. Her crepe frock in three
shades of green was good-looking, very, her hair went
rather well with it, her skin—

"Needs powder," she told her reflection. Would Geoffrey—Geoffrey! enchanted color stole from the base of
the looking-glass girl's throat to the uneven line of her
ruddy hair—his eyes, his voice when he had inquired,
"Coming?"—had seemed to draw her heart up into his
arms. She looked at her double and demanded, as Betty's
favorite Alice had demanded of the Cheshire cat;

" 'Would you tell me please which way I ought to walk
from here?' "

The question spun through her mind again when after
a delectable dinner served by a servant who might have
stepped out from one of the books which lined the walls,
Geoffrey suggested that the view outside was worth
seeing. She looked appealingly at her father. He shook
his head.

"I've seen it. With my love of the sights and sounds of
a city it was like being led up into a high mountain and
shewed all the kingdoms of the world in a moment of
time. I want to examine these wonderful books and
'phone to my old parish."

With lingering care Geoffrey adjusted a Chinese Mandarin coat heavy with gold embroidery over her shoulders.

"You'll need this outside. Must have had a premonition
when I selected green," he observed cryptically as he
opened the long French door to the roof. Past a pocket-
handkerchief of a lawn, past flower-beds, a few dwarf
cedars, she followed him to a stone parapet. A delicate
breeze touched her face with velvet fingers.

"How wonderful!" she breathed softly.

Far below lighted canyons, gleaming with asphalt ribbons which were streets, crossed and recrossed. Murmurous as the Sunnyfield river rose the hum of traffic.
Far away the Brooklyn Bridge, crowned, shod with topaz
lights, girdled the dusk. A black bulk, gold trimmed,
thrust its bold accent among the castellated walls of giant
buildings. Windows gleaming. Signs flashing. The illuminated backdrop of a mammoth pantomime. Splendor.
Beauty. Ugliness veiled by the golden mystery of a city
night. In contrast the over-head stars seemed but pale
spatters on a sable canopy. Nancy softly voiced her appreciation;

"I love it. Dad is right. We are city people."

With his face in shadow Geoffrey reminded;

"You had planned to live in the country for Betty's
sake. The wheel of fortune turns. You are free to leave it.
I am pledged to stay."

He laid his hand with its curious seal ring over hers
resting on the stone parapet. Her pulses thrilled to his
touch. Even when she had thought she disliked him, she
had loved his hands, she remembered.

"You told me once that you thought of me as a patch
of hard-caked earth which needed a tremendous stirring
before it could produce anything worth while. You stirred
it. It's all yours. What will you plant in it—Garden-
maker?"

She fought against the tide of feeling sweeping her
toward him. She inquired with tormenting charm;

"You have a conundrum complex, haven't you?"

His laugh caught at her breath.

"Have I? I'll ask you another. You've known all the
time that I loved you, haven't you?"

The huskiness of his voice sent her heart winging to her
eyes but she kept her lids lowered as she demanded;

"How could I know? You told me that I was the most
disagreeable, most unlovable girl you had ever met."

"Protective coloring. You held me off with the tips of
your cool, slender fingers." With sudden hungry passion
he caught her close, so close that it hurt, pressed his lips
against her eyes, her throat. "You'll never do it again
after this—will you?"

Her heart passed forever into his keeping as she parried and acknowledged with unsteady gaiety;

"Another question. Now I'll ask one. How did you know I loved you?"

The chimes of a clock in a distant tower brought them back from their flight into an enchanted future.

"So late! Dad will think we have deserted him," Nancy reminded.

"He knows. I told him that I love you. He approves—dear."

Noah Caswell regarded them quizzically as they entered the book-lined living room.

"I began to fear that you'd fallen from the roof."

His daughter became absorbed in rebowing the dangling ends of his tie.

"We . . ." she began valiantly and stopped.

"You needn't tell me, Nan. I can guess. Your eyes surpass in glory all the stars in the Milky Way. I thank God for your happiness, my dear." He wiped his eyes before he added practically, "If you expect to reach Sunnyfield tonight we should be starting."

A half hour later as they approached the limousine waiting at the curb, Noah Caswell announced with an attempt at gaiety;

"You young people won't miss me on the way home. Decided that this was the psychical moment to visit my old parish. 'Phoned there while you were on the roof. Two of what Nan disrespectfully calls my 'down and almost-outers,' are coming for me. Here they are now," he added as a dilapidated flivver—looking as out of place on the gleaming avenue as would be a gasoline tractor in an Italian garden—drew up at the curb and stopped a few rods distant.

"Good-night, dear. I'm trusting the best of my life to you, Geoffrey." His voice broke. He turned away. Nancy, watching wistfully, saw two men tumble out of the car to greet him. Under a street lamp he turned and raised his broad-brimmed black hat. The light illumined his silver hair, the dusky beauty of his eyes, the pathetic eagerness of the life-battered faces gazing adoringly up at him. Under her breath the girl said softly;

" 'I have set watchmen upon thy walls, O Jerusalem.' "

Every person with high ideals of living was a watch-man upon the walls of righteousness, her father had said. She looked up at Geoffrey Hilliard through a mist of tears;

"He's—a saint!"

There was infinite tenderness in his voice as he com-forted;

"A happy saint, Nan."

He opened the door of the car, held out his hand.

"Coming?"

Before the shining steadiness of his eyes, the shaken ardor of his voice, the clouds of disillusion and unhap-piness of the last months rolled back as had the clouds of that first storm they had watched together. She put her hand in his. Her lovely voice was buoyant with hap-piness, gaiety, as she declared;

"Something tells me that I am."